WHO MOVED MY BLACKBERRY™?

Who Moved My BlackBerry™?

Lucy Kellaway

with

"Martin Lukes"

NEW YORK

Book Design by Gretchen Achilles

Library of Congress Cataloging-in-Publication Data

Kellaway, Lucy.
    Who moved my BlackBerry? / by Lucy Kellaway.—1st ed.
    p. cm.
    ISBN 1-4013-0251-3
    1. Office politics—Fiction. I. Title.

PR6111.E49W48 2006
823'.92—dc22

                                2005044780

Hyperion books are available for special promotions and premiums. For details contact Michael Rentas, Assistant Director, Inventory Operations, Hyperion, 77 West 66th Street, 12th floor, New York, New York 10023, or call 212-456-0133.

FIRST EDITION

1 3 5 7 9 10 8 6 4 2

To my dearest mum,
my #1 fan

WHO MOVED MY BLACKBERRY™?

Prologue
DECEMBER

DECEMBER 4

From: Martin Lukes
To: Sylvia Woods

Hi Sylvia
   What's this message to call Sebastian Fforbes Hever? Did he say what it was about? I'm going out now for a spot of lunch. If he calls back, I've got my mobile, pager and BlackBerry with me.

Martin

From: Martin Lukes
To: Jenny Lukes

Darling—
   Sorry about last night . . . had a few too many. Will try to get back early tonite to make amends.
   btw one of the top headhunters at Heidrick Ferry has been trying to get hold of me(!) . . . dunno what it's about.

Love you, M xx

From: Martin Lukes
To: SebastianFforbesHever@HeidrickFerry

Hi Sebastian

Thanks for your most intriguing e-mail. Yes, indeed, I could find a window to meet up with you tomorrow. I'll have to juggle a couple of meetings, but should be doable—could see you at your offices in Buckingham Palace Road at around 3ish.

Bestest
Martin Lukes
Marketing Director, A&B (UK)

From: Martin Lukes
To: Jenny Lukes

Darling—

Guess what?? I've been approached to be director of marketing and strategy at a major retailer!! All very hush hush . . . the head-hunter wouldn't say which one over the phone, but I'm going to meet him tomorrow.

I know you're really up against it this pm but wld be v grateful if you'd pick up my gray Hugo Boss suit from the cleaners.

Love you M xx

DECEMBER 6

From: Martin Lukes
To: Sylvia Woods

Hi Sylvia, I'm popping out now. If anyone wants to know where I am, say I'm at a forward planning meeting with Tim at Boogie Gargle Fink.
Will be back 5ish.

Martin

From: Martin Lukes
To: Jenny Lukes

Darling—FANTASTIC meeting with Sebastian just now. The job is marketing director of Sainsburys!! The role's heaven made for yours truly—I'd be in charge of 350 people globally, $1bn annual budget. Very high profile.
Sebastian didn't mention the package at this stage, but said it wouldn't be an obstacle to finding the right person. I assume at least twice what I'm on now . . . It's got my name all over it—what they want are unrivaled communications skills, out of the box thinking, results driven mentality and an outstanding track record in driving performance . . . I've got ticks in all the boxes. Coming straight home now.

Love you M xx

Sent from my BlackBerry Wireless Handheld

DECEMBER 7

From: Martin Lukes
To: Sebastian Fforbes Hever

Hi Sebastian

Great to meet with you yesterday—I felt we were very much singing from the same hymn sheet. I just wanted to reiterate how positive I am about this position, and how much I have to bring to the party.

Just to recap: I'm very can-do, very get-up-go—I operate very well within a large company—but have a pronounced entrepreneurial streak that keeps me thinking outside the box.

Look forward to hearing from you.

All my very bestest
Martin

From: Martin Lukes
To: Jenny Lukes

Darling—

I'm on the short list!!! I'm going to meet all the top bods at Sainsburys on Monday. I've got to prepare a presentation on how I would transition the marketing strategy onto a higher plane. Should be no problem, though I'm a bit out of the loop on food shopping—you've deskilled me on that one. As a shopper, have you got any pointers on supermarkets—from the consumer's perspective? Debrief tonite?

Love you, M xx

PS I'll be working flat out all weekend . . . so don't think I'll be able to make it to yr parents on Sunday.

From: Martin Lukes
To: Jenny Lukes

Darling—don't think you understand this is the biggest inflexion point in my career to date. I'm sure your parents won't mind—they don't like me anyway . . .

DECEMBER 12

From: Martin Lukes
To: Jenny Lukes

Darling—total triumph!! The chief executive of Sainsburys has the IDENTICAL take on the future of marketing to yours truly. I gave them my spiel on how we have gone beyond traditional marketing into a new age of synchronicity across functionalities. The interview was meant to last an hour, but I got the feeling they had made up their mind after 15 minutes, and after that it was more like a relaxed friendly chat than your bog-standard interview.

My presentation on their marketing strategy was 110 percent on the button. I decided not to pull my punches, and I was pretty critical—though obviously in a very positive sort of way. Basically I said that in the past they've relied too heavily on Jamie Oliver—they need to have a more flexible approach to winning hearts and minds of today's shoppers.

See you later
M xx

From: Martin Lukes
To: Sebastian Fforbes Hever

Hi Sebastian

Just wanted to touch base to find out how you think that went? Have you had any feedback from your client? From my point of view it was very positive indeed . . .

Bestest
Martin

From: Martin Lukes
To: Jenny Lukes

Darling—Just had a brief chat with Sebastian—and he says they are "very interested" in me. Re package, we're talking of something in the region of 350k, plus bonus which could be same again. Obviously share options, pension, health insurance, gym club membership. Car allowance would be double so that we could trade in the Mitsubishi Shogun and get a Porsche Cayenne V8 Turbo S.

We could also think of moving. I could see us in one of those 8-bed detached jobs on the common itself—near where George and Stacey live. I just called the estate agent, and there's one on the market for 3.2mil, which would be do-able.

Love you M xx

From: Martin Lukes
To: Jenny Lukes

Darling—Yes, I know I shouldn't count my chickens. And I'm not. I'm simply repeating what I've been told. In any case in this market milieu if you don't have a positive headset you don't get anywhere.

M

DECEMBER 13

From: Martin Lukes
To: Graham Wallace

Hi Graham

Did you notice that I wasn't firing on all cylinders in the board meeting just now? Between you and me and the gatepost, that could be the last one I'm ever going to attend. I'm up for a big job. It's as good as in the bag, though can't tell you what at this juncture. But put it this way. Think supermarket. Think Jamie Oliver. Think Chief Marketing Officer . . .

Mart

From: Martin Lukes
To: Graham Wallace

Cheers, Graham. Yes obviously I am totally over the moon. I had started feeling very stuck here—but I suppose I've been in denial about it. At the end of the day, being marketing director has been a load of fun, but I've outgrown it.

Mart

PS Keep this under your hat till it's greenlighted. Then monster drinks in order.

From: Martin Lukes
To: Sylvia Woods

Hi Sylvia

I think I should let you into a little secret. I'm afraid our ways are about to part. I've been headhunted for a very senior job, so looks like this might be my last week here. If anyone from Sainsbury or Heidrick Struggles calls in the next hour when I'm in the budget meeting come and get me out.

M

From: Martin Lukes
To: Sylvia Woods

Anyone called?

DECEMBER 14

From: Martin Lukes
To: Sebastian Fforbes Hever

Hi Sebastian
    I don't want to hassle you, but I just wondered if there was any news?

Bestest, Martin

From: Martin Lukes
To: Sebastian Fforbes Hever

I don't understand. That wasn't what you implied earlier. I thought the Sainsburys board loved me. Is this a joke, or what?

From: Martin Lukes
To: Jenny Lukes

I don't fucking believe it. They've gone and fucking given it to someone fucking else. Sebastian is a fucking lying sod. He said they LOVED my presentation—practically said the job was in the bag. And now he's saying I didn't have the right skillsets, fit not quite right, better qualified candidates . . . blah blah. I think the guy who got it is head of marketing at Tesco or Asda, so I suppose that means the idiots have gone for the safe candidate rather than the best candidate. I still just can't fucking believe it. It's so unfair. My dream job.

M

From: Martin Lukes
To: Sylvia Woods

Sylvia I'm feeling very unwell. I think I'm coming down with the flu. I'm going home now.

DECEMBER 15

From: Martin Lukes
To: Graham Wallace

Just to check—you haven't told anyone about that job, have you? As it happens I've decided against.

Basically, I've always believed that work is all about the people. And although it was very flattering to be offered such a mega job at Sainsburys, at the end of the day I didn't want to work with them. Apart from anything else fun wasn't part of their DNA at all.

Feeling a bit rough this am. Hair of the dog later?

M

1

JANUARY

Myself—The Basics

JANUARY 1

From: Martin Lukes
To: Pandora@CoachworX!

Hi Pandora

I'm jotting down a few key facts re myself, so that we'll be able to hit the ground running when we have our first Coachworx! session on Wednesday.

But first I'm going to be up front about the key learnings I want to take out from the coaching experience. For me, it's about achieving peak performance. At the end of the day, it's about winning. And that's what I want to do—to win.

So, with that out of the way, who am I ?

Basically, I'm a board director of A&B (UK). Our parent company is based in Atlanta—and I'm Director of Marketing here in London. It's an exciting and challenging leadership role, and I feel I play a critical role in shaping the business going forward. I have always seen myself as a high-octane player. I'm very results driven, very can-do.

However, over the last year I feel I have hit a plateau careerwise. Last month I was headhunted for the position of Marketing Director at Sainsburys. I was way out in front of the field in terms of skillsets, but at the end of the end they went for the safe choice—someone less talented but who had retail experience.

Frankly, following this setback, I am faced with a choice. Do I hunker down here, or do I play the field? I've thought deeply about this and have decided to stay at A&B for now, as my values are well aligned with the company—and at 43 I feel I still have a huge amount to contribute.

I think you wanted to know a few key facts re my home life? I've been married for 17 years to Jenny and we have two smashing boys. Jake is 15, and Max is 12. Jake is highly creative, though has some issues around behavior—which makes him typical for a youngster of his age. Max is a highflyer across the board—a chip off the old block, if you will. He's doing Common Entrance this year—we've put him down for Eton, and according to his head teacher, he's expected to walk it.

I'd say the marriage is definitely a happy one, albeit with the usual ups and downs. The only thing I'd flag up is that in the last couple of years Jens has been getting stressed about her career— she works part-time for a pr agency. Frankly I sometimes wonder if there are time of life issues at play too—I mentioned it to her the other day, but she didn't see the funny side! She's a year older than me, but she takes good care of herself, and is still a perfect size 4!

Home is in Wimbledon in a six bed villa we bought back in 1993 for £250,000, and has just been valued (conservatively for insurance purposes) at £1.9 mil!

You ask about my personal health and fitness, exercise regime, diet and alcohol levels. Basically I'm in reasonable health—if you push yourself as hard as I do, your immune system has to work 24/7! I try to get to the gym as often as possible—I'm in between personal trainers at the moment, but obviously would like to start again asap, time permitting. I've put on a bit of weight recently, and for Christmas Jens gave me Atkins Made Easy—The First Two Weeks. I've tried Atkins before but not stuck to it. This year it's going to be different, and today is Day One!

Drink? I'm a great believer in the value of alcohol as a stress buster, but I don't drink to excess. Probably in the region of 14–17 units a week, or thereabouts.

Smoking—no way. I'm very anti smoking. In fact this is something I'm totally passionate about. I've told both my boys that if they get to 18 without smoking I'll give them both £1,000 cash in hand. At the end of the day, getting the incentive right is key. What do I get up to in my spare time? I don't have any! Joking aside, I'd say it's divided in three.

1. Golf—though I don't get to play nearly as much as I'd like. Currently got a handicap of 14, which I'm not at all happy about.

2. My family. Of course they are mission critical in every sense of the word.

3. The culture scene. Theatre, opera, cinema, reading. Words mean a lot to me. I sometimes think I would have liked to be a writer, and have got lots of book ideas. But at the end of the day there are only so many hours available.

Hope that's enough for now. I'm eagerly anticipating speaking with you on Monday at 3:30.

All my very bestest
Martin Lukes

JANUARY 2

From: Pandora@CoachworX!
To: Martin Lukes

Thank you for that Martin! It is always good to know as much about my clients as possible! We are embarking on an exciting life-changing journey together and I have the highest expectations of you. I'll be your number one fan and I believe in your phenomenal potential to do, to have and to be whatever and whoever you want. Look forward to talking to you on Monday.

Strive and thrive!
Pandora

From: Martin Lukes
To: Sylvia Woods

WHERE THE HELL IS MY TIGER WOODS MUG? IT'S BLOODY TYPICAL—YOU GO ON HOLIDAY FOR A COUPLE OF DAYS, AND COME BACK TO FIND SOMEONE HAS TAKEN YOUR SODDING MUG.

From: Martin Lukes
To: Sylvia Woods

Hi Sylvia

False alarm—mug found. Happy New Year, hope you had a good one.

Would appreciate if you could get my expenses done this am, as Christmas cost me an arm and a leg. There's a pile of receipts on your desk—some of which are blank—please make sure the total comes out slightly higher than this time last year, though not out of the ballpark.

Ta muchly, M

PS When you've got a mo, could you get me a latte and a bar of Green and Blacks white chocolate. Alas, no more almond croissants for me, as this is day two of Atkins!

From: Barry Malone, CEO
To: All Staff

Howdy!

First up, Happy New Year! This is a particularly joyous occasion as it is my first at the helm of this fine company.

New Year is a time for a new beginnning, not just for us as individual leaders but for us together, as a global family.

Over the festive holiday I met up with Chuck P. Stallone, the best coach basketball has ever seen. We got talking about what he had done to keep his team at the top for nearly two decades. Chuck said something to me that made a whole lot of sense. He said it wasn't about getting to the top—but staying at the top. The name of his game is not "peak performance," but Peak Performance—Permanently. And that is my dream for us. That we will peak perform not just this year, but every year going forward.

I want to share with you the image of stonemasons building a cathedral. Their task is no different to ours here at A and B. Why did they chisel that stone? Because their bodies and their souls bought into the idea.

I am asking you to be like the stonemasons. If you have faith in our great company, if you buy into the idea of PPP, we can build our cathedral together.

Have a joyful new year. One of the things that makes me proudest about this company is you all. This company would not exist without the passion and the sweat of every one of you. So if any of you have any ideas, or feelings you would like to share, please e-mail. Or just e-mail to say Hi! That sustains me.

I love you all
Barry

From: Martin Lukes
To: Graham Wallace

Hi Graham—how goes it? Our Christmas was a classic of peace and harmony. Jake got pissed on Christmas day and threw up on the in-law's new Axminster carpet. Btw, can't remember if I mentioned to you that I've signed up with a top life coach? I've got Pandora Barry—she was trained up by the guy who did Chelsea Clinton, Nelson Mandela and Bill Gates. First session this pm—watch this space!!

Have you read BM's seasonal twaddle? A classic of its kind.

Mart

PS Fancy a drink later?

JANUARY 5

From: Martin Lukes
To: Sylvia Woods

Sylvia—what the hell is this budget meeting in my diary for 3pm?
I've blocked out that hour to talk to my coach on the phone.
E-mail Roger I can't come.

Can you get me two liters of mineral water and a latte?

M

From: Martin Lukes
To: Pandora@CoachworX!

Hi Pandora!

Great to talk to you just now. I was impressed at how quickly
you got my number—I can actually be quite awkward at times—
but when I click with someone then the sky's the limit!

As we discussed, the top-of-the-range Coachworx! Platinum
Service would be most appropriate. As I understand it, you would
be available on a 24/7 basis on the telephone and by e-mail and
face 2 face to coach me through ongoing issues as they surface,
and would bill A&B @ £300 per hour.

I need to get our finance director Roger Wright to greenlight
the expenditure, but I anticipate that as a formality.

All my very bestest
Martin

From: Martin Lukes
To: JennyLukes@PRPalace

Darling—First coaching session was SENSATIONAL! Pandora
clearly thinks I'm destined for the very top.

She's a fascinating woman—used to be a ballet dancer but then had a breakdown and got cancer—was given six months to live, but basically coached herself into remission.

She says I have this amazing power inside myself. I just have to learn how to unlock it!

Only issue was that I ate four bourbon biscuits while talking to her—which was very bad news with the Atkins. Will tell all tonight.

Love you, M

From: Martin Lukes
To: Jenny Lukes

Actually, darling, I think you've got it arse around tit. Coaches aren't "untrained shrinks"—they're experts in lifting performance. Pandora says lots of the people she's coached have increased their income ten times as a result of the program!!! Do you have any IDEA what that would mean for you? You could chuck in your job and become a Lady Who Lunches! And we could have our garden relandscaped with the Chatsworth style water feature that you admired at Chelsea last year—only ours could be bigger.

See you 9 ish—
Love M

PS Big juicy steak would be nice . . . quite fancy a slab of dolcelatte for afters and that lovely chocolate cake of Nigella's that doesn't have any flour in it . . .

JANUARY 6

From: Martin Lukes
To: Roger Wright

Hi Roger
   Yesterday I had the first complimentary coaching session with
Pandora Barry of CoachworX!, and would like to proceed with
the Executive Platinum Coaching Program. I am attaching the fee
schedule.

Bestest, Martin

From: Martin Lukes
To: Roger Wright

Hi Roger
   You ask: why do I need a coach? You're probably thinking that
as I'm highly successful already, I don't need one. But look at it
this way—Tiger Woods has a coach. Wayne Rooney has a coach.
They don't need one, but they have one because they feel more
comfortable with the career success that a coach can provide. Even
Pandora herself has a coach because she is committed to consistently beating her best.
   I realize she charges a premium price, but in this business if
you pay monkeys you get peanuts.

Martin

From: Martin Lukes
To: Pandora@CoachworX!

Hi Pandora
   Some bad news, I'm afraid. I have been informed by Roger
Wright, our autistic finance director, that due to ongoing restric-

tions to our operating budget, he's only prepared to greenlight the Bronze Program, which I understand is coaching by four monthly e-mails.

This is obviously a blow. And it's bloody typical of this place, if you'll excuse my French. Spends a fortune on moronic diversity training programs, and then as soon as you suggest something good, there's no money. Also typical of Roger—who thinks blue sky is what you can see on a sunny say.

Bestest, Martin

From: Pandora@CoachworX!
To: Martin Lukes

Hi Martin!
One of the things I will teach you on this journey is that everything is possible. I'm going to teach you to say goodbye to negative feelings and get back to your childlike optimism. The Executive Bronze Life Coaching Program is going to help you get there!

Now a lesson for you. Where we at CoachworX! differ from other coaches is that they teach you to be the very best you can be. We think you can go further. This program is about being *better* than your very best. I'd like you to meditate on that, and think of a quantifiable target that you think is achievable. We will then assess your progress against this target every month. I think it is fair to say that I have never had a coachee that did not finish the year ahead of their targets!

Pandora

From: Martin Lukes
To: Pandora@Coachworx!

Hi Pandora
What you say makes a lot of sense to me—in the kind of hypercompetitive field I operate in, the best is an entry ticket, if you

like. I've always said to the people who have worked under me: keep pushing the envelope until it falls off the table!

So, this is the goal I am signing up to.

By year end I will achieve performance levels that are 5 percent better than the very best I can be.

Certainly this journey will take me way outside my comfort zone, but I'm ready for that.

Bestest
Martin

From: Pandora@CoachworX!
To: Martin Lukes

Hi Martin!
You are starting to think big—but not BIG enough! I am going to help you make a quantum leap in your self belief. I, your greatest fan, sincerely believe you can beat your best by 50 percent by year end. What is stopping you?

Strive and thrive!
Pandora

From: Martin Lukes
To: Pandora@CoachworX!

Hi Pandora
It's energizing to realize how much you believe in me, but I wonder if your metrics are a bit high. Can we compromise and say that I'm going to aim to be 22.5 percent better than the very best I can be? I think that's probably scalable!

22.5 percent better than my bestest!
Martin

From: Martin Lukes
To: Keith Buxton

Hi Keith

I have just visited the staff canteen and found that there was not a single menu choice consistent with the Atkins diet.

Today there was pigs in a blanket, or mushroom risotto, or chicken pie. All of the above combine carbohydrates and protein.

Many of the more senior members of the staff follow Atkins and we should be encouraging them to use the canteen. It is only by the mingling of staff that knowledge is shared.

All my very bestest
Martin

JANUARY 7

From: Keith Buxton
To: All Staff

Dear all—I am delighted to inform you that Cindy Czarnikow, Global Head of Strategic Marketing, is to join us in London on a two-month assignment. Cindy will be spearheading Project Rebrand, a global drive to reinvigorate the A&B corporate personality. She will be working closely with Barry Malone and the top team in Atlanta, who have been working on plans to rebrand the company for six months. I know you'll give her every support in this exciting initiative.

Additionally, Martin Lukes has been tasked with leading a brainstorming group on how to improve the staff canteen. Any thoughts about delivering uplift to the current service should be addressed to him.

Keith

From: Martin Lukes
To: Graham Wallace

Fucketyfuckingfuck. I didn't opt for a high flying career in order to discuss pigs in a sodding blanket.

What do you know about Cindy Czarnikow?? My sources in Atlanta say she's shagged her way to the top—possibly having a scene with Barry Malone . . .

Drink later?

M

From: Martin Lukes
To: Jenny Lukes

Darling—fraid I won't be back in time to talk to Jake about his behavior tonight. Will send him a motivational e-mail when I get a window.

Love you, M

JANUARY 8

From: Martin Lukes
To: Jake Lukes

Jake, old man. Sorry I didn't touch base with you yesterday. I just wanted to reinforce the ground rules we agreed before Christmas. This term is make or break for you academically but also for your future, and I'd like to share some advice with you. In this life, you get out what you put in—and you are not putting enough in.

Set yourself a stretch goal and then stick to it. I'm not asking you to be your best—think BIG Jake! Push the envelope! Be BET-TER than your best! Agreed?

C u later!
Love Dad

From: Martin Lukes
To: Jake Lukes

J—No I haven't lost the plot, as you so charmingly put it. I was merely passing on to you some advice my coach has given me. I suppose it was asking too much to expect you to buy into the philosophy behind it.

Dad

From: Martin Lukes
To: Sylvia Woods

Hi Sylvia—when you've got a window can you make me a big laminated sign for my wall that says:
BY YEAR END I WILL ACHIEVE PERFORMANCE LEVELS THAT ARE 22.5 PERCENT BETTER THAN THE VERY BEST I CAN BE.
Also plse cancel Christo—I was meant to be having my first session mentoring him, but I'm too busy. See if you can schedule something for next week or the week after.

Ta muchly
Martin

PS I've got about 400 e-mails complaining about the canteen food. Can you reply to all, saying thanks for feedback, I'm looking into it.

From: Martin Lukes
To: Sylvia Woods

WHAT'S ALL THAT BANGING?? I CAN'T HEAR MYSELF
THINK. PLEASE CALL BUILDING SERVICES AND TELL
THEM TO STOP IT.

From: Martin Lukes
To: Graham Wallace

Hi Graham—Cindy's taken the partition walls down and has com-
mandeered twice as much space as my office. I've just sent Sylvia
out to count the ceiling tiles. I've got 49 and she's got 63!! She's
got no desk, just squashy sofas—perfect for her favorite pastime.
Though, without walls she's not going to be able to get up to
much!

    Have you clapped eyes on her yet? Check out the teeth and
smile—she's got the classic American look—a ton of makeup,
perfect grooming, really skinny with a massive arse. Not my scene
at all.

Cheers, Mart

From: Cindy Czarnikow
To: All Staff

Hi everyone!
    *It's phenomenally exciting to be with you here in London
town! I am humbled to be heading up such an exciting project as
Project Rebrand. We have many image consultants working on
this project in Atlanta, but we also want to tap into our own creative genius globally!*
    We are taking the A&B footprint and we are going to re dream

it! Task One is to draw a road map. This is going to be an inclusive bottom-up rebrand, and I want to hear from you! I want each of you to come up with five unbeatable words that you think describe the A&B corporate DNA going forward! These will form the building blocks for the new identity.

Please e-mail me, or come see me! I'm right by Martin Lukes' office on the fifth floor. You'll find it looks a bit different up here. I've taken down the walls, chucked out the desk, and put in two white leather couches! This is going to be a space where we can hit ideas around and make it happen!

I'm smiling at you
Cindy

From: Martin Lukes
To: Cindy Czarnikow

Hi Cindy

Welcome to London Town! I'm sure we are going to enjoy working together. A word of advice, if I might make so bold. While I, more than anyone, believe in open lines of communication, I find that at the end of the day one does need to get some work done. And for that I find that a door which closes and a desk have their uses!

As I'm sure you appreciate, I am presently snowed under with work. However, I will do some blue sky thinking on the five traits as soon as I've got a window.

Martin

From: Martin Lukes
To: Cindy Czarnikow

Graham—Five traits of a certain person: Dumb. Big bum. Phony. Devious. Dangerous.

I'm leering at you!
M

From: Martin Lukes
To: Cindy Czarnikow

Hi Cindy—I think I may have sent you something in error. It was meant for Graham . . . Plse ignore. Martin.

From: Martin Lukes
To: Graham Wallace

Fucketyfucketyfucketyfuckingfuck. Just done something that would be funny if it weren't so awful. Will fill you in over a large one . . . M

From: Pandora@CoachworX!
To: Martin Lukes

Hi Martin!
   I just wanted to check that you are doing what we agreed. Keeping it professional. Staying proactive. Thinking positive.

Strive and thrive!
Pandora

From: Martin Lukes
To: Pandora@CoachworX!

Just seen your message. Yes, I was doing really well until this morning. Unfortunately I now seem to have got into a spot of hot water due to a technical problem. I sent a message to Graham Wallace, who's my opposite number in sales. I can have a good laugh with him—he's no rocket scientist but after a jar or two he's a lot of fun. Basically, I sent him an e-mail which I believe may have been read and misinterpreted by Cindy Czarnikow, a seriously humorless colleague from the US of A.

Martin

From: Martin Lukes
To: Sylvia Woods

Can you check and see if Cindy's on her sofa—I need to pop out for a second, and would rather not bump into her just now.

From: Martin Lukes
To: Jenny Lukes

Hi Jens—Just seen your message re Jake's phone bill. How the bloody hell did the little bugger manage to run up £495 in three months????

M

JANUARY 13

From: Martin Lukes
To: Sylvia Woods

Morning Sylvia! Why does Keith want to see me urgently? Any idea what it's about? Large latte would be nice. M

From: Martin Lukes
To: Graham Wallace

Hi Graham

Just had the biggest bollocking of my life from Keith. Now I've got to grovel to Cindy, and I'm being threatened with a gender awareness course called Sex@Work which sounds rather fun, though have a very nasty feeling it's going to be anything but.

Martin

From: Martin Lukes
To: Cindy Czarnikow

Hi Cindy—

First let me apologize for any embarrassment I might have caused you by my misdirected e-mail, which was far more innocent than it may have seemed!

I realize there are large cultural differences between us people on either side of the pond, and we all need to be cognizant of these 24/7!!

I also wanted to point out that you seem to have got the wrong end of the stick re myself having issues around women. In fact I'm one of their keenest champions, as any of the girls here will tell you. Far from trying to undermine you, I have actively supported your Rebrand work, and it goes without saying, I think you're doing a terrific job.

Would be delighted to give you any advice going forward, on matters marketing or otherwise.

You suggest a breakfast—I can do next Tuesday, though could we make it 8am rather than 6:30?

All my bestest, Martin

JANUARY 16

From: Cindy Czarnikow
To: All Staff

Hi everyone!

Project Rebrand is a total blast! First up, the personality trait that most of you mentioned as being associated with the new brand was joy! Our new corporate personality is going to be like a joyful smile! The smile is the strongest form of human communication we have, and we are going to harness its power!

I am also phenomenally excited to say that we have hired Beyond the Box presently which has a team of 12 rebranding consultants dedicated to our assignment, and have come up with in excess of 1,000 corporate names. They are assisting our search to find a new name that will create brand empathy and position us as a company that Peak Performs—Permanently!

I'm smiling at you,
Cindy

From: Martin Lukes
To: Jake Lukes

Jake—I've just seen the itemized bill for your mobile. Your mother is on a total bender. EXPLANATION PLEASE.

Dad

From: Martin Lukes
To: Graham Wallace

Hi Graham—You are bloody lucky that you've got daughters. Jake seems to have been doing phone sex on his mobile. When we were his age Penthouse was good enough for us.

Drink? I need a large one.

Mart

Text Message to Jenny. Sent 07:43

What do u mean, where am I?? Am having v quick drink w Graham, and then on my way home pronto. Is that a prob? M x

Text message to Jenny. Sent 07:45

How was I supposed to know that? It wasn't in my calendar. M x

From: Martin Lukes
To: Sylvia Woods

WHY WASN'T MY SON'S SCHOOL PLAY IN MY CALEN-DAR??? I was meant to be there this evening seeing him star in Romeo and Juliet, and am now in a lot of trouble with the ladywife. I gave you a list with all his school fixtures on it. What did you do with it?

Martin

JANUARY 18

From: Pandora@CoachworX!
To: Martin Lukes

Hi Martin
One of the most important things I am going to teach you on this course is how to turn your stumbling blocks into stepping stones.

I will show you how to stop thinking about obstacles and problems, and start seeing them as opportunities to improve yourself. Let's start today. Tell me about a stumbling block, and I'll show you how to transform it!

Strive and thrive!
Pandora

From: Martin Lukes
To: Pandora@CoachworX!

Hi Pandora
Frankly, it's occurred to me that one of my biggest stumbling blocks may be my PA Sylvia. She's been with me for two years, but simply doesn't see the point of going the extra mile. Instead she loses things, has cocked up my calendar arrangements and had the nerve to say that I never gave her the dates. I've given her a bit of a pep talk, but no effect.

Martin

From: Pandora@CoachworX!
To: Martin Lukes

Hi Martin

You are a great leader. Great leaders have great followers, and it may be that Sylvia isn't a great follower. But you need to ask yourself: Is she ready to change? Is she ready to get rid of her limiting beliefs? You need to take the time and work through these issues with her.

Strive and thrive!
Pandora

From: Martin Lukes
To: Sylvia Woods

Hi, Sylvia

I've been mulling over what happened last week and I suggest we turn you into a stepping stone. I believe that you need to ask yourself some pretty big questions: Do I want to change? Am I ready to get rid of my limiting beliefs?

Shall we discuss over breakfast tomorrow?

Martin

From: Martin Lukes
To: Sylvia Woods

What did you want to see me about? Can't it wait? I'm writing what may be a career changing memo . . . M

From: Martin Lukes
To: Barry Malone

Hi Barry

Let me introduce myself. I'm Martin Lukes and I'm Marketing Director in London. I just wanted to touch base, first of all to say hi, and also to say how very inspirational I find our new Peak Performance Permanently culture. It has always struck me that what matters is winning—not just now but going forward. You may be interested to know that I am actually going through something similar with my coach on an individual level. The best, I passionately believe, is only an entry ticket!

All my very bestest
Martin

From: Martin Lukes
To: Sylvia Woods

You want to QUIT? But you can't when there's so much on! I'll get you a pay raise.

Martin

From: Martin Lukes
To: Faith Preston

Faith,

Sylvia's threatening to resign, which is obviously highly inconvenient. I think she's at 20k—can you up it to 20.5k effective at once?

Martin

From: Martin Lukes
To: Faith Preston

I see. So what did she say about me? Sylvia and I have had our differences at first but recently we've had an excellent working relationship. And I'm always very appreciative whenever she makes a special effort—which, to be perfectly honest, doesn't happen every day. I've already given her a massive coaching pep talk. Maybe a box of chocs would do the trick.

All my very bestest
Martin

JANUARY 21

From: Martin Lukes
To: Phyllis Lukes

Dear Mum

Many thanks for your message which I got yesterday—in fact I got six of them!! You only need to press the send button once! How are you? Have you been getting out in this cold weather at all?

Boys are both really well. Max was brilliant as Juliet in the school play—looked quite convincing as a girl! Jake beavering away at his GCSEs. Otherwise not much is happening on the family front, Jens is a bit tired and hacked off with her job—but has decided to redo the kitchen (again!). She's fed up with the stainless steel and we're getting something more authentic. But for now it means total chaos chez nous!

Fraid we're not going to be able to get up to see you at the weekend. Hope you don't mind. I've been invited to play golf at Wentworth, which is too good to turn down!

Sorry to hear that the shelves I put up last time have come down. As I said to you at the time, you didn't have the right plaster screws, and that wall isn't really suitable. I'll sort something out next time I come.

Your loving son
Martie

JANUARY 22

From: Cindy Czarnikow
To: All Staff

Hi everyone!

I am phenomenally excited to announce that today we are inviting all of you, the people of our global family, to choose A&B's new name via an on line jamming session, led by Christo Weinberg, our brilliant UK brand ambassador. This is going to be a high-engagement, high-energy, all-employee process. We have chosen a competition because we want to make sure our new name is not just best of breed but uniquely fits our culture.

Does this mean that the work with Beyond the Box has been wasted? Far from it. We have learned a lot from the process, but now feel it is time to move on.

Some co-colleagues have asked me what the winning name will be like. That's up to you!! But I hope it will be global, pro-active, hypercreative and caring.

There are some phenomenally exciting prizes including a workshop in circus skills, and a free feng shui makeover of your master bedroom.

I'm smiling at you
Cindy

From: Martin Lukes
To: Cindy Czarnikow

Cindy—Can I just correct something in your message? Christo is not our brand ambassador. As director of marketing that role falls to me. As you know, from a hierarchical point of view, I don't mind about these things—I only mention it because it is best to avoid confusion where possible. I've been mentoring Christo since the beginning of the year, and would be delighted to help keep him on track with this new assignment!

All my very bestest
Martin

JANUARY 23

From: Christo Weinberg
To: All Staff

Hi!
There are unbelievable riffs coming out of this process! I'm forwarding to you some of the on line jamming session. Really mellow! Keep it coming!

I'd like to kick things off by suggesting "a and b global." It is a win win name. Modern, traditional and global . . . (Keith Buxton, UK chairman)

I'm comfortable with it. It clears my two hurdles—it underlines our commitment to diversity, and is passionately caring. (Faith Preston, Director for People)

Re: a and b global, it takes a long time to say (5 syllables), it involves too many key strokes. (Roger Wright, Finance Director)

How's about "a.b. global"? It's funkier than Keith's suggestion and shorter, authoritative, and has instant impact. (Christo Weinberg, marketing manager)

Thank you Christo! I buy into that! That sure has made my pulse race. (Cindy Czarnikow, Leader of Rebrand)

I feel this debate goes to the very heart of what we are trying to do as a company. Let me suggest an alternative: a-b global. The hyphen has more heart than a full stop. It shows that we can move quickly and that we are unerring in our attention to detail. (Martin Lukes)

The hyphen has no place in the company history. (Roger Wright)

This discussion is ongoing. Please continue to add riffs of your own.

Keep it mellow!
Christo Weinberg

From: Martin Lukes
To: Sylvia Woods

Sylvia—If you are determined to leave us, I can't stop you.

Martin

PS I found that list of school dates at the bottom of my briefcase. All forgiven! Mea culpa!!!

From: Cindy Czarnikow
To: All Staff

Hi!
This is an exciting day! The Rebrand Steering Committee, in conjunction with Barry, have considered two sensational options: a.b. global, and a-b global, and I would like to give you a heads up that we have decided the name best aligned with our PPP

*values is a-b global. When the designers have worked on a logo we
will be ready to start rolling it out!*

I'm smiling at you!
Cindy

From: Martin Lukes
To: Barry Malone

Hi Barry

I'm delighted that you like a-b global—you may not be aware
that I am actually the man behind the hyphen! As my coach says,
sweat the small stuff—the devil's in the detail!

All my very bestest
Martin

JANUARY 29

From: Martin Lukes
To: Rebrand Steering Committee

I've seen the roughs of our new logo from the design team and the
designers have put the name under a square root sign, which,
though innovative, represents a cultural dissonance with our core
values.

I suggest that we build on the success of the hyphen by having
a circumflex over the a and an umlaut over the o, so that the name
would appear: a-b glöbâl. This is an exhilarating option that
would provide a feelgood factor for our stakeholders globally.

All my very bestest
Martin

From: Roger Wright
To: Rebrand Steering Committee

Hi! Although I am not myself a student of modern languages, I understand that the umlaut suggested by Martin Lukes would make the word pronounced "gloerbal," which does not work in any language. The circumflex is now obsolete in France and as a forward-looking company, we are not seeking association with the past.

Roger Wright
Finance Director

From: Cindy Czarnikow
To: Rebrand Steering Committee

I love Martin's solution! I think it's really cool! I think these accents will encourage our global stakeholders to want to love, and live, our brand!

Cindy

From: Martin Lukes
To: Pandora@CoachworX!

Hi Pandora!

Sorry I haven't been in touch. This rebrand project is seriously eating into my time! Things are getting better with Cindy—she is finally buying into my charisma! Christo is getting a bit big for his boots. As his mentor, I should probably try to gently take him down a peg or two...

I've had some enormous wins on Rebrand—and now looks like the final name will have three vital components supplied by yours truly—a hyphen and two accents. Must dash—will e-mail at greater length when (if) things aren't so hectic!!

22.5 percent better than my very bestest
Martin

PS Thanks for sending me audiotape of Why Men Lie and Women Cry, started listening in the car, though Jens objected!

JANUARY 30

From: Barry Malone
To: All Staff

Hi everyone!

A&B is starting the New Year way ahead of the curve. We have chosen a sensational new name for ourselves—a-b glöbâl— we have harnessed our own dreams and sustained and renewed ourselves from within.

Our rebranding process has been a case study in how to make it happen. It demonstrates how a close-knit team—led by Cindy Czarnikow, ably assisted by Christo Weinberg—has brought about a best of breed outcome. It has shown just what can be done within our community when we are all reading from the same road map.

I would like to offer heartfelt thanks to Cindy, who will be coming back to Atlanta a month early in her new role of Chief Morale Evangelist!

Have a phenomenal week,

I love you all
Barry

From: Martin Lukes
To: Graham Wallace

IT'S FUCKING BRILLIANT . . . I DO ALL THE WORK AND DON'T EVEN GET A MENTION . . .

From: Martin Lukes
To: Keith Buxton

Hi Keith

Just seen your message re the progress on Project Eat Well! I have done some interesting preliminary work on this project, though due to my increasing interest in Project Rebrand I have not had the resources to devote to it. However, Eat Well will become top of mind for me going forward.

Bestest, Martin

From: Martin Lukes
To: Pandora@CoachworX!

Hi Pandora!
Here is my first report card for the month of January.
MY WINS!

1. Basically I have taken control of the rebranding platform. I contributed the bulk of the winning name.

2. I have put myself on the map with Barry Malone.

3. I have managed to get rid of a PA who was blocking my energy, leaving the path open to a better partnership going forward.

4. I have seen Cindy off to Atlanta. We had our ups and downs but I think she has a greater respect for myself going forward.

5. There have been some ongoing issues at home with my son Jake. I have made a good start with applying coaching techniques to him, but there is some way to go.

6. Project Eat Well has been a tough learning experience. My strategy is to assume that Keith will eventually forget about

it . . . In future I'll think twice before mentioning the canteen's offering again!

22.5 percent better than my bestest
Martin Lukes

From: Pandora@CoachworX!
To: Martin Lukes

Hi Martin
Congratulations on completing the first month! You've had some great wins.
Before we wrap up for January, can we just take a minute to make a commitment to each other? I find this really helps build trust between us. Can you sign your commitment, date it, and return it to me?

COACHING CONTRACT

I, Pandora will

1. Believe in you totally, and be your #1 Fan!

2. Consistently feed your self belief so that it will grow and flourish.

3. Help you define a plan of action to achieve your goals and desires, and keep you on track to achieve them.

I, Martin Lukes, agree to demonstrate my commitment to myself and to the coaching relationship by

1) Carrying out the challenges and assignments that my coach sets for me—without delay.

2) Choosing to adopt a more enthusiastic, optimistic perception on my life from this moment onwards.

3) Spending a minimum of 35 minutes a day in silent contemplation of the day's goals and learnings.

Signed

Pandora Barry   Martin Lukes

FEBRUARY

My DNA

FEBRUARY 1

From: Pandora@CoachworX!
To: Martin Lukes

Welcome to month two of the CoachworX! Executive Bronze Program.

Last month you thought long and hard about where you are now. And that's not a bad place, is it Martin? This month we are going to dig a little deeper. We are going to find out about your values and your essential DNA. Let's start with an exercise! I want you to imagine that you are a number, a building and an animal. Which animal, building and number would you be? Don't think too long about this, Martin. I want to know what first comes into your head.

Strive and thrive!
Pandora

From: Martin Lukes
To: Pandora@CoachworX!

Fascinating questions, Pandora. I will answer as soon as I get a window.

I'm actually feeling a bit rough this morning—had a couple of drinks last night as today is my first day on the wagon.

Did I tell you I always go on the wagon in February? It's an interesting fact to flag up about myself—as it speaks volumes both for my self-control, and for my desire to stand out from the crowd. I know a lot of people do it in January, but I believe that if you can find your own niche in life, you get noticed. February is also the shortest month!!

22.5 percent better than my very bestest
Martin

From: Martin Lukes
To: Sylvia Woods

Hi—I see Cindy has left all her clobber outside my office. Call building services and tell them to remove it. I'll keep the sofas, but tell them to take away that awful picture of the eagle with DARE TO SOAR written underneath.

Also see if you can get the partition wall of my office shifted out to include some of Cindy's old area. Also, when you've got a mo I'd like a double espresso, a bacon sandwich and some Alka Seltzer.

Martin

PS You don't know anything about modern buildings do you?

PPS. Assume I don't need to remind you that even though you've given in your notice, you are expected to deliver 120 percent effort until the very end!!

From: Barry Malone
To: All Staff

Howdy!

Today is the happiest day of my life—with the exception of that sunny day 31 years ago when I made love for the first time. This morning we committed our company to a migration path that will sustain and renew us going forward. I feel proud and humble to announce this historic, momentous change in our corporate mark from A&B to a-b glöbâl.

If we all strive together, this company will peak perform—permanently.

I love you all
Barry

From: Martin Lukes
To: Graham Wallace

Hi Graham—Terrifying to think of the first shag of BM's life . . . rather more information than one strictly needs.

Feeling a bit rough this am—went for a few jars last night to escape Jens' women's reading group. When I got home they were all going on about this book written by a 15 year old autistic boy about a dog at night—or something. Whatever turns you on . . . I'm reading something brilliant at the moment, How We Won the Ryder Cup—The Caddies' Stories. Have u read it?

M

PS No can do drink tonight. Am on the wagon for the month of Feb.

From: Martin Lukes
To: Sylvia Woods

Sylvia—thanks for the tip, though when I googled Mease van de Rower just now, I couldn't find any matches. He's obviously too modern by half—can you think of any other architects?

Martin

From: Martin Lukes
To: Jenny Lukes

Darling—Sorry about last night. Got the feeling that you and your girlfriends didn't appreciate my comments re autism . . .

I know you're hard up against it today, but could you help me with something? I'm trying to dig down to the bottom of my essence, and I wondered if you can think of any leading edge modern buildings that remind you of yours truly?

Love you
M

From: Martin Lukes
To: Jenny Lukes

It's an exercise of Pandora's. Actually quite interesting . . . It's a long time since I've had to think on such a philosophical level re myself, and I'm struggling a bit.

I've got a lot on today—having to sort out a new personal assistant, and being nagged by Rog for new metrics for this year's operating plan. See you late tonight.

Love Mx

PS It's Sylvia's last day tomorrow. I haven't got time to get anything. Would be eternally grateful if you could find a minute to sort some flowers or something?

FEBRUARY 2

From: Martin Lukes
To: Faith Preston

Hi Faith

Attached is the revised text for the ad for my new PA. I've made some changes and taken out "sense of humor required" as that sounds as if working for myself might be frustrating! Can you get it into crème de la crème section of The Times soonest?

PA to DYNAMIC LEADER Culturally diverse! Ever-changing and Evolving DNA! Ours is a fast-moving innovative culture. Can you keep up with us? In this high-profile Personal Assistant position you will provide a range of support and administrative functions to a dynamic leader on the board of a-b glöbâl (UK). Do you have phenomenal interpersonal, communication and appointment book management skillsets? A can-do headset? Unrivaled problem-solving skills? £££ Highly competitive + perks!! YOUTHFUL ENERGY A MUST!!

From: Martin Lukes
To: Faith Preston

Faith—What do you mean, it's illegal to say youthful?? All I am saying is that I have very high levels of energy. And anyone who is going to be working for me must be able to take the pace.

Best, Martin

FEBRUARY 4

From: Martin Lukes
To: JakeLukes@MillgateSchool

Hi Jake—No, you can't go to Amsterdam with Tarquin at half term. You are meant to be studying. Remember?

If you want to make yourself useful—you could answer a question. Can you think of an animal that reminds you of yours truly?

Love Dad

From: Martin Lukes
To: Pandora@CoachworX!

Hi Pandora

Here you go—the answers to your questions. Sorry it took a while—I'm someone who likes to get things right first time!

1. If I was a number, I would definitely be the number one. Partly because that is the only position I'm comfortable with, but also because the number is straight and upright and has a kind of understated simplicity.

2. re buildings—I've being thinking outside the square on this and can see some interesting parallels between myself and the more innovative modern structures. My first thought was the World Trade Center's twin towers. Although they were very tall (which I'm not!!) and there were two of them, and, obviously, they were blown up by Osama Bin Laden (which I haven't been—as yet!!) there are some revealing areas of overlap. They were very competitive. They wanted to be the tallest in the world. They wanted to be noticed and stand out from the crowd. Again, there was this understated simplicity about them, that is very much my style too.

   But after some research I found a building that captures

my essence exactly. It is Farnsworth House, built by one of my favorite architects, Mies Van der Rohe. At the time it was controversial, and was way ahead of the curve. It wasn't frightened to offend. Simple yet revolutionary. It's also stood the test of time, and is still as relevant as when it was built!

3. As for animals—I've been doing some 360 degree brainstorming on this. My son Jake suggested some parasite that gets into your bowel, and makes you flatulent!!! Jake's got a great sense of humor—a brilliant mind, he just has issues with harnessing his natural talent to his schoolwork!

   Seriously, though, if I was an animal I'd be a sheepdog. They are intelligent and are catalytic, they are natural leaders and they know how to drive a team to achieve peak performance.

Hope that helps

22.5 percent better than my very bestest
Martin

FEBRUARY 6

From: Keith Buxton
To: All Staff

Hallo everyone

Many of you will have seen hostile articles in the media over the weekend, accusing us of having squandered $38m of shareholders' money and wasting valuable senior management time on our new corporate name, a-b glöbâl. As you know, this is far from the truth—the global figure on our rebranding bill is coming in south of $20m and the management time expended on the project has enabled us to think deeply and strategically about the nature of the business we are in.

The key learning we should take out from this is to examine the interface between us and the press. Until now most of our PR has been handled out of Atlanta. I believe we must now strengthen our capability in London.

Bestest, Keith

From: Martin Lukes
To: Jenny Lukes

Sorry, darling—now isn't the best time to discuss this. I'm totally snowed under on something mission critical.

But basically—yes—I do think you should tell pr palace to stuff their stupid job. You're never going to be able to work with Rowena as a boss. She's got issues with you because you are smarter than her—and a lot sexier. There's no problem moneywise if you do decide to quit—we could save on the cleaner and the au pair?

Love, M xxx

From: Martin Lukes
To: Jenny Lukes

No, of course I don't have an issue with you as a career woman. I'm just saying that if you are not comfortable with where you are—change it! As Pandora would say, the only person who can re-dream your life is you! Anyway, let's discuss later.

M xx

From: Pandora@CoachworX!
To: Martin Lukes

Hi Martin
How are you? The last exercise you did for me obviously got your creative juices flowing! Now I'd like you to try something a bit harder. I want you to tell me about the four brilliant characteristics that you think define yourself—and the four brilliant characteristics others would say defined you.

Strive and thrive!
Pandora

From: Martin Lukes
To: Pandora@CoachworX!

Hi Pandora
Interestingly, I don't think there's a gap between others' perception of myself and my own perception. I've always been realistic about myself—maybe it's in my DNA, or maybe it's because my family keep me down to earth!

1. The most noticeable thing about yours truly is creativity. This is a very important part of myself, and has driven my success in the marketing space.

2. Communication skills. My style is very easy, very natural, very empowering.

3. I see myself as a hub. I am a born networker, and like nothing more than getting people together.

4. Emotional intelligence. As I said earlier, I've got a very high EQ—self-knowledge and empathy are both big things for me.

22.5 percent better than my bestest
Martin

From: Pandora@CoachworX!
To: Martin Lukes

That's great Martin! Well done! Now what I want you to do is to Live your DNA! Each time you have had a major win using your key skills, send me an e-mail, telling me which skill you are using and rank it with 1 to 4 stars. That way we can monitor your progress!

Strive and thrive!
Pandora

FEBRUARY 10

From: Martin Lukes
To: Keith Buxton

Hi Keith
 I've been doing a little blue sky thinking, and have come up with a phenomenal idea about how we can win back hearts and minds, and prove that we care about the communities we serve. We have a supply of sweatshirts, boxer shorts etc with the old A&B logo, which I suggest we give away to charity. If the public can see us handing out goods free to the homeless it could go a long way to reversing the brand damage suffered by the name change.

All my very bestest
Martin

From: Martin Lukes
To: Sylvia Woods

Hi Sylvia—One last task! Can you go through Yellow Pages and find a list of all the homeless charities in London.
 Really sorry we're not going to have time for a drink before

you depart for pastures new. But I wish you all the best of British. We'll all miss you here, and hope things really work out well for you at Beyond the Box. You and I have been an unbeatable team, and I want to thank you for your unstinting passion and contribution. Keep in touch and all the best.

Cheers, Martin

PS Can you leave details for your unlucky successor sharing your ancient wisdom on how to get along with yours truly?

FEBRUARY 11

From: Martin Lukes
To: Jenny Lukes

Darling—
Just had a brain wave. Here's evidence of how much I support your career: why not come back here? Following the issues around our media coverage, we've decided to beef up the PR department. We're in the market for two or three extra bods, some of whom will be at a fairly junior level. There's bound to be something part-time. As Pandora says: Dream it! Plan it! Do it!

Love M

PS May be a bit late tonight—Can you get me something nice for supper—chicken korma with pilau rice would go down nicely. M x

From: Martin Lukes
To: Jenny Lukes

Glad you like the idea. And I know that's not Atkins, but I can't do that and the booze. In any case booze is so fattening, that the pounds will fall away. I'd also like some naan bread and an aloo gobi.

Love you, M xx

From: Martin Lukes
To: Keith Buxton

Hi Keith—
My God, the ladywife moves quickly! I only mentioned the job to her half an hour ago! Yes, she used to work here, long before your time . . . in fact we met here—I thought you knew that. For the last few years she's been working two days a week for a small company called PR Palace but wants to quit as she doesn't get on with her boss. Something relatively unstressful and part-time may suit her. Obviously I think she's a great girl, but then I'm partial!

All my very bestest
Martin

From: Martin Lukes
To: JennyLukes@PRPalace

Jens—Frankly I was a bit taken aback to get a message from Keith saying you had contacted him already. If we're to work together, we can't have you dashing off e-mails to my boss without me being in the loop . . . Will be very late as I'm interviewing new PAs.

M

FEBRUARY 12

From: Martin Lukes
To: Faith Preston

Hi Faith—Feedback on the PA interviews: yesterday I met Keri Tartt and Preetha Patel. Both girls were aligned with our values though I have a preference for Keri who has a can-do headset and seems very results-driven. I felt Preetha, though clearly stronger on paper, didn't have the requisite passion quotient. Can we get Keri to start asap? I've attached her CV for your files.

Martin

Keri Tartt CV

Age: 29
An energetic, fun-loving PA with loads of get up and go!!!
Place of Birth: Wellington, New Zealand
Education: Wellington Girls High School
Trained: Physiotherapist Module 1

WORK
PA to Marketing Director *Esquire* Magazine
Ticket sales Glastonbury
Hobbies: Windsurfing, Crystals, Life saving, Holistic healing, Travel

From: Martin Lukes
To: Graham Wallace

Graham—eat your heart out . . . I'm getting a gorgeous new PA. She looks a bit like Goldie Hawn, trained as a physio, tall, slim . . . very tasty. Mart

FEBRUARY 16

From: Martin Lukes
To: Jenny Lukes

Darling—

I've been doing some detective work re your schedule for this pm. You'll be seen first by Lucinda Mogg-Watson, our PR girl.

She's sweet, in a posh sort of way. She's no rocket scientist—I think you'll like her. Then you're being interviewed by Faith Preston, Director for People. She's hell on wheels—aggressive, humorless, seriously pc—and has me down as some sexist, racist bastard. Let me know how you get on. Fingers crossed!

Love you, M xx

From: Martin Lukes
To: Graham Wallace

Graham—No yr eyes didn't deceive you. It was Jenny—being interviewed to work for Lucinda in PR. If she gets the job, she'll only be part-time, so I doubt that our paths will cross much. In fact, it might make things better between us. At least she'll be able to see for herself how hard we all work and how much pressure we're under.

Cheers, Martin

PS I've done two weeks without a drink!! Am feeling pretty good—or would be if I could get rid of this flu.

From: Martin Lukes
To: Lucinda Mogg-Watson

Hi, Lucinda

How are you getting along fixing up media interest for our drop of obsolete A&B boxer shorts and sweatshirts to homeless charities? I personally will be taking a parcel to Arlington House in Camden Town next arriving 3pm.

I gather you are interviewing my wife this pm. She's quite something—though I would say that, wouldn't I?

Martin

From: Martin Lukes
To: Jenny Lukes

Darling—glad it went so well—extraordinary that Keith wanted to see you, as he normally only interviews people of department head level and above. Did he mention me? I should have warned you about him in advance. He's intensely ambitious and political. Your best mate one minute then stabbing you in the back the next. Btw, you're also way off beam on Faith. She's neither intelligent nor well-meaning.

M xxx

From: Martin Lukes
To: Graham Wallace

Graham, am having second thoughts about the virtues of working alongside the ladywife. She informs me that Faith is a fine, intelligent woman. She also had an hour-long session with Keith! He never gives me more than 10 minutes. I sometimes think that if we were women we wouldn't have to work our arses off.

Martin

FEBRUARY 17

From: Keith Buxton
To: All Staff

Hallo everyone!
   I am delighted to announce that Jenny Withers has been ap-
pointed to our rapidly growing External Relations team. Jenny
joins us from PR Palace where she has built up an unrivaled track
record in delivering exceptional pr solutions. She will be reporting
to Lucinda Mogg-Watson, and will be helping on all aspects of
our press strategy.

Bestest, Keith

From: Martin Lukes
To: Jenny Lukes

Jenny—I've just seen Keith's message—and so far so good! You're
honored that he's making such a big deal of this. But why are you
using your maiden name? Before you say anything, I don't have a
problem with it—you can call yourself whatever you like. But I
don't understand the rationale. M

From: Martin Lukes
To: Jenny Lukes

That's ridiculous!! Why wouldn't people take you seriously as my
wife? Is being married to me so bad?

From: Martin Lukes
To: Keith Buxton

Hi Keith

Thanks for your message! Dinner would be great!! What sort of time?

Bestest, Martin

From: Martin Lukes
To: Jenny Lukes

Darling—We've been invited to dinner with Keith and his wife on Monday—just the four of us at his place!! He said it'd be v informal, v low key. We're honored!

Love you, Mxx

FEBRUARY 18

From: Martin Lukes
To: Lucinda Mogg-Watson

Hi Luce

Wow! The six o'clock news and all the broadsheets?? I thought they weren't supposed to be interested in reporting good news?!

I've decided the occasion calls for a speech—which I'll write tonight and send you for the press pack. I think it should also include a copy of my CV. Do we need a mug shot, or will the papers all be sending their own photographers? Might be worth getting a pic done just in case. Can you contact a good portrait photographer?

Martin

From: Martin Lukes
To: Jenny Lukes

Lucinda says there's massive media interest in Project Boxer Shorts!

What do you think I should wear? I think suits work best on TV, but might not strike the right note with the drunks and nutters at the shelter. I thought my new Paul Smith polo shirt—the pink one with Serenity written on it would be just right. Casual, informal but with a hint of difference? What do you think?

M xx

FEBRUARY 19

From: Martin Lukes
To: Pandora@CoachworX!

Hi Pandora

I've had two huge wins since I last e-mailed.

Jens and myself have been invited to dinner with Keith. This reflects partly his excitement at Project Boxer Shorts. It may also be because his radar has picked up on the New High Achieving Me.

Even more exciting is the head of steam behind Project Boxer Shorts. Half the nation's press is going to be there—which makes it the perfect opportunity to position myself as a national thought leader. I'm attaching my speech—wld be v grateful for feedback. I made it humorous but with a serious message—Hope you like it.

```
          SPEECH TO HOMELESS
        (ML mounts the podium)


Ladies and Gentlemen of the media, homeless persons,
social workers,
```

First let me introduce myself—I'm Martin Lukes and, for my sins, I'm Marketing Director of a-b glöbâl uk. I've been fortunate enough to be one of the team working on the rebranding project that has seen our famous brand A & B transitioned into a-b glöbâl.

In your press packs you will find details of the new logo, a story about the journey that took us there and a brief bio of myself.

But while the glamour of our rebranding gets the headlines, underneath we are tirelessly thinking: what can we give back? Here at a-b glöbâl, this duty is always front of mind. So what we are doing today is giving back to you, the homeless. We are providing high-quality merchandise, free of charge, with no strings attached.

I know you sometimes read biased reports in the press (and I shouldn't say this with so many journos here!) about fat cats and big companies riding roughshod over the lives of decent ordinary people. But at a-b glöbâl we are here for all members of the community that we serve.

Today isn't just about merchandising. Remember the saying "Give a man a fish and you feed him for a day. Teach him to fish and you feed him for life?" Well, today I'll be sharing knowledge—not on how to fish!!!— but on how to rebrand yourselves. I will be challeng- ing your mind-sets to rethink the homeless brand, if you will. There is a lot of negative baggage around the term "homeless," which I hope I will help you leave behind. There is a need for a root and branch rebrand, and I hope today will be a first step on that exciting journey.

Thank you for coming today, and I hope you'll stay

behind to ask me further questions over tea and biscuits.

[applause—(I hope!). ML gets down off the podium]

22.5 percent better than my bestest
Martin

FEBRUARY 24

From: Martin Lukes
To: Keith Buxton

Good morning Keith! Many thanks for a great dinner last night.
You really are the chef!

Much enjoyed meeting your ladywife . . . didn't realize what a
successful woman she is in her own right. Had a very interesting
intellectual discussion with her, please pass on thanks.

All my very bestest
Martin

PS Hope we didn't outstay our welcome!

From: Martin Lukes
To: Graham Wallace

Graham—Did I tell you that I supped with the boss last night? It
was a great evening . . . only slight blight was that Keith was all
over Jens—I wonder if he fancies her??—they talked about books
half the night. I really liked Mrs. B—she's something big at Channel Five. I said how much I liked topless darts—obviously in an
ironic sort of way—I think she found me a breath of fresh air after
all the PC idiots she has to put up with.

Cheers, Mart

From: Martin Lukes
To: Jenny Lukes

Darling—just had a nice message back from Keith. You were quite wrong to say that I disgraced myself for being pissed. He said they enjoyed it, and he's now thinking of starting a men's book club!

We should have them back soon. Might be an idea to invite someone from the "arts world" with them. Did you mention meeting Ian McEwan's agent's wife at a school thing of Max's?

Love you, M xx

From: Martin Lukes
To: Jenny Lukes

Oh, she's his agent in her own right? Good for her!! All the more reason to ask her. What does the husband do?

FEBRUARY 25

From: Martin Lukes
To: Keri Tartt

Hi Keri—welcome to a-b glöbâl! I hope Sylvia has left you a list of tasks . . . fraid I'm not going to have a window to show you the ropes.

You'll have to excuse us today because everything is going to be totally crazy—though if I'm frank, every day in marketing is crazy, as we like to push ourselves to the limit and beyond. Tomorrow afternoon I'm doing a major media event—might be a good learning experience for you if you'd like to come along.

M.

PS Have you changed your hairstyle? Very fetching, if I might make so bold.

From: Lucinda Mogg-Watson
To: All Staff

Calling all couch potatoes!!!! Program your VCRs for tomorrow night! Our own Martin Lukes will be on the Six O'clock News giving away our old A&B boxers and tops to poor people!

Luce (Mogg-Watson)

From: Martin Lukes
To: Jenny Lukes

Darling—Thanks for the pearls of wisdom, but frankly you're getting a bit ahead of yourself. You haven't even started the job yet, and you're not up to speed on the background, so I really wish you'd stand back, and leave Project Boxer Shorts to myself and Lucinda.

In any case, your concerns are totally off piste—we've sold the story to the media as a colorful example of how big business really cares at the grassroots level—and they've bought into that. In fact they can't get enough of it. Don't forget to watch—I've sent Jake a text too. He'd probably be quite pleased in front of his mates to see the old man on the box.

M x

From: Martin Lukes
To: Graham Wallace

The ladywife is really getting on my tits. She's already started telling me how to do my job!! I bet Lynne doesn't give you a hard time about your sales figures . . . (though the way they are going, maybe she should!!)

M

From: Martin Lukes
To: Phyllis Lukes

Dearest Mum

Don't forget to watch the six o' clock news tonight. I am going to be on—helping the homeless improve their lives. I know your views about the homeless, mum, and up to a point I totally agree. A lot of them are just wasters and spongers—but you need to understand that the media doesn't see them like that, and we need to reflect public opinion.

Boys both doing fine. Did I tell you Jens has finally quit her job and is going to work here? I know you don't approve of her working, but at the end of the day it's her call. In any case it's going to be very part-time. I swung it for her—it was really getting to me how miserable she was.

Will try to get down at the weekend. Jake's going to be back for half term, and I've been banned by Jens from playing golf. Not sure I'll be able to fix the tap, but I'll have a go, if you've got the right tools.

Yr loving son
Martin

FEBRUARY 26

From: Martin Lukes
To: Keri Tartt

Hi Keri. Trust all set for later today. Can u call a cab for 3:30? M

From: Martin Lukes
To: Jenny Lukes

I'm off now—should be back home by 6, in time to see myself on the news! Wish me luck

Love you M xx

Text message to Jenny. Sent 16:17

ohgodgodgodgod. . . . run the bath. pour me a large whiskey . . . i'm on my way home.

FEBRUARY 27

From: Keith Buxton
To: All Staff

Hallo everyone! Last night, as many of you will be aware, a-b was the victim of a concerted attempt to damage our reputation as a global company that cares passionately for the local community. Martin Lukes was ejected from a hostel and set upon by the homeless and by antiglobalization protesters. One hostel resident put a pair of A&B boxer shorts on his head and jostled him in front of the camera. Another set fire to a bundle of our A&B sweatshirts. These are attacks that we cannot tolerate.

The key learning that I, personally, take out of this is that our mission has not been universally understood by the public at large. We must think clearly about our target audience and how best to connect with them emotionally.

Bestest, Keith

From: Martin Lukes
To: Pandora@CoachworX!

Hi Pandora—Basically, long story short, it was the most humiliating day of my life. When I got there, no one seemed to know I was coming. Eventually this news reporter turned up—looked really young and cute, but then started asking me all these really cynical and ignorant questions. I feel I gave some pretty good answers, but they were all cut out.

She insisted on filming me with this homeless woman—probably a crack addict, with multiple body piercings, who picked up our fleecy sweatshirt and said "I'm not wearin that, innit?" I told her that she was being ungrateful, and then a riot started.

And the tragedy was that I didn't get the chance to give the rebranding seminar. Keith isn't being at all supportive—he's going through the motions but when I saw him just now he was pretty standoffish.

22.5 percent worse than my bestest (!)
Martin

From: Pandora@CoachworX!
To: Martin Lukes

Hi Martin
Can I say one thing to you? NO FAILURE ONLY FEED-BACK. Repeat this mantra. It's really important. Failure has no place in your life. There is no such thing as failure. Only feedback.

Yesterday was a positive for you. There were some big key learnings there. What do you think they were, Martin?

Strive and thrive!
Pandora

From: Martin Lukes
To: Pandora@CoachworX!

Hi Pandora—Frankly it's hard to feel positive when drug addicts are pelting you with rotten eggs. But you're right that this wasn't a failure of mine, and you're right about the key learnings. I can think of at least four.

1. The homeless don't give a shit about anything apart from themselves.

2. Frankly it is no surprise to me at all that they are homeless. There wasn't a can-do headset between them.

3. I also feel really angry about having been forced to this by Lucinda and Keith. It was always obvious to me that there were going to be serious risks associated with this project, but they were insistent on getting the publicity at all costs.

4. Giving back isn't all it's cracked up to be.

22.5 percent better than my best
Martin

3

MARCH

My Dream

MARCH 1

From: Pandora@CoachworX!
To: Martin Lukes

Hi Martin!

Give yourself a big pat on the back for reaching month three! This is one of the most vital months of the whole Executive Bronze Program. You have your DNA under your belt and now its time to dream!

You may not believe this, Martin, but many people do not actually know what their dream is! They need a little help to reach out and touch it.

The first exercise should be great fun. I want you to get a big piece of paper. Place it landscape and then get some Magic Markers. I want you to draw your dream. You need to let your conscious mind go blank and let your subconscious mind get to work!

Strive and thrive!
Pandora

From: Martin Lukes
To: Keri Tartt

Hi Keri

How are you this morning? Great outfit! I need a big bag of Magic Markers—I'd like some thin ones and some of those big chunky highlighters and some A3 paper.

Tx Martin

From: Jenny Withers
To: All Staff

Hi

I should introduce myself—I'm Jenny Withers, and this is my first week working in external relations with Lucinda Mogg-Watson.

Over the coming weeks I shall be looking at ways of promoting our ethically and socially responsible strategies.

Already this morning people have told me about ways in which they are generously giving their time to worthwhile causes. What I want to do is to bring all this good stuff together, and show the outside world what we are doing.

After the events of last month, there is a public perception that we are not entirely committed to the Coporate Social Responsibility agenda. We need to prove that we are. I shall be holding a Lunch and Learn session on Friday. Please bring your sandwiches and your ideas!

Jenny Withers

From: Martin Lukes
To: Jenny Withers

Darling—

Brilliant memo, well done! A couple of tiny points. First, not sure you've got the tone and the vocab quite right. You sound a bit—how should I put it?—downbeat.

I'm also concerned that you misunderstood what I was going on about last night. When I said that in order to get noticed in this place you have to be very visible, I didn't mean that you start cluttering up people's inboxes on Day One. There's a lot of resistance here to creating company spam. I have a rule which I find quite helpful: before I send out an e-mail, I always think: does this pass the need-to-know test? And then, and only then, do I press send.

Obviously it's too late to take this morning's missive back. But worry not, everyone will be very forgiving on your first day!

M xx

PS Could do lunch later if you like?

From: Keith Buxton
To: All Staff

Hallo everyone

I would like to congratulate Jenny on a best of breed memo. It is always a pleasure when individuals who have just joined the company buy into our values from Day One!

Being seen as a socially responsible company is top of our agenda going forward.

All the best,
Keith

From: Martin Lukes
To: Graham Wallace

Hi Graham

Just called a chum in the headhunting community who says Keith's in line for the number one job at Boots!! Which would be win-win—he'd stop ogling my ladywife . . . and his job'd be up for grabs. You heard anything?

Mart

From: Martin Lukes
To: Keri Tartt

Hi Keri

Can you bring me some more A3 paper? Drawing my dream is actually much more challenging than you'd think. The trouble is that when your mind is as full as mine, it's very hard to empty it. Have you got any tips of what I could draw?

Martin

From: Martin Lukes
To: Keri Tartt

Wow! Thanks for that, but I'll stick with the basics!!!

Can you keep everyone out of my office for the next half an hour? If my ladywife comes round, tell her to wait. I'm having lunch with her later . . . maybe you'd like to join us?? The two of you will need to bond. I should warn you she likes to keep a close eye on my calendar. There were issues with Sylvia over communication . . . dates went missing, yours truly in deep trouble. Sure that won't happen with you!

Martin

From: Martin Lukes
To: Pandora@CoachworX!

Hi Pandora
    Just sent you the picture. I did spend a tiny bit more than five minutes on it, but I think in the end I got pretty close to something. Though I'm no Picasso, I'm actually quite pleased with the end result!

22.5 percent better than my bestest
Martin

From: Martin Lukes
To: Jenny Withers

Darling—How's your first day been? Shall we leave together? I could go home early for once—see you downstairs 6ish.
    What did you think of Keri? She is a bit flaky, but willing. She lost me at lunchtime when she was going on about chakra gemstone kits. But she's much nicer to work with than Sylvia. And, no, I don't fancy her.

Love you Mxx

MARCH 3

From: Pandora@CoachworX!
To: Martin Lukes

Hi Martin
    Thank you for sharing your dream with me. It is always fascinating watching coachees' dreams take shape, and yours is a uniquely special one. Your road symbolizes your journey, the castle is your home life—those walls are very thick and solid, which is a

great sign! However, this may also be a reflection of you as a defensive adult, with a vulnerable child within.

The white circle in the corner is your true North. This is your guiding star. It shows that whatever you do, you want it to be for a bigger purpose. Yes you want success—but you want it because it helps you achieve immortality.

Now Martin, I want you to break your dream down into achievable targets. Tell me your specific dreams. And I will help you make them come true.

Strive and thrive!
Pandora

MARCH 5

From: Barry Malone
To: All Staff

Howdy

Everywhere I go in this company I get fired up by how you are living by our five values, Purpose, Practice, Potency, Performance, and People.

Of these the most important is People. And that is why I am today announcing a new board level position, Chief Talent Officer. The CTO will focus in on our people globally and ensure we have the very best talent mix we can. I am delighted to tell you that this position will be filled by Keith Buxton who is currently chairman of a-b glöbâl UK. Keith has an unrivaled track record in managing talent. He will add unique leadership and powerful insight to all our talent nurturing initiatives going forward.

I love you all
Barry

From: Martin Lukes
To: Graham Wallace

Talent officer? Is that glorified HR or what? Sounds v flakey to me.
So are you going to apply for Keith's job??

From: Martin Lukes
To: Keith Buxton

Hi Keith

Congratulations! Really well deserved promotion. I've always passionately believed that the talent space is very underdeveloped. Get the talent pool right and everything else flows from that. When are you off?

Any news yet on a successor? I've got some views on this. Could we have some face time soonest?

All my very bestest
Martin

MARCH 8

From: Martin Lukes
To: Pandora@CoachworX!

Hi Pandora—

Sorry it's taken me a while to get back—I've just learned that Keith is going to Atlanta, so the top UK job is up for grabs.

So that's my number one dream—to be chairman of a-b glöbâl (UK). Timing is perfect for me—this time I'm going to come out on top.

Btw You were spot on re my artwork. The only thing I'd say is that when I drew the white circle I meant it to be a golf ball, but you're right, it works just as well as a guiding star!!

22.5 percent better than my very bestest
Martin

From: Pandora@CoachworX!
To: Martin Lukes

Hi Martin
I love your dream! I love your confidence! What you need is a plan to ensure you succeed. Remember you can have whatever you want. You need to want it enough, and you need to follow the GROW! model.
This is a four step process. Goals, Reality, Options and Will.
Under each of these titles I want you to tell me how you are going to get this job!

Strive and thrive!
Pandora

PS Can you check with your payments department if there is a problem. In the contract it specifies that payments must be made AT THE BEGINNING of the month.

From: Martin Lukes
To: Pandora@CoachworX!

Hi Pandora
Here is the outline of my GROW model. Just a first draft at this stage.
GOAL
To be appointed chairman of a-b glöbâl UK
REALITY
There are six possible internal candidates—Roger, Faith, Graham, Cindy, Christo and myself. Rog is too much of a numbers

man, Faith is totally ignorant of everything outside HR, but has got one massive thing going for her—she's a woman. Cindy is a possibility, though if she's having a scene with Barry (which is what my Atlanta sources tell me) he won't want her 4000 miles away. Graham doesn't have the skillsets. Christo's a total outsider, though very much flavor of the month. He's my mentee, so this would be worst case for me.

Which leaves myself, with well aligned skillsets, comprising the obvious choice!

OPTIONS

I need to lobby relentlessly with Keith and Barry. Although Keith won't be making the choice, Barry will certainly listen to what he says.

WILL

I have the will to do this. I will turn all stumbling blocks into stepping stones. I believe in myself, and I believe this job will be mine!

22.5 percent better than my bestest
Martin

MARCH 9

From: Faith Preston
To: All team leaders

Hi!

A reminder that all Work and Development Plans MUST be signed off by the end of the day today and returned to myself. These documents are the most important score card of all co-colleagues' performance.

Faith

From: Martin Lukes
To: Keith Buxton

Keith—That's great! What can I say? I'd be delighted to stand in for you! It's ages since I was last at St. Andrews.

On a different matter, could we share some face time soonest? I'd like to talk through my ideas for a-b glôbâl (UK) going forward. Have you got a window to discuss today or tomorrow?

Best, Martin

From: Martin Lukes
To: Jenny Withers

Darling—Keith has just asked me to take his place at the St. Andrews Old Course this weekend!! It's a charity do—it's going to be brilliant networking!

The fact he's picked me to replace him on the golf thing strongly suggests that I'm his chosen successor!! Graham and Roger will be FURIOUS!!! Sorry about leaving you in the lurch with Max.

Love you M xx

From: Martin Lukes
To: Max Lukes

Max old man

Sorry I'm afraid I'm not going to be able to take you to Stamford Bridge for your birthday on Sat. But worry not, Svetlana will go instead. Will make it up to you next weekend. Promise.

Dad xx

From: Keith Buxton
To: All Staff

Hallo everyone!

Many thanks to all of you who have offered me congratulations on my promotion. I am, of course, extremely excited about this opportunity.

Next week our CEO, Barry Malone, will be visiting us from Atlanta. The time frame is very tight. Barry has requested that this day be highly informal. He is here to listen and to learn. Attached is his schedule.

```
7:30 BSM arrives Wharfside. Briefing by KB
8:00 BSM and CC have working breakfast with depart-
     ment heads
9:00 Walkabout with KB and JW
10:00 Informal briefing by BSM "5Ps to achieve PPP."
12:00 Action meal attended by cross section of staff
2:00 CC to all staff on "Pushing the Morale Envelope
     in Europe"
4:30 BSM debriefed by KB
```

I know I can count on all of you to make the day a great success.

Keith

From: Martin Lukes
To: Jenny Withers

Jens—How come you get to show him around??

Mx

From: Martin Lukes
To: Barry Malone

Hi Barry

Delighted to hear that you are crossing the pond next week. I wondered if I could beg a few minutes of your time to tell you about some blue sky thinking I've been doing re the role of a-b glöbâl UK. As marketing director I am uniquely well placed to assess our strengths and weaknesses as a corporate brand. I believe that we are currently at an inflexion point—the challenge is to harness our talent to create a proactive headset that will take us from good to great.

I would be delighted to meet with you when you are in London to discuss these ideas.

All my very bestest
Martin

From: Martin Lukes
To: Phyllis Lukes

Dear Mum

Sorry I couldn't get down to see you at the weekend. Happy Birthday for next Tuesday. Great news about the knee op . . . you'll be a new woman once it's done!

I've got some very good news too. You know I've been a bit cheesed off at work recently? Well I'm in line for a big job, running the whole outfit in the UK. That means 1,000 people, and your loving son would be in charge of all of them!

I know you think all this coaching stuff is just mumbo jumbo, and obviously I was pretty skeptical at first, but I actually think Pandora's doing me a lot of good.

Boys are both fine. Max is on the school debating team, and is leading a debate on immigration. "This house believes immigration has undermined the nature of Britishness." You'd be right behind him on that!

Don't go on fussing about the shelves, mum. I'll do them next time, but for now can't you get the home help to pile all the stuff into the cupboard, and I'll sort next time I come?

Lots and lots of love
Martin

MARCH 10

From: Martin Lukes
To: Jenny Withers

Darling—Jake's housemaster just left a message saying that Jake and Tarquin have been drinking Bacardi Breezers on the school premises, and they are both suspended. Next time either of them steps one foot out of line, they get expelled. Can you sort it? He needs picking up this pm. M x

From: Martin Lukes
To: Jenny Withers

Jens—No I can't ring Tarquin's mother. I don't have her number, and I'm preparing one of the most important presentations of my life, and I still haven't got these sodding WDPs done for Faith.
     I know you've got your Lunch and Learn today, but can't Lucinda do it instead?
     The little bugger has picked the worst possible time to do this.

M

From: Martin Lukes
To: Christo Weinberg

Christo—Attached is your latest Work Devleopment Plan. Let me know if you are in agreement, and I'll sign off on it. Martin

Name: Christo Weinberg
Position: Assistant Brand Evangelist

Christo has achieved some creative successes over the past six months; he develops own capabilities, and improves business processes. However, there are issues around his ability to work effectively with others. He needs to demonstrate integrity and high personal standards, and needs to support the development of others' creativity. He shows enthusiasm in giving time to non-work activities. While this is to be encouraged, it is a pity if it is allowed to interfere with his work. I recommend he attends a refresher course in Teamskills and three-day residential seminar on How to Work Effectively with Others. His progress will be reviewed at the next WDP in six months' time.

Signed by
Countersigned by

From: Martin Lukes
To: Christo Weinberg

Hi Christo

I'm sorry that you are not comfortable with the WDP. This is actually a highly balanced assessment, with positives and negatives.

As we discussed in our mentoring session, you need to get better at receiving feedback. It is only by recognizing weaknesses and building self knowledge that one shifts performance onto the next level.

Martin

From: Martin Lukes
To: Jenny Withers

OK—I'll deal with the headmaster, but frankly, Jens, I think we need to talk about this. Basically, I don't feel you're being at all supportive of me. I sometimes get the idea that you don't care if I become the next UK chairman or not. I also think you're getting a bit over-intense about your job. At the end of the day, no one ever said on their deathbed: I wish I had spent more time in the office!

Martin

From: Martin Lukes
To: Headmaster@MillgateSchool

Dear Mr. Pitman

Thank you for your message. I'm very sorry to learn about the incident this afternoon, concerning my son, Jake. I would like to take this opportunity to personally thank yourself and the school for taking swift action.

You ask if there is anything wrong at home that might explain the lad's behavior. As you are probably aware, we are a very tight-knit, supportive family, with traditional values. The only change since last term is that Jake's mother has recently had a career change that has resulted in her being more preoccupied than before.

Rest assured that she and myself will talk to Jake when he gets home. I am certain that this is a one-time thing and will ensure that this unfortunate type of occurance does not happen again.

Jake, as you know, is an exceedingly talented lad who needs the right sort of motivational program in order to unleash his true potential, which I am confident is very substantial.

Yours very sincerely
Martin Lukes

From: Martin Lukes
To: Jake Lukes

Jake—
   I have just had to grovel to your headmaster on yr behalf which is NOT an experience I enjoy. You are a complete idiot, and are now grounded. You have no allowance, no telephone. You are going to spend the rest of the week at home, working. Svetlana will pick you up at about 4ish.

Dad

From: Martin Lukes
To: Barry Malone

Barry—That's great! A 6am power hour briefing is good for me, too. I've always been an early riser! Looking forward to meeting with you.

Martin

MARCH 15

From: Martin Lukes
To: Graham Wallace

Graham—
   Great weekend at St. Andrews. The course was in fantastic condition and the weather also came up trumps. Some of the tee shots are semi-blind which adds to the enjoyment. But my driving was in good nick, and best of all, I birdied the last after hitting a drive and a 9 iron to six feet!!! A small crowd around the 18th will bear witness to my score.
   And guess who I bumped into at the 19th hole? Lord Browne! I actually felt pretty sorry for him, BP's obviously got succession

problems of its own. He's actually a nice guy, and we really bonded. I gave him some advice on how he should rebrand himself to get back on top. He hinted that if things don't work out for me here, there might be openings at BP . . . though Keith has indicated to me in private that they have already made up their minds . . .

M

PS Are you meeting BSM when he's over? He's requested an audience with yours truly . . .

MARCH 17

From: Martin Lukes
To: Barry Malone

Hi Barry

Just to say how very stimulated I was by our discussion this morning. These are all issues that are very close to my heart—I am highly passionate about a-b glôbâl (UK)—as you may have gathered!

Here in London we are a close-knit high-performing team. All credit to Keith, who has done a better-than-excellent job as chairman. However, as I said to you, I believe there is still plenty of low-hanging fruit that we can use to leverage our performance still more, and I would like to drive that process.

All my very bestest
Martin

MARCH 18

From: Martin Lukes
To: Pandora@CoachworX!

Hi Pandora

Had a very interesting pre-breakfast meeting with Barry yesterday. The day started badly—the minicab driver didn't turn up, so I had to drive in, and then I got a bloody wheel clamp. I find it hard to function at 120 percent at 6am, but Barry was firing on all cylinders—the man's a human dynamo—having been up since 4am running and training.

Unfortunately there was something wrong with the power supply to my laptop, so I couldn't give him the power point presentation I'd spent the whole weekend preparing. Potential disaster, but actually I think it worked out for the best. Barry's so informal that he probably preferred just listening to me kick ideas around. I told him about my concept for repositioning a-b glöbâl UK at the heart of Europe. He kept nodding and saying "Uh huh! Uh huh! I can feel your passion."

He didn't ask any questions at all about me, which you might think was a bad sign, but we really bonded on an intellectual level, which was more important than anything.

I did exactly what you said and was focused, focused, focused! My creativity came across strongly as did my communication skills. Not sure about my humor. I made a couple of good jokes which he didn't laugh at, but then Americans don't have a sense of humor. I sent Barry a message immediately afterwards saying how much I enjoyed our meeting, but have got nothing back, as yet.

I've now got to go to Jake's school to grovel to his headmaster.

22.5 percent better than my bestest
Martin

From: Barry Malone
To: All Staff/London

Howdy!

First up I'd like to say how much of a kick I have gotten out of my visit to London yesterday. There is a load of passionate, diverse human capital in this company and it has been a unique privilege to interact with it.

At a-b glôbâl we know how to play the game. We know how to stay in the game. However, having skin in the game is not enough. To achieve PPP what we must do is shape the game.

I know there is some uncertainty over leadership issues, but I would like to reassure you that we are working on this, and will make an announcement soon!

I love you all
Barry S. Malone

From: Martin Lukes
To: Jenny Withers

Jens—Not sure what to think about that . . . At first I thought it was a bad sign he didn't send me anything personally. But actually I think he probably needs to tell the people who aren't getting the job first. So no news may be good news.

M x

MARCH 22

From: Barry Malone
To: All Staff/London

Howdy!
In the coming weeks we will be kicking off root and branch reassessment of our talent pool. Ahead of this we believe it would be premature to appoint a permanent successor to the position of chairman of a-b glöbâl UK. I am today delighted to say that Roger Wright is appointed as acting chairman to a-b glöbâl UK until a permanent replacement is found.
I know you will give Roger every support in this function.

I love you all
Barry

From: Martin Lukes
To: Graham Wallace

AAAAAAAAAAAAAAAAAARRRRRRRRRRRGGGGGGGGGG-GHHHHHHHHH
I've lost the will to live. Think I'm going to ask out that gorgeous Suzanna to cheer myself up.

From: Martin Lukes
To: Suzanna Elliott

S—Fancy a quick drink tonight? Could meet you at All Bar One at 6:30. M

MARCH 30

From: Martin Lukes
To: Suzanna Elliott

Morning, Suzanna. Did you get home all right? Am feeling a tad rough . . . Hope I didn't go on too much!

Martin

From: Martin Lukes
To: Jenny Withers

Darling, really sorry about last night. I went out for a drink with Graham to drown my sorrows. I know I was in no fit state to drive home. Sorry. Hope I cleaned up the mess ok.

Love you M xx

From: Martin Lukes
To: Graham Wallace

No nothing happened. I'm sure she would have been up for it, but I wasn't in the mood. As I say, I've lost the will to live.

M

From: Martin Lukes
To: Pandora@CoachworX!

Pandora—
    Terrible news . . . They've given the job to Roger, admittedly only on a temporary basis, before appointing an outsider. I did everything you told me to. I polished up my self belief. I prepared

some unbeatable ideas. I positioned myself perfectly—and did I get my dream?? No, I got fuck all, if you'll pardon my French. What this proves is that to get anywhere in this place you must either be a box ticker, or a woman. A man who can think outside the box is going to lose out over and over again. I am so hacked off. I'm getting in touch with the headhunters today—I'm leaving this company, and frankly, I think I can do that without your help.

Rgds
Martin

From: Pandora@CoachworX!
To: Martin Lukes

Hi Martin!
Thank you for sharing that with me. Even negative thoughts are better shared. What you are going through now is a natural part of the SARAH cycle. When you have difficult news you feel Shock, Anger, Resentment, Acceptance and Hope. I am here to get you into the second part of the cycle as soon as possible.

I think you're forgetting your mantra—NO FAILURE ONLY FEEDBACK. Say it after me.

One learning I've taken out of this is that you don't like yourself enough. People who like themselves are lighthearted and optimistic. They have magnetic personalities. Do you like you? Are you genuinely grateful to be you?

Strive and thrive!
Pandora

From: Martin Lukes
To: Pandora@CoachworX!

Of course I bloody like me. That's not the issue. The problem is that no one bloody else seems to. You ask if I'm grateful to be me. With the greatest respect, Pandora, that's about the stupidest thing anyone has ever asked me. I've just been stitched up. I feel that whatever I do goes pear shaped. So am I grateful to be me?? No, surprise, surprise, I'm not at all grateful. And why the fuck should I be??

Frankly, I don't want to go on with this coaching program. My faith in you, and in your entire philosophy, is zilch. You said that I could get this job, and like a complete idiot I believed you.

Please send your closing account to Roger Wright—my new sodding boss.

Rgds
Martin

APRIL

My Negative Energy

APRIL 1

From: Martin Lukes
To: Stewart@harleystreetclinic

Dear Dr. Stewart,

Over the past few days I have been experiencing the following worrying symptoms: my heart is beating excessively fast, I've got low back pain, and am having trouble digesting my food.

I fear I have bowel cancer. I've looked up the condition on the internet and I seem to have ticks in all the boxes—though no bleeding rectum, as yet.

Can you fit me in for an urgent appointment at your earliest convenience?

Yours sincerely
Martin Lukes

From: Pandora@CoachworX!
To: Martin Lukes

Hi Martin!

How are you today?

I hope you are rested and are reconnecting with your optimistic, magnetic personality. And that you are ready to start on month four of our program! This month we will be consolidating the learnings from months one to three, and pushing forward towards even greater success and happiness for you!

Strive and thrive!
Pandora

From: Martin Lukes
To: Pandora@CoachworX!

Pandora—I think there is some misunderstanding. As far as I am concerned, I terminated this coaching relationship last month. That means that no, I am not ready to start on month four.

Rgds, Martin

From: Pandora@CoachworX!
To: Martin Lukes

Hi Martin

It always makes me very sad on the exceedingly rare occasions when coachees fail to complete the Executive Bronze Program. This program has been carefully designed as a holistic package which lasts for 12 months. If you only complete part of it you may actually be in a weaker position than when you started. However, if you do decide to take this backward step, I'd like to refer you to my contract which states that you will be liable to pay the outstanding full year's fee on termination.

Pandora

From: Martin Lukes
To: Jenny Withers

Jens—Am feeling worse by the minute. I've just googled bowel cancer again and found that one in 18 men in their mid-40s have it—it's the second biggest killer in men.

My athlete's foot has also flared up horribly. Do you think this is connected to the other symptoms?

Love you, M x

From: Roger Wright
To: All Staff

Re: weekly HODs meeting
As you know, Barry Malone has invited me to act as Chairman of a-b glöbâl (UK) until further notice. I shall be convening the first in a series of regular weekly meetings for all heads of department to discuss forthcoming issues in Meeting Room 305 at 08:15hrs tomorrow. There are 39 items on the agenda and it is imperative that everybody attends promptly.

Roger Wright
Chairman, a-b glöbâl (UK) (Acting)

From: Martin Lukes
To: Graham Wallace

Hi Graham—Rog's dictatorial tendencies to the fore . . . would make me feel ill if I wasn't so ill already.

Martin

APRIL 2

From: Barry Malone
To: All Staff

Howdy!

This morning I issued an announcement to the SEC that our earnings for the first quarter would show an 18 percent decline on last year. This is due to adverse exchange rate movements, and to hypercompetitive conditions in our market space. Our underlying position remains strong and I would like to thank each of you for making this happen and for bringing your passion and integrity to work every day.

Today I am delighted to announce the next step on our journey towards achieving Peak Performance Permanently.

Our number one goal is to raise the talent bar. At a-b glöbâl we should have zero tolerance of low bench strength. We are a home for A players and B players. C players do not belong here.

In alignment with our caring values, we will treat every existing a-b glöbâl coworker with human dignity. Those of you who stay will be rewarded by working with highly motivated colleagues. Those who do not stay will be free to pursue jobs someplace else where you will feel more passionate and more effective.

I have tasked Keith Buxton, Chief Talent Officer, with implementing the program. He will contact you shortly.

I love you all
Barry S. Malone

From: Martin Lukes
To: Graham Wallace

Graham—Don't like the sound of this ABC thing . . . share price tanking, which means my options are all underwater—but as I'll probably be dead by the time I can exercise them, it doesn't make much difference.
Drink later?

Mart

From: Martin Lukes
To: Keri Tartt

Hi Keri—
I'm really impressed at how perceptive you are about my illness. I agree this is my body giving me a major wake-up call about the multiple stresses I am under. You can't go on firing 120 percent on all cylinders indefinitely, can you?
I'm off to see the doctor in half an hour, so we'll see what he has to say. Can you call me a cab?

M

PS Ta muchly for the crystals . . . really sweet of you.

From: Martin Lukes
To: Jenny Withers

Darling—

Just seen Dr. Stewart, and the news is very bad. Obviously he couldn't say anything about the bowel cancer at this stage, but he's sending me to a top specialist for a colonoscopy. Am feeling very poorly indeed. Would appreciate high-fiber supper and then whiskey and bed.

M xx

APRIL 5

From: Martin Lukes
To: Pandora@CoachworX!

Hi Pandora

A query from left field: I remember you telling me that you were diagnosed as having cancer, and that your doctor gave you six months to live but you coached yourself out of it.

It appears that I may have contracted bowel cancer myself, and would be interested in a program of coaching targeted specifically at helping me towards remission.

Bestest
Martin

From: Pandora@CoachworX!
To: Martin Lukes

Hi Martin!

I am delighted to see that you are working through the SARAH cycle, and have reached the resentment/acceptance stage. Yes I would be delighted to recommence our program. However it is im-

perative that you sincerely renew your commitment to me and to the Executive Bronze Program. Coaching is not something that you dip in and out of. For it to succeed you must commit now to completing the course, and to striving to being 22.5 percent better than the best you can be.

You mention your cancer. Yes, I can certainly help here. However, there is not a special cancer coaching module—instead, the principles of self love and self belief that I teach strengthen the body both inside and out.

Strive and thrive!
Pandora

From: Martin Lukes
To: Keri Tartt

Hi Keri—I'm working from home today. I feel really awful, so I'd rather that people didn't ring or e-mail. I put the crystal healing thing by my bed last night, but alas no improvement yet!

M

From: Roger Wright
To: All Staff

Re: working from home
It has been drawn to my attention that we currently have no binding guidelines covering arrangements for working from home. I would like to remind all members of staff that working from home is only permissible in exceptional circumstances, and then requires written approval from a line manager.

Roger Wright
Chairman, a-b glöbâl (UK) (Acting)

From: Martin Lukes
To: Roger Wright

Roger—I am somewhat surprised at your memo. I believe that trust should be the cornerstone of our culture, and we should trust our team members to select the work schedule that suits them best.

You may be interested to know that today I am working from home because I will shortly be having hospital tests of a serious nature. Instead of taking the day off sick, I am actually finding that the quiet headspace offered by the home environment enables me to continue to work as per usual.

Martin

APRIL 6

From: Roger Wright
To: All Staff

Re staff changes

Lucinda Mogg-Watson will be leaving us at the end of the month to pursue other options. I would like to extend thanks to her for the work she has done with us, and offer her every success with her future career.

Jenny Withers has been appointed Head of External Relations. The appointment of a new assistant will be announced shortly.

Roger Wright
Chairman, a-b glöbâl (UK) (Acting)

From: Martin Lukes
To: Jenny Withers

I DON'T BELIEVE THIS!! When we discussed it last night I thought we agreed that it would be a very bad idea for you to take on additional responsibilities given my health issues—which you seem in total denial about??? M

From: Pandora@CoachworX!
To: Martin Lukes

Hi Martin

How are you today?

At this stage in the program we would normally be looking at your energy levels holistically. However I think it would be better if we commenced with your negative energy.

Many of my coachees find this a difficult concept to grasp. The easiest way of understanding this, Martin, is to think of yourself like a colander. Energy is poured in, but pours out again through the holes. This is your negative energy. We need to find where those holes are, and find ways of blocking them.

Close your eyes and think of that colander. Can you see where the negative energy is gushing out? E-mail me between five and ten of these "holes," and we'll find a way of blocking them!

Strive and thrive!
Pandora

From: Martin Lukes
To: Pandora@CoachworX!

Hi Pandora. I have been trying to find some holes (as it were!!). I have come up with the following list which is by no means comprehensive, but I hope will be a start.

1. My bowel situation

2. Roger

3. Cindy

4. Christo

5. Jake's issues around work, drugs/alcohol etc

6. Jens' issues around my cancer, around her career etc

7. When Arsenal beats Chelsea

22.5 percent better than my very bestest
Martin

From: Pandora@CoachworX!
To: Martin Lukes

Hi Martin!
Well done! Can I make a suggestion on how we can take this forward? Many of your holes are related to other people. These people have very high levels of negative energy and are toxic to people like you, Martin, who are committed to being Better than your Best.

There is only one thing to do with toxic people. Ignore them! And if this is difficult, explain to them that they are toxic to you, and that you need to limit your exposure.

Strive and thrive!
Pandora

From: Martin Lukes
To: Jenny Withers

Just seen your message. Just because I'm at home doesn't mean I can be a tutor to Jake. In fact I have to be careful at the moment because Jake is connected to my negative energy, which impacts adversely on my health. What time you coming home?

M

From: Martin Lukes
To: Jenny Withers

No of COURSE I am not saying Jake's caused my cancer. He's one of the holes in my energy colander, if you will.

M

From: Martin Lukes
To: Jenny Withers

No need to be sarcastic about it . . . it's a useful concept of Pandora's—at the end of the day we're all just colanders, energy goes in and comes out. Jake just happens to be one of my holes.

M

APRIL 7

From: Keith Buxton
To: All Staff

Hallo everyone
You will all by now have seen Barry's memo unveiling our exciting program for upgrading our talent pool.
As Chief Talent Officer I shall be overseeing this program, which is code-named Project ABC, and which will sort our coworkers into three grades—A, B and C. This sorting will be

done in a scientific, highly objective way that will assess each indi-
vidual against target behaviors. Phase One will commence this
week, and will consist in designing a customized Matrix of Key
Behaviors. Further details on the intranet site.

Keith

From: Martin Lukes
To: Keith Buxton

Hi Keith!
    Great to hear from you! Yes, I'd be only too delighted. I have
lots of ideas about our target behaviors, but will of course make
the consultative process here as inclusive as possible. Needless to
say, I am 110 percent behind this initiative.

All my very bestest,
Martin

From: Martin Lukes
To: Jenny Withers

Darling—Keith's asked me to head up the Key Behaviors Task
Force in London!!!! It's incredibly visible—a huge break for me. I
must have really impressed Malone last month after all.

M xx

From: Martin Lukes
To: Stewart@harleystreetclinic

Dear Dr. Stewart
    I am due to go to the US next week on mission critical busi-
ness. As you know my colonoscopy is scheduled for next Wednes-

day. Could you arrange for it to be moved forward to the tail end (no pun intended!!) of this week?

Yours sincerely
Martin Lukes

From: Martin Lukes
To: Jenny Withers

Darling—Just got v cryptic msg from Stewart. For what it's worth, he says it doesn't matter if I postpone the colonoscopy for three and a half weeks. I suppose he thinks I'm toast anyway. They are unbelievably casual, these doctors. If I was that slack I would have been struck off years ago . . .

M x

APRIL 8

From: Martin Lukes
To: Behaviors Focus Group

Hi, Suzanna, Matt, Graham and Nigel
    Thank you for agreeing to join me on the Key Behaviors Task Force. Ahead of the first session in my office tomorrow at 10am I'd like each of you to think of the six behaviors that you personally think are the key drivers for every individual in the a-b glöbâl family to ensure that we as a company excel at every point in the value chain. It should be a highly stimulating session. See you tomorrow.

Martin

APRIL 9

From: Martin Lukes
To: All Staff

Hi Everybody

The Key Behaviors Focus Group had its first meeting yesterday and surfaced many innovative ideas. So far we have identified the following target Behaviors: Courage, Citizenship, Playfulness, Wisdom, Win-win Headset, and Hi-trust. I think you will agree that this has been an outstanding start. Now it's over to you—we want to hear your views!

My best, Martin

From: Jenny Withers
To: All Staff

With my Communications hat on, I'd like to suggest we present each behavior as a personal statement: "I am courageous," "I am a good citizen," "I am playful." That way we align them more closely with the values of each individual coworker.

Best, Jenny

From: Christo Weinberg
To: All Staff

Hi!

I think we can kick this baby up a notch. What we are doing is creating riffs which we all play together. This isn't about "I." It's about "we." "I" is a feeble solo, "we" is a monster big band jamming session. If we say "WE are good citizens," "WE are play-

*ful," then that creates an inclusive formula we can all feel passion-
ate about!*

Cheers, Christo

From: Suzanna Elliott
To: All Staff

*Hi!! What about making the behaviors all begin with the same let-
ter? It would help us create a really powerful behaviors brand.
Two of them already begin with C, so we could convert all the
others to C words. Instead of "win-win headset" we could have
"can-do headset." Instead of "wisdom," "cleverness." And instead of playfulness we could have "clowning." I know it's a bit
outrageous, but you can't accuse me of thinking inside the box!!!*

Suze

From: Martin Lukes
To: Suzanna Elliott

Suze—you're a STAR!! That is brilliant, really creative. Just been
thinking about this, and it has given me a breakthrough idea: given
the quality of your work, I'd like you to clear your calendar and
come with me to Atlanta next week for the big presentation.

M

APRIL 12

From: Pandora@CoachworX!
To: Martin Lukes

Hi Martin

Now you know where your negative energy is, you are ready to start managing it. One easy win is to look at the words you use that drain your energy—Killer. Bad. Worse. Life Sentence. Awful.

These words are all about pain. And pain has no place in your life.

Don't say you're exhausted. Say you're RECHARGING. Don't say you're snowed under—say that you're IN DEMAND or that you're STRETCHING. See the difference? Don't say I hate. Say I PREFER. Don't say failure, say LEARNING. Don't say sick, say CLEANSING. Don't say oh shit! Say OH POO! Don't say angry . . . say A LITTLE BIT CONCERNED!

When you are dealing with the people who sap your energy it is vital to use these empowering words. Try it for a day or two, and tell me about the difference!

Strive and thrive!
Pandora

From: Roger Wright
To: All Staff

I fear inadequate consideration has been given to the metrics of the matrix. These behaviors are intended to be the subject of objective measurement. I cannot see which metrics would be used to measure "playfulness." Neither do I see how this is a useful addition to our global behaviors set.

Roger Wright, Acting Chairman

From: Martin Lukes
To: Roger Wright

Roger—Thanks for sharing your thoughts with us. Can I make a small point? This behaviors matrix is about change, changing behavior from the negative to the positive. Negative words like "fear" and "cannot" have no place in the debate!

All my very bestest
Martin

APRIL 14

From: Martin Lukes
To: All Staff

Hello everybody
I am delighted to say that the Key Behaviors Focus Group has completed its work and I am now in a position to offer you a preview of the behaviors matrix before I unveil it in Atlanta next week. After much highly inclusive debate we have decided on six positive behaviors that define us at a-b glöbâl UK.

Why CONVERSATION? Because this is how we touch each
  other's souls.
Why CONNECTIVITY? Because no man is an island. We are
  teams that connect with each other.
Why CRAZINESS? Because without a bit of craziness we would
  be the same as everyone else.
Why CARING? Because we are global citizens who love each
  other and the communities we serve.
Why COACHING? Because this is how we nurture each other
  and pass on our key learnings.
Why CREATIVITY? Because without this we could never change
  our DNA.

You will notice that the behaviors begin with the same first letter, which gives them a powerful internal brand. I would like to thank my team for going the extra mile to reach what I am sure you will agree is truly a caring, creative and crazy matrix!

All my very bestest
Martin

APRIL 15

From: Martin Lukes
To: Keri Tartt

Hi Keri—Can you get the travel arrangements for Suzanna and myself sorted asap? We need to leave mid-morning Thursday. Plse check that British Airways has beds in Business Class on its 747s—I want the window seat in the bubble. In Atlanta, plse book us into the W. Preferably a suite for myself.

Ta muchly, Martin

From: Martin Lukes
To: Jenny Withers

Jens—I DID tell you I'm leaving on Thursday—you weren't listening. Yes, I do realize Jake will be home for Easter. What do you expect me to do about it—tell Keith I can't come because I need to make my delinquent 15-year-old son study for his GCSEs?

And yes, Suzanna is coming with me. The only reason I didn't mention it to you was because you've shown no interest whatsoever in this trip. Suze has done a better than excellent job on the focus group, and I really don't see what yr problem is . . . You're always moaning about the glass ceiling and how women don't get a chance in this company.

Love you
M

APRIL 17

From: Martin Lukes
To: Phyllis Lukes

Dearest Mum
    Sorry I haven't been in touch for a bit, but I've had a blow on the health front recently. Long story short, it seems very likely I have bowel cancer.
    Don't know what the prognosis is, my strategy for dealing with it is to be very honest about it, and to keep on absolutely as normal. Did I tell you that Pandora is very knowledgeable on matters cancerous, having had a brush with it herself? She say's its all about balancing the positive and negative energies, which makes a lot of sense when you think about it.
    Am off to Atlanta on important business tomorrow so fraid I won't be able to come down at the weekend to help prune the shrubs. Will see you when I'm back.
    Try not to worry too much.

Your loving son
Martin

APRIL 19

From: Martin Lukes
To: Keri Tartt

Keri—travel department has booked us into the HOLIDAY INN!!
I am a director of this company and traveling on the most important business. Tell them to upgrade my hotel to the W. This is absolutely bloody typical.

M

APRIL 20

From: Martin Lukes
To: Jenny Withers

Darling—Plane delayed three hours at Heathrow . . . I'm totally shattered. Or, as Pandora would have me say, I'm recharging.

There's been a massive cock-up over hotels—everyone else is staying at the Holiday Inn, and no one told me. Suzanna and I are in the W, miles away from the action. Trust all OK at home. I had an e-mail from Max asking me for help with his algebra paper for Common Entrance—told him I'm a bit up against it. Can't you do it?

M xx

From: Keith Buxton
To: UPBOB

Hello everyone! Let me say how delighted I am to see so many of you from so many different geographies gathered here for the Project Uplift Brainstorm on Behaviors (UPBOB).

Tomorrow we kick off with a pre-breakfast Show and Tell, and I will be asking each of you to share with us something personal about what the key behaviors mean to you. You will notice that the walls of the meeting room are draped in brown paper. During all sessions, I'd like you to write any thoughts you may have on the walls. Whatever comes into your minds, write it down! It's going to be a lot of fun!

Keith

APRIL 21

From: Martin Lukes
To: Jenny Withers

Darling—just got yr message. Jake's totally out of order. However, it's a pity that you went apeshit at him—I think it's much more motivational to use more empowering language.

Will send him an e-mail tonight if I have a mo. Just ran into BSM—he said he was really looking forward to my presentation! K's gone native, acting like touchy-feely American. Ugh.

Love you, M XX

From: Martin Lukes
To: Jake Lukes

Jake—I am a little bit concerned to hear from your mother that you stole some money from Svetlana, which has resulted in her threatening to leave.

I must be honest with you: my initial response was "Oh poo," but I have now reflected on the situation, and feel you need to think about changing your behaviors.

Jake, can you do an exercise for me? Can you to think up six key behaviors that will help you going forward, and e-mail them to me? Then I can help you learn to live them. Let's make a new start!

Love, Dad

From: Martin Lukes
To: UPBOB

Hi everyone!

I'm sorry I'm not at the pre-breakfast Show and Tell. I'm stuck in traffic. I didn't realize it would take so long to get across town! Should be with you in half an hour.

Cheers, Martin Lukes

Sent from my BlackBerry Wireless Handheld

From: Keith Buxton
To: UPBOB

Hallo everyone! Thanks to one and all for a stimulating day's discussion. I have never seen so much passionate graffiti in one place! Thanks also to Martin Lukes for joining us eventually and sharing the interesting story of how he is using a behaviors matrix as a tool to motivate his son. I really believe that Project Uplift behaviors matrices have great potential both in the work and the home arenas! Please be prompt for this evening's networking drinks. 6:30pm in the Printemps Suite.

Keith

From: Martin Lukes
To: Jenny Withers

Darling—really energizing day. We had a very intellectual discussion about the link between behaviors and values. Will tell all when I get back. Am forwarding Jake's response to my motivational message. Any idea what he's on about?

Love you, M x

From: Jake Lukes
To: Martin Lukes

```
Dad, you're gay. J
```


APRIL 22

From: Martin Lukes
To: Keri Tartt

Hi Keri
    Just arrived at Heathrow—am off home to recharge and renew. I've got a couple of key memos I need to write . . . Tell Rog that whatever it is, I can't see him today. M

Sent from my BlackBerry Wireless Handheld

APRIL 26

From: Martin Lukes
To: All Staff

Hello everyone

I wanted to debrief you on an incredibly exciting few days in Atlanta. There is huge momentum behind UPBOB, and our committee's input went down extremely well. Suzanna gave a better-than-excellent presentation that left all the others standing! We are expecting that the UK contribution will be well represented in the ultimate outturn!

Best, Martin

From: Martin Lukes
To: Keri Tartt

Hi Keri

Can you put through my Atlanta exes asap? If Rog gives any trouble you might point out Suzanna and I worked 14-hour days while we were in Atlanta. We were putting the UK in the driving seat on our most important global initiative since Project Rebrand.

Martin

From: Barry Malone
To: All Staff

Howdy!

First up, I wanted to say thank you to all those who came to Atlanta last week for UPBOB. There is an amazing amount of passion and love being shown on this project. Over the next few days Keith Buxton and myself will be finalizing the matrix based

upon last week's inputs, and then we will be able to commence the
global rollout of Project Uplift!

I love you all,
Barry

APRIL 30

From: Pandora@CoachworX!
To: Martin Lukes

Hi Martin
When we started the program I said I was going to be your
greatest fan. And let me tell you that the way you have got back
into the Bronze Program has been exceptional. The Old You is
dead. New You is alive and growing!!
Can I ask you to jot down some of the advances you've made
this month, and then give yourself a big round of applause?

Strive and thrive!
Pandora

From: Martin Lukes
To: Pandora@CoachworX!

Hi Pandora
If you'll excuse a literary reference, April is the cruelest month.
As the poet Robert Frost predicted, this has been a hyper challenging month for myself, though I have notched some wins that I
am very proud of. I am interacting less with people who impact
negatively on my energy levels.
I am also making progress with the words I use. I am avoiding
disempowering words and words full of pain. This has been highly
successful except possibly with my son, who seems to have de-

cided that I'm a shirtlifter. Which is quite ironic, when you think about it(!).

This month I have made a good start in coming to terms with bowel cancer. To have scored a major career win under these circumstances is no mean feat.

I am distressed that not much progress has been made on the home front. Jens is burying herself in her career, in order to avoid confronting various issues. I see this as a growing problem.

Basically, going forward I need to look after number one and take things one day at a time!

22.5 percent better than my bestest
Martin

5

MAY

My Heart and My Head

MAY 3

From: Pandora@CoachworX!
To: Martin Lukes

Hi Martin

Welcome to Month Five!

This month we are going to focus in on your heart. But before we do that I want you to stand in front of a mirror very close, with your nose almost touching the glass, and then slowly walk backwards. I want you to describe the man in front of you using a fun test of mine called KWYA. It's pronounced choir, because it is like your inner choir singing in harmony about the New You.

K stands for your kindness to yourself. W is your wisdom. Y is Your values and being true to them. A is your aims and ambitions.

So look in the mirror, Martin, and tell me about the KWYA you see reflected there. We need to check that your inner choir is singing from the same hymn sheet.

Strive and thrive!
Pandora

From: Martin Lukes
To: Jenny Withers

Jens—Just looked at the hospital letter and seems I'll be practically on nil by mouth for 36 hours before the colonoscopy, and have to take three batches of laxatives. I'll stay home tomorrow and the next day, and probably best if I don't go to Max's debating contest tonight . . . Mx

MAY 4

From: Martin Lukes
To: Pandora@CoachworX!

Hi Pandora

I am trying to do your tests, though finding it hard thanks to some of the strongest laxatives on God's earth which I've taken ahead of my colonoscopy tomorrow. Still, to the best of my current ability, here we go on my KWYA thingy.

KINDNESS to myself—Yes, I think I'm doing well on this. I'm learning to like myself much more. I'm broadly speaking pleased with what I see in the mirror—could be a bit thinner (though today alone I must have lost half a stone). I see a decent, funny person, good to have around.

WISDOM—Yes, I think the guy in the mirror has it. It's not just wisdom about stuff I know, it's wisdom about what makes me tick, and what makes others tick, too.

YOUR VALUES—Not sure that I can actually see my values in the mirror. As you know, I want to use my creativity, my networking, my sense of fun to make the world a better place. But not quite sure I can pick that up from my reflection.

AMBITION—I can certainly see that—this guy is already successful and is on the way up. It's a look of determination in the chin. He wants to be a leader.

That's about it. Though if I am being 140 percent honest there is something else I see—I can sense that this guy in the mirror is ill. But we'll find out more about that tomorrow.

22.5 percent better than my very bestest
Martin

From: Martin Lukes
To: Phyllis Lukes

Dear Mum

Thanks for your e-mail. Yes, I survived the US trip well. Basically, I'm like you mum—tough as old boots, so no need to worry. My strategy is not to think about it, and to carry on as per normal. Colonoscopy tomorrow, so will keep you posted.

On a happier note, we should be hearing if Max has got into Eton in a few days. The lad seemed really confident after the exams and his last school report (did I show it to you?) says he's a total all rounder—he's a very useful spin bowler in cricket, on the first eleven rugby team, top set for maths, english, latin. He's a chip off the old block, though possibly a tad more motivated than I was at that age.

Yesterday he reached the finals of the school debating competition (he's got his mother's argumentative streak!!) all foreigners are Wogs. Unfortunately I was too poorly to go, but Jens went and said he was brilliant, even though as a bit of a leftie she was on the other side of the argument. You would have been v proud though.

Keep your fingers crossed for me tomorrow. Will be in touch afterwards.

Much love
Martie

PS I can't believe that your knee op has been put back again. It's beyond a joke. I've really had it with the National Health Service. I think you should go private, and I'll pay.

MAY 5

From: Roger Wright
To: All Staff

Re: a-b glöbâl 1st Q earnings
Today you will have seen the announcement out of Atlanta of our Q1 earnings. These show a continued squeeze on margins. It is imperative in this tough climate that we continue to contain costs. To that end I am today announcing the following measures, effective at once.

1. *Cuts to travel budget. All air travel must be in economy class. There will be no exceptions to this.*

2. *Our contract with Bloomin' Krazy has been terminated. In future we will have a display of imitation flowers in the 1st floor reception space only.*

3. *Headcount. Project ABC will reduce headcount by an estimated 15 percent. In addition I am today announcing a hiring freeze.*

4. *Vending machines. The 3p subsidy per cup will be rescinded, effective immediately.*

Roger Wright
Acting Chairman

From: Martin Lukes
To: Graham Wallace

Trust you've seen Rog's memo. Frankly, sometimes dying seems like the easy option.

From: Martin Lukes
To: Roger Wright

Hi Roger

I am extremely concerned at the hiring freeze. I should not need to remind you that the marketing department is the engine room of this company. If we do not have top talent in this department, we have zero chance of maintaining/enhancing our pole position as one of the creative engines in the a-b glöbâl family.

You will be aware I am currently looking for a Senior Brand Evangelist. This is a pivotal position and I am not aware of any internal candidate with the appropriate skillset.

Best, Martin

From: Martin Lukes
To: Jenny Withers

Darling—I'm back at home feeling very dopey after the sedative. Dr. Gorton may be the top bowel cancer bod in the country, but even he was defeated by my case. He claimed not to be able to find any cancer in the colon at all—which frankly, I find very worrying. Have just watched the video of my bowel and I'm 280 percent certain there's a nasty shadow lurking on the bowel wall. I've phoned his office and spoken to one of his dopey assistants who says that shadows are "perfectly normal"(!) God knows where they get these people from. I'm definitely seeking a second opinion.

Come home quickly and watch it with me.

Love M xx

PS I'm very very hungry after my purge. Can you pick up a large Indian takeout on yr way back?

MAY 6

From: Martin Lukes
To: Pandora@CoachworX!

Hi Pandora

The medical profession are completely baffled by cancer and tests ongoing. The results have left me feeling very low and confused. When your cancer was diagnosed did you come across any medical experts prepared to think out of the box on this? Not 22.5 percent better than my bestest (if I'm honest!)

Martin

From: Martin Lukes
To: IT Department

ARE WE THE ONLY COMPANY IN THE WORLD WITHOUT A FUNCTIONING SPAM FILTER??? I AM TOTALLY FED UP WITH ALL THIS SPAM. I DON'T NEED VIAGRA, OR PENIS ENLARGEMENT—CAN SOMEONE IN THE IT DEPARTMENT GET THIS SORTED—NOW.

MAY 7

From: Pandora@CoachworX!
To: Martin Lukes

Hi Martin!
The great news is that your KWYA is in perfect harmony, and you are now ready for the next module, which is all about your heart.
Like many highly successful men, Martin, you let your head work overtime. You are extremely intelligent, Martin, and very

logical, but unless you let your heart talk, you will achieve your goals, but you won't be fulfilled, and you will have a working style that will veer on the demanding and the bullying.

So I am going to show you how to build a little bridge between the left side of your brain, which is the logical side, and the right side, which controls your feelings. Close your eyes, Martin. Imagine a red rose in the right side of your brain. Imagine a white rose on the left. Can you see those roses, Martin? Now swap them over.

The power of this exercise is amazing. If you do it every hour for the next four weeks, you will find the bridge is there and the difference in your decision making will be amazing.

Strive and thrive!
Pandora

From: Martin Lukes
To: Keri Tartt

Keri—do you mind if I ask you something? I'd really like your honest answer. Do you think my management style can be demanding, or even bullying?

Martin

From: Martin Lukes
To: Keri Tartt

Very kind of you to say so! Thank you! Next odd request. Can you come into my office and help me perform a little trick with roses?! A large latte and an almond Danish would be nice . . . it's something that may require a little sustenance!

M

From: Martin Lukes
To: Pandora@CoachworX!

Hi Pandora

For what it's worth, you have got me wrong if you think I'm purely a "head" person. Certainly logical thought is extremely important to myself, but I reject 120 percent the idea that I am bullying. I've just asked for some honest 360 degree feedback from members of my team, who do not buy into the idea at all! That said, I'll practice the tests and see what happens!

22.5 percent better than my very bestest
Martin

MAY 10

From: Martin Lukes
To: Phyllis Lukes

Dearest Mummy

Can you send me the name of your knee doctor and I'll investigate the private option?? Really don't worry about the money. Obviously I'll pay for it. I thought I had already said that. Yes, the Eton fees are going to be an arm and a leg (assuming he gets in), but I've only got one mum, and I'm going to walk the extra mile to look after her!

Martie

From: Martin Lukes
To: Keri Tartt

Hi Keri

Great trousers! Very fetching!

Can I ask you to do a little something? Can you find out who is in charge of our health insurance? I want to wangle my mother's op onto my policy. I know it normally only covers wife and kids . . . but I think I might be able to swing something . . . M

From: Martin Lukes
To: Roger Wright

Roger—You suggest Bettina Schmidt as a satisfactory candidate for Senior Brand Evangelist. I know that she has worked on some leading edge marketing projects for a-b glöbâl (Germany) before her maternity leave, but I understand she will only be working four days a week. We are all working 24/7 as it is—and a new member of the team must be 120 percent committed.

Rgds
Martin

MAY 12

From: Keith Buxton
To: All Staff

Hi everyone
I wanted to update you on where we are with our behaviors matrix. We must not lose sight that the purpose of it is to divide all our family into three streams—A, B and C. We feel it would therefore be inappropriate if our target behaviors are branded around the letter C, as these are the co-colleagues who do not have a future here.
I am delighted to say that we will unveil the matrix next week. In advance of that time, if any co-colleague would like to feed into the process please feel free to contact me.

Keith

From: Martin Lukes
To: Graham Wallace

Graham—Jesus fucking wept. I despair over this place. Rog is fobbing me off with some German girl as the new Suzanna who has just had a baby and who will have fried brains and be dribbling milk and dashing off home the whole time. Now bloody Keith has decided he doesn't like my matrix after all. Drink later?

Martin

MAY 13

From: Martin Lukes
To: Keri Tartt

Keri, can I try something out on you?

When I was in the shower this morning I was thinking about the behaviors matrix, and this word came into my mind. Creovation. Cre-ovation—half creativity and half innovation! What do you think?

M

From: Martin Lukes
To: Keri Tartt

Thanks, Keri—I thought you'd love it! Jens doesn't get it, or at least she pretends not to. Obviously I'm not going to say anything as clichéd as my-wife-doesn't-understand-me, but last night she had the nerve to suggest she is the only one who is doing real work and I'm just faffing around. Keri, you are a massive reality check for me, you remind me that my creovative juices are flowing!

M

From: Martin Lukes
To: Jenny Withers

Jens—I know it's your book club tonight, but I don't think I'll be able to make it back in time to hold the fort. I need to prepare something for Keith and BSM on creovation. With respect, I don't think you quite grasped the point of it this morning—you were too busy giving orders to Svetlana and looking for Max's cricket jumper.

Will probably be back 10ish.

Martin

MAY 14

From: Martin Lukes
To: Barry Malone

Hi Barry

Just wanted to say that I strongly agree that it's inappropriate to have all our behaviors start with a C. I should explain how the suggestion came about—It was surfaced by a junior member of my team, and I included it in my presentation as I passionately believe in order to get a team to co-create effectively, you have to throw everyone's ideas in the pot, stir them around before you start weeding the weaker ones out.

However, it's important we don't throw out the baby with the proverbial bathwater. The most important C on the list is creativity. This is our tool kit for changing our dna, if you will. I've been thinking about what sets the truly creative co-colleagues apart. It isn't simply creativity. Neither is it innovation. What the highest flyers do is combine the two into a single behavior that I call Creovation. A Creovative idea is both out of the box and actionable. It is bolt-on and blue-sky. I passionately believe it should form the heart of our matrix.

All my very bestest
Martin

From: Martin Lukes
To: Barry Malone

Hi Barry!
    Thanks for getting back so quickly! I'm totally delighted that you think Creovation is phenomenal. Can I revisit your image of the stonemason? If the stonemasons building the flagship St. Paul's cathedral in London had been a bit more creovative, they might have come up with something less of a cliché than a bog standard dome!

All my very bestest
Martin

From: Martin Lukes
To: Keri Tartt

Hi Keri
    I've got a challenging one for you. Can you find out how to register something as a trademark? I want to protect my intellectual capital in creovation, before someone nicks it.

Ta muchly M

From: Martin Lukes
To: Phyllis Lukes

Dear Mum

How are you? Glad to hear your roses are looking lovely.

I've got some great news re your knee op. It's all sorted, you're going to have it done at the Wellington, they'll ring with a date later today. I'm still pretty hacked off with the medical profession—they still haven't traced the source of my cancer. The only person who is being remotely helpful is Pandora, who is teaching me how to tackle it by exercising the right side of my brain. I know you think all of this is mumbo jumbo, and at one level I do too, but I've decided to give it a try. Let's face it, I haven't got much to lose.

Despite all this, everything is going v well workwise. I've come up with this new concept called creovation, which is going down a storm here. Which is ironic in a way given that my back is against the wall heathwise. Or maybe it's not so ironic. Didn't Beethoven write his finest unfinished symphony on his deathbed?

Hope to see you at the weekend.

Lots of love
Martie

From: Martin Lukes
To: Phyllis Lukes

Dear Mum,

You're such a one for the Queen's English!! It means part creativity and part innovation. Really mum, I think it's time to wake up and smell the coffee. Times change, and you have to creovate!!

Much love
Martie

From: Martin Lukes
To: Keri Tartt

Thanks Keri, you're a star! Question. Does the £125 buy me the tradmark in the world or just in the UK? I'm going to need global protection for this, as the market in these ideas doesn't respect national boundaries!

M

MAY 17

From: Martin Lukes
To: Jenny Withers

Jens
   Don't forget that we're going to Chelsea Flower Show tomorrow pm with my friend Tim from Boogie Gargle Fink . . . Is my Hugo Boss pale gray pinstripe at the dry cleaners?

Mart

From: Martin Lukes
To: Jenny Withers

I told you about Chelsea MONTHS ago. What is this Eve-o-lution cocktail party? Is it some women's networking thing? If it's networking you want you can't do better than Chelsea . . . all the great and the good from the advertising fraternity are at our table.

M

From: Martin Lukes
To: Keri Tartt

Hi Keri

How do you fancy going to the opening night of Chelsea Flower Show with me tomorrow? We'd be guests of BGF, which always pushes the boat out on these occasions . . . bubbly . . . nice eats. Hope you can make it. Posh togs the order of the day.

M

MAY 18

From: Martin Lukes
To: Bettina Schmidt

Hi Bettina

I understand you're returning from maternity leave next week, joining us in marketing. I'm sure you'll notice the buzz after Germany!

I believe you have requested Fridays off, but unfortunately I shall be starting a regular weekly team briefing, which it would be a shame to miss.

My bestest
Martin

From: Martin Lukes
To: Bettina Schmidt

Bettina—As anyone on my team will tell you, I'm a passionate believer in work/life balance, but at the end of the day your child minder's schedule isn't my business. Can I give you some advice? If you want to thrive here in the marketing department, you must leave family problems behind you. The winners on my team always give 110 percent, minimum.

Bestest, Martin

From: Martin Lukes
To: Graham Wallace

Graham—Do you ever wish you were a woman?

From: Martin Lukes
To: Graham Wallace

I didn't mean that, you pervert!!!
   I meant we men are a disadvantaged species. On one hand I have Bettina expecting me to arrange team meetings for her child minder's convenience. On the other, there is my ladywife forming a women's networking club to give themselves even more unfair advantages . . . Drink later? M

From: Pandora@CoachworX!
To: Martin Lukes

Hi Martin
   I can see that "creovation" is the product of head AND heart. I'm impressed! You are starting to build that bridge between the left and right chambers but I think you can develop your right side more. You are still intellectualizing everything. Lead more with your heart, Martin!

Strive and thrive!
Pandora

From: Martin Lukes
To: Pandora@CoachworX!

Hi Pandora

Small point. I've actually trademarked creovation™, so would you mind putting the ™ sign on it after you've used it? As you say, I've got to look after yours truly first!

22.5 percent better than my bestest
Martin

From: Martin Lukes
To: Keri Tartt

Sensational dress! You look so much like a flower that someone might pick you!! Can you call a cab downstairs for 6:30??

MAY 19

From: Martin Lukes
To: Jenny Withers

Darling—what time did you leave the house this morning? You were already gone when I woke up. Sorry I was a bit late back—I had to go for a nightcap with Tim and his team afterwards. You didn't miss much—usual crowd, usual gardens, though there was one I liked that was all brushed steel and water. It was very attractive in an elegant, urban way. Food for thought for when we re-landscape ours. Love you

Martin x

From: Martin Lukes
To: Keri Tartt

Keri, thanks for an amazing evening, and I hope you're not feeling as rough as I am this morning!! Hope also you didn't think I was a bit forward in the cab on the way back from Anabel's, or that I make a habit of that sort of thing.

It's a long time since I let my hair down and bopped like that—you're a great mover!

Martin x (if allowed!)

From: Martin Lukes
To: TimZadek@BoogieGargleFink

Hi Tim

Many thanks for a great bash last night . . . Good crowd of people . . . sorry we had to slip off a bit early . . . Let's do lunch soon.

Bestest, Martin

From: Martin Lukes
To: Keri Tartt

What was that sideways look meant to mean this morning?? Can I buy you lunch?

MAY 24

From: Keith Buxton
To: All Staff

Hallo everyone!
It is with great pride that I am today unveiling our key behaviors matrix. I would like to offer sincere thanks to coworkers from all over the globe who participated in the inclusive process that has created a matrix that will make a-b glöbâl unbeatable. The six behaviors that define our essence going forward are IN-TEGRITY, LOVE, DELIGHT, DETERMINATION, CREOVA-TION AND DARING.

To introduce these behaviors I am asking colleagues to choose one that they feel passionate about, and explain how we can use it to sort out our A, B and C players. Barry will kick off, then Martin Lukes will explain his creovation concept, but after that the field is wide open!

All my very bestest,
Keith

From: Martin Lukes
To: All Staff

Hi co-colleagues
A big thank-you to Keith for inviting me to describe creovation™. Can I first say that I do not think of the idea as "mine." This sort of not-invented-here headset is the enemy of creovation™. Ideas are everywhere. They are free. Creovation™ is about grabbing them, harnessing them. Living them.
Question: What is creovation™? A players won't need to ask this. Deep inside they have always known what it is and recognize it in themselves. Creovation™ takes the best blue sky element out of creativity. It takes the bolt-on, results-driven part of innovation. It's a perfect partnership, if you will.

People often ask me: Is creovation™ something learned, or something you are born with? The answer is both. A players are born creovative™. B players have worked hard to acquire the skill. Some C players can innovate, and some can even create, but they struggle to walk the extra mile to creovate™.

All my very bestest
Martin

From: Martin Lukes
To: Keri Tartt

Keri—

How about doing something tonight?? Jens has got her book club—they are discussing something called Reading Lolita in Baghdad—which promises to be such a stimulating read they'll be nattering away half the night. She won't be back til late, so we could make an evening of it . . . M xx

MAY 25

From: Martin Lukes
To: Keri Tartt

Dearest Keri—It's 3 am and I've just got back. I don't even know if you check e-mails at home, but I just wanted to say what a GREAT LOVELY FANTASTIC time I had tonight.

Jens is fast asleep, so I didn't have to explain why I only had one sock on and was smelling of your perfume. What is it by the way? Can I buy you some? I'm going to bed now, but I don't know if I'm going to be able to sleep. Good night to you, you sexy thing!

M xxxxxxx (I wish I could give them to you in person)

MAY 26

Oh God . . . Just got a message to call Jens—urgent. Nightmare . . . she can't have found out already?? M xxx

From: Martin Lukes
To: Keri Tartt

Keri—catastrophe averted! She wanted to tell me Max has just got a scholarship to Eton!! Don't know if that means anything to a Kiwi, but it's the best school in the country, ergo in the world! Can you come into my office for a second now . . . xxx

Martin

From: Martin Lukes
To: Jenny Withers

Darling—Of course I'm pleased!! The reason I seemed a tad distracted earlier on is that I've got a lot on my plate. This is the most fantastic news—Max is a total star! How much money do we get off the fees?? M xxx

From: Martin Lukes
To: Keri Tartt

God that was dangerous—but I couldn't resist. You really are the sexiest thing I've ever ever seen. Next time we better stick something over the peephole in my door . . . or find somewhere safer. M xx

From: Martin Lukes
To: Max Lukes

WELL DONE MAX!!!!!!! You're a chip off the old block! . . . I knew you could make it!! You've learned a really important lesson that I didn't learn till much later in life. You know how to be your own greatest fan and how to be better than your best. If I had worked that stuff out when I was twelve, I'd be running the country by now!!! I've bought you a present—Eminem's CD Encore. I've taken advice from someone in the office who is a bit closer to your age . . . and it's the hottest CD of the moment. See u later.

Dad

From: Martin Lukes
To: Max Lukes

For Godssakes Max, Eminem is supposed to be hyper cool . . .

From: Martin Lukes
To: Keri Tartt

Keri—you might be the perfect being, but I'm afraid you bombed with Eminem. I've just had a lecture from a 13-year-old on how this sort of music shows no respect for women! Can I respect you a bit more later on?

Martin xx

From: Martin Lukes
To: Graham Wallace

Hi Graham—Max won a scholarship to Eton!! Obviously I'm really pleased for him, as he'll be a round peg in a round hole. But personally I don't really hold with all the elitist nonsense . . . tailcoats and royalty and all that malarkey. And God knows what they get up to in those houses—probably all rogering each other(!) Still, it's a great place for super bright super sporty kids. Did Fergus pass common entrance?

Martin

From: Martin Lukes
To: Graham Wallace

Oh dear . . . is that a local school? I'm a great believer in horses for courses . . . I'm sure he'll be v happy. Can't have celebratory drink as am off home for monster celebrations.

M

MAY 27

From: Martin Lukes
To: Faith Preston

Faith—I strongly object to the tone of your message. You imply that I am discriminating against Bettina as a mother. The facts are: 1. I have been highly supportive about her baby to date. 2. I offered her advice on how to be more successful, and told her she needed to make work number one priority. I did this in my capacity as coach and mentor.

Martin

From: Martin Lukes
To: Keri Tartt

Keri—let's meet at the fire escape in half an hour. I've checked it out—leave through the fire doors on the fourth floor . . . I'll go first—leave it a minute or two then you come.

M xx

From: Martin Lukes
To: Keri Tartt

Wow! That was amazing . . . Do I look a bit sweaty??

From: Martin Lukes
To: Bettina Schmidt

Bettina—I am sorry to hear from Faith that you have some issues surrounding your return from maternity leave.

As I told you last week, work/life balance is very close to my heart. Can I tell you a highly personal story? You may not know that I am married to Jenny Withers who works here in PR and has a career in her own right. Issues on the domestic front crop up from time to time, and we take it in turn to solve them. If I need to go home, or go to one of the boys' schools, then I do that. I quite understand that home life matters. Work hard, play hard—that's my watchword. If Fridays are a problem for you—then let's set up a video conferencing link so that you can participate from home.

Bestest, Martin

From: Martin Lukes
To: Keri Tartt

My lovely sexy Keri

Jens has just popped her head around the door and asked me what I'm doing. I've said I'm writing a message to BSM.

I have been thinking about you all evening. I love the way you flick your hair around your ears. I love the butterfly you have tattooed on your left buttock. I want to kiss it right now. I love the way you feel. I love the way you taste. Corporal Cock and Private Pussy are made for each other.

When I'm with you, I feel I can do anything or be anything. These last two weeks have been so fantastic for me, and I wanted you to know that.

Love xxx

MAY 31

From: Pandora@CoachworX!
To: Martin Lukes

Hi Martin

I'm just checking up on you—I haven't heard from you for a couple of weeks but I get this sense that you are following two key messages—Love like you've never been hurt. Dance like no one is watching.

Please share with me your wins—month five is nearly at an end, and we need to measure how you've done . . .

Strive and thrive!
Pandora

From: Martin
To: Pandora@CoachworX!

Hi Pandora

Has someone said something to you??? I thought the deal with coaching was that it was totally confidential?

Martin

From: Pandora@CoachworX!
To: Martin Lukes

Hi Martin!

I'm puzzled . . . Yes, confidentiality is the cornerstone of the Executive Bronze Program. I was simply asking if you were growing your heart, and doing the exercises I gave you regularly. Is there something else happening in your life you would like to share?

Strive and thrive!
Pandora

From: Martin Lukes
To: Pandora@CoachworX!

Hi Pandora

Sorry—total misunderstanding! Yes, I have been doing the red and white roses test a couple of times, and I am very impressed at the power of the right side of the brain as a work tool!

For me this has been a great month for both head and heart. My win with creovation™ was a classic bridging exercise. I have also used my heart to make a very difficult situation with a new employee better. I have shared a personal story with her, to help her shift her performance and team loyalty onto the next level.

Above all I have used my heart to make myself more in tune with, and more stimulated by, the working environment. No question.

22.5 percent better than my bestest
Martin

6

JUNE

My Body

JUNE 1

From: Martin Lukes
To: Keri Tartt

Pinky
Meet you on the fire escape in five mins . . . I'll go first, and text you if the coast is clear . . .

Perky

PS The corporal is standing to attention already!!

From: Pandora@CoachworX!
To: Martin Lukes

Hi Martin
One of the biggest wins we have got out of Executive Bronze so far is your great new attitude towards yourself! This month we are going to focus in on your body, and I am going to teach you how to look and feel marvelous—forever! First, let's draw the baseline—tell me how you feel about your health, your diet, your

fitness, about how you look, and we'll take it from there!

Strive and thrive!
Pandora

From: Martin Lukes
To: Keri Tartt

Hi Pinky—you've exhausted me! You've got some stamina!

You'll be glad to hear that Pandora is going to work on my body this month—that spare tire may soon be consigned to history!!! I may not be your porky Perky for much longer!!

PPxxxxx

From: Keith Buxton
To: All Staff

Hallo everybody

I am proud to be able to announce the first step in the rollout of ABC.

Over the next two weeks all co-colleagues will attend an ABC workshop which will kick-start the segmentation process. It is imperative that every co-colleague attends the workshops, which have been designed to be rich learning experiences as well as a lot of fun!

Keith Buxton
Chief Talent Officer

From: Martin Lukes
To: Pandora@CoachworX!

Hi Pandora

It's weird that you don't even know what I look like, so am attaching a picture of myself taken for our annual report. It's a bit cheesy—I had to stand there laughing into the phone for yonks while some idiot photographer faffed about. Still, all things considered I don't think I look too bad for 43—or 44 as I'll be in two weeks. On the upside, I've got a very good head of hair, hardly receding and hardly any gray which is more than most men of my age can boast, and 20-20 vision.

Weight—I've put on a bit of weight around the middle and maybe a tiny bit on the face since that pic was taken. Just weighed myself on Jens's scales and apparently I weigh 14 stone 2—which I don't think can be accurate . . .

I've got an exercise bike and rowing machine in my study at home which I use as much as I can, though I've never found the home the right environment for a workout, so I work out at the gym on my own, as and when.

I'd say I'm pretty health conscious foodwise. Occasionally I eat a Twix or a Bounty, but that is mainly as a result of my highly pressured lifestyle which means I often need to grab a bite on the run. I'm a total water addict. I aim to drink 5 liters for my daily detox. I'd like to start with a personal trainer again, and build up fitness, and should also try to cut back on the snacks, where possible.

22.5 percent better than my bestest
Martin

From: Pandora@CoachworX!
To: Martin Lukes

Hi Martin—

The bad news is that I am hearing a lot of double talk from you. You say you want a better body, but then you offer me a lot of excuses.

The good news is that I can help you reprogram your mind. There is a little word that begins with f. We are frightened of the f-word, and we teach our children to be frightened of it too.

I can feel that word undermining everything you say about your body. I want you to turn your back on the f-word. Once you do that, you will succeed!

Strive and thrive!
Pandora

From: Martin Lukes
To: Pandora@CoachworX!

Pandora—Frankly, I'm confused. That word is quite important to me, especially at the present time, and we certainly haven't taught our kids to be scared of it . . . on the contrary Jake (at nearly 16) seems to think of nothing else. He even tried to jump on our fat Russian au pair the other night. I just don't see how turning my back on sex is going to help my body. Quite the reverse, in fact.

22.5 percent better than my bestest
Martin

From: Pandora@CoachworX!
To: Martin Lukes

Martin—you have a great sense of humor! I didn't say anything about sex! I have no issues with that at all! Sex is great—it's one of the body's natural ways of reenergizing itself.

My f-word is fear! Listen to yourself talk, Martin. You are afraid of your body, afraid of not getting it into perfect shape. You make excuses for not going to the gym, for eating fatty foods. New You doesn't recognize fear. You are not going to fail to rebuild your body, Martin. You are going to succeed!

Strive and thrive!
Pandora

From: Martin Lukes
To: Phyllis Lukes

Dearest Mum

Thanks for your message. It is nice to think of you sitting up in your hospital bed with your laptop on your knee. I hope those nurses are treating you well. Best of British with the op tomorrow. Will come and visit in the evening, schedule permitting. I've told them that there's no hurry for you to come out. I want you to enjoy being pampered for a bit. Don't worry about the money, I've implied that Phyllis Lukes is my daughter and now seems it's all on my health insurance!

Yr loving son
Martie

From: Martin Lukes
To: Phyllis Lukes

Dearest Mum

No, I haven't lied, though maybe a smidgin economical with the truth! In any case, you shouldn't worry about insurance companies. They are all parasites, they don't add value . . . not a creovative™ individual in the entire industry . . .

Your loving son
Martie

JUNE 8

From: Martin Lukes
To: Pandora@CoachworX!

Hi Pandora

Have had my first session with Donna at the gym, who says my upper body strength is pretty good for my age! She made me do 10 mins on the cycle machine, 10 mins on the treadmill and 10 mins on the crosstrainer then we did pecs, quads, curls and stretching. Donna says the key thing is for me to learn how to exit my personal comfort zone . . . she's very motivational. I'm going to see her every day, so watch this space!

22.5 percent better than my bestest
Martin

JUNE 9

From: Martin Lukes
To: Keri Tartt

Pinky—I'm hurting . . . I ache all over . . . can you pop in and give me a little rub . . . also if you are going out could I have six liters of Evian water? Perky

JUNE 14

From: Cindy Czarnikow
To: All Staff

Hi everyone. As chief morale officer, I have been tasked with ensuring that the morale implications of Project ABC are phenome-

nally positive. I know some of you have surfaced some issues with the process, which I hope this FAQ will solve!!

Q: Are the people who are As better than the Bs and Cs?

A: No way! Everybody in this company is a uniquely talented individual. All we are saying is that the talents of A workers are supremely well aligned with our core purpose. Bs are well aligned, and Cs are not so well aligned.

Q: Are the Cs being fired?

A: I'm glad you asked that! The Cs are NOT being fired! We love them and we are deeply appreciative of all the fine work they have done here. However, we believe that in their own best interests they would be happier working someplace else.

Q: Will the senior people all be As?

A: Uh-uh! All the top people have been appraised like everyone else. As I said, the process has been incredibly fair. If I myself am a B or a C I would have no problem with that because I know I have always given this job my love and my passion.

Q: Is my grade going to be made public?

A: It's up to you! Only you and your senior manager will know your grade. If you want to cherish your grade to yourself then we don't have any problem with that!

I'm smiling at you
Cindy

From: Martin Lukes
To: Phyllis Lukes

Dearest Mum

So sorry not to have seen you last night. I came round a tad late and some mini Hitler refused to let me in as you were sleeping off the anesthetic. Will stop by today after work.

I can't believe that they got you out of bed on the first day, and that you're walking already! I told Pandora, and she said it showed that your energy levels are in balance!

See you later
Love Martie

JUNE 15

From: Martin Lukes
To: Keri Tartt

Pinky—Can't face the fire escape—it's still pouring with rain. Shall we try the Canning Town Novotel at lunchtime?

Btw you must stop being paranoid about Jens. I went on and on last night about how gorgeous Donna is which puts her off the scent (literally!!) Though actually she's so far from suspecting anything it's almost insulting! It simply hasn't occurred to her that anyone might find her husband devastatingly sexy.

Porky

From: Martin Lukes
To: Keri Tartt

No of course I don't! Donna's got hairy arms, and a minute arse.

From: Martin Lukes
To: Keri Tartt

My kinky pinky
      You really need to stop this. No I am not saying you have a big bum. As you may have noticed, I think your bum is absolutely to-

tally the perfect size, and in three hours the corporal and myself will be examining it in a proper bed!!

Porky Perky

From: Keith Buxton
To: All Staff

Hi! Next week we will be holding a brainstorming session for directors and senior department heads on the aim, scope and practice of Project ABC.

We will be kicking off with an ice breaking exercise—I'd like each of you to come up with something that's surprising about yourself.

We'll follow up with some role-play exercises. I want each individual to think of a famous person that exemplifies one of the behaviors and act in character. I know this is going to be a uniquely rewarding learning experience.

Keith

JUNE 16

From: Martin Lukes
To: Keri Tartt

Sweetest Kinky Pinky. Please don't nag me about this. I want to spend more time with you, too. It's just really hard to get it sorted. We mustn't be silly about this. We've taken a lot of risks . . . it is really important we don't get found out . . . I'll see what I can do, maybe try to get J to go away for a bit.

Porky Perky x

From: Martin Lukes
To: Graham Wallace

What are you doing for this role play? I was going to do Einstein for creovation™, but I think it's too obvious. Instead I've decided to show that I also have some of the other values, too, so am going to do Gandhi for Integrity.

Mart

From: Martin Lukes
To: Graham Wallace

Yes, I know Gandhi didn't have a beer belly. You obviously haven't noticed that I've lost 4 lbs already this month.

From: Martin Lukes
To: Jenny Withers

Darling, sorry if I was a bit short with you at breakfast. I know you find my relationship with mum difficult, but I had to ask her to convalesce with us. It won't be for long—she'll keep herself to herself, and she loves the boys.

A thought has occurred to me—why not get away from it all for a weekend to destress and detox? I could easily hold the fort, and Svetlana could help me. I'd quite like some quality time with the boys, anyway.

Martin

From: Martin Lukes
To: Jenny Withers

Jens—it saddens me that when I try to support you, you start looking for secret agendas. I simply suggested that you do something that might boost your positive energy flow. You clearly need to de-stress, but at the end of the day, it's your call.

M xx

From: Martin Lukes
To: All Staff

Pinky—It's proving harder than I thought but I'm still trying. Can't wait till later.

Perky

From: Martin Lukes
To: Keri Tartt

Fucketyfuckingfuck . . . I've just sent an e-mail to you to the whole bloody office . . . oh god oh god, my whole life is flashing before my eyes . . .

From: Martin Lukes
To: All Staff

Hi—co-colleagues may have been as surprised as I was re an e-mail sent out this afternoon under my name to all staff. This message mentioned the children's characters, Pinky and Perky. I'm mystified as to the meaning of this and can only assume that some prankster was at my terminal. If anyone has any light to throw on the matter, please contact myself, or my PA, Keri Tartt.

Best, Martin

From: Martin Lukes
To: IT Director

Hi, can you get one of your team to investigate the issue of security. I have just had someone else sending out e-mails apparently from me. In this department alone we have much intellectual capital with untold value. It is IMPERATIVE that we have adequate fire walls in place.

Martin

JUNE 21

From: Keith Buxton
To: All Staff

Hi!

The first ABC workshops have been exceeding expectations. I was privileged to attend the London one—where everyone got a lot closer to each other. In the course of the day Roger Wright shared the interesting fact that he collects first world war helmets, Jenny Withers told us that her ambition is to write a novel, and Faith Preston told us about her gold medal in salsa dancing.

The power of the role play exercise to unleash the spirit was phenomenal. It would be invidious to single out the performance of any individual, but Christo Weinberg as Frank Zappa for creovation was inspired. Jenny Withers was a fabulous Pollyanna, and Martin Lukes' Gandhi was unforgettable—as was his Indian accent!

It is now time to move on to the next plank of the project, which is a 360 degree exercise. I would like everybody to ask three colleagues to grade them on a scale of one to 10 on the six behaviors, and then e-mail the grades to me. Choose one person who reports to you, one who you report to, and one who is a peer.

And then I will ask you to assess yourselves, before embarking on a thorough scientific assessment of all team members.

Keith

JUNE 22

From: Martin Lukes
To: Pandora@CoachworX!

I'm a bit down because it's my birthday today. At the end of the day, I don't want to be 44. I hate birthdays at the best of times, but this year I got no cards at all. I asked Jens for a juicer, so that I could make celery and fennel pick-me-up, but she got me something that squeezes oranges, which is hopeless, as Donna says citrus is much too acidic for me.

Martin

From: Pandora@CoachworX!
To: Martin Lukes

Hi Martin
Where's the positive headset?? The passing of another year is a HUGE celebration, not something to be depressed about.

Did you know you have three ages, Martin? Your chronological age, your biological age, and your mental age. Only by the first measure are you getting older. The other two measures are much more important, and if you focus on them you can get younger, as young as you like. By self care you can roll back your biological age. You can also turn back your psychological age by surrounding

yourself with younger people. By rethinking your wardrobe. Martin you are not 44. You are whatever age you want to be!!
Happy Birthday!

Strive and thrive!
Pandora

From: Martin Lukes
To: Jake Lukes

Hi Jake
Good to get your message, though can I remind you that the traditional way of celebrating someone's birthday is to give them a present, not to ask them for more money. The answer is no, your allowance must last till the end of the month. But once your exams are out of the way, I may give you a little extra.

Love Dad

From: Martin Lukes
To: Keri Tartt

Dearest Pinky. Thank you so much. I've never worn combat trousers before, but it's going to be my new look—Pandora says that by being with you and wearing younger clothes I am making the clock go backwards. Can't be bad! Don't sulk at me about this evening—Jens has invited friends round for a not very surprising surprise party. Can't we celebrate at lunchtime?

M xx

From: Martin Lukes
To: Graham Wallace

Graham—

Ha, ha very funny. Actually Keri thinks they look great on me. Just because I'm 41, doesn't mean I have to dress it.

Am assuming that you and I are doing each other's ABC forms? Let's agree on a marking system: no marks lower than 7 and an average of about 8.5. Are you going to get Rog to do it as your boss? As I've completely blown it with him, I may have to ask Keith.

M

From: Martin Lukes
To: Keith Buxton

Hi Keith

I just wanted to touch base to say what a sensational job we all think you are doing with Project ABC. Btw, I wondered if you could do my behaviors rating for me? I feel that you know my strengths (and weaknesses!!!) better than anyone—I'd be delighted to return the favor.

All my very bestest
Martin

JUNE 23

From: Martin Lukes
To: Keri Tartt

Pinky—Boring horrible evening, and cost me an arm and a leg. I thought about you all the time. This mate of mine from Goldmans went on and on about how much money he's making, and Jens was tired and bad tempered.

I'm filling in your ABC form—can u do mine??

Love you
Perky

From: Martin Lukes
To: Faith Preston

Hi Faith—I don't understand your message. I haven't got a daughter, and she hasn't had an accident . . . ???

Cheers Martin

JUNE 24

From: Martin Lukes
To: Jenny Withers

Darling—

That's fantastic! OF COURSE you should go. West Midlands CBI is a fantastic forum for you! Don't worry about me—I can hold the fort and make sure Jake is prepared for his GCSEs. It's only one night. Go and show them what you're made of!

Love you
Martin

From: Martin Lukes
To: Keri Tartt

Kinky Pinky—

Perky's got some fantastic news! J is off to Birmingham tomorrow night to keynote to some boring midlands businessmen about pushing the communications envelope, or something.

I need to pop into the hospital to see mum, then will meet you at One Aldwych. The au pair knows I'm going to be out . . . so long as I'm back by 2am . . . should be ok . . . we can have 7 whole hours together . . . can't wait . . . Corporal v excited.

Porky Perky xxx

JUNE 25

From: Martin Lukes
To: Jake Lukes

Hi Jake

How was your history GCSE today? Hope not too horrendous.

Fraid something has come up at work . . . probably won't be back till late. Svetlana will make supper, make sure you get to bed at a reasonable time . . . and are fresh for your maths exam tomorrow.

Dad

JUNE 26

From: Martin Lukes
To: Jake Lukes

WHAT THE BLOODY HELL DID YOU THINK YOU WERE DOING LAST NIGHT????? SVETLANA SAYS YOU WENT OUT DRINKING, GOT HOME DRUNK AFTER MIDNIGHT, THREW UP AND WERE LATE FOR YOUR EXAM THIS MORNING. THIS WAS UNBELIEVABLY STUPID, EVEN BY YOUR RECENT STANDARDS.

DAD

From: Martin Lukes
To: Jenny Withers

Hi Darling—hope your speech went well last night, was keeping my fingers crossed. Sorry I wasn't at home when you called . . . I had to pop out for a swift half with Peter next door. Everything fine this end. See you later.

Love you M xxx

From: Martin Lukes
To: Jake Lukes

I don't like the tone of your message—it is not your business where I was last night, though if you must know I was out with Graham and some clients, missed the last train so stayed at his place.

Can I suggest a deal? Your mother is going to go absolutely ballistic when she finds out about your GCSE. So I suggest that we do not tell her. In return I would be grateful if you did not mention that I was out all night. Your mother doesn't approve of Graham, so it might make life easier if she didn't know.

Is that a deal?

Dad

From: Martin Lukes
To: Jake Lukes

What do you mean "whatever"? This matters. Do we have a deal?

Text message to Svetlana. Sent 10:42

Best not to mention anything about yesterday to Jens. I know nothing was your fault, but she might blame you . . . Martin

JUNE 28

From: Martin Lukes
To: Keri Tartt

Pinky—Probably best if we cancel our afternoon assignment. I'm meant to be writing my own assessment so I need to give it some serious headspace . . . Don't put any calls through to me, and if any team members try to see me, tell them to go away.

From: Martin Lukes
To: Keri Tartt

Kinky pinky, don't be silly. You of all people should understand how important being an A is to me. The corporal is sulking, but I've told him he'll see some action tomorrow.

Love you
(still) porky perky

From: Martin Lukes
To: Jenny Withers

Darling—how are you going to approach this self assessment thing? If I give myself 10 for everything, do you think they might smell a rat? But if I give less I might lose out to people like Graham and Christo who are so boastful . . . how are you going to play it?
M

From: Martin Lukes
To: Jenny Withers

What do you mean: "just be honest"????? That's no help at all.

From: Martin Lukes
To: DonnaAdonis@Bodybuild

Hi, Donna.
  I'm afraid I'm going to have to cancel tonight. I'm totally snowed under here, but will work out at home tonight.
  See you tomorrow. Martin

From: Martin Lukes
To: Graham Wallace

Jesus, I've just seen the ABC forms we're meant to fill in for our teams. They are 62 pages long and I've got 37 people to do! Don't these consultants realize we have work to do?? Mart

Shall we have a large drink?

JUNE 29

From: Martin Lukes
To: DonnaAdonis@Bodybuild

Hi Donna—really sorry am going to have to cancel again. Rest assured, I'm working hard on my machines at home. This week I'm concentrating on the isolation, definition intensity and focus of my abdominals.

Will do Tuesday without fail.

Martin

From: Martin Lukes
To: Bettina Schmidt

Hi Bettina

In reply to your message, yes I shall be doing an assessment of you. I know that you have only been on my team a short while, but don't worry about that—I'll talk to your line manager in Düsseldorf . . . and we can build up a behavior profile of you together. If you want to talk, my door is always open.

Cheers, Martin

From: Martin Lukes
To: Bettina Schmidt

Sorry, can't do now—make an appointment with Keri.

From: Martin Lukes
To: Christo Weinberg

Christo—Thanks for sending me the reminder of all your wins in the last year. I shall of course take them all into account.

Martin

From: Martin Lukes
To: All Marketing

Team—Various members of the team have expressed concern at the ABC procedure. I appreciate that this is an uncertain time for everybody. However, I hope I don't need to tell you that I shall be thinking long and hard about each of the forms. I suggest that for the time being you channel your concerns into your work. We don't want to let anyone accuse this team of taking its eye off the ball!

Best, Martin

From: Pandora@CoachworX!
To: Martin Lukes

Martin,
    Congratulations! You have reached the halfway mark of Executive Bronze. This is always a moving moment. Half the program in the past, and the other half still in the future! I feel that you have come such a very long way. Your body is stronger and more grounded. You are getting younger. When I first met you, you were

someone who used the word can't. I haven't heard you say that in ages.

I want you to give yourself a treat or a present. You deserve it, Martin. And when you give it to yourself I want you to say: I love me. I love my body. I look and feel fantastic, over and over.

Strive and thrive!
Pandora

From: Martin Lukes
To: Keri Tartt

Pinky—I've booked us the bridal suite at the Canning Town Novotel for the afternoon. Champagne, rich chocolate fudge cake, the works. Pandora says I deserve it.

Perky

JUNE 30

From: Martin Lukes
To: Keri Tartt

Pinky—Yes, I am cheesed off. It was meant to be a treat for me, and after the grim evening on my birthday I felt I deserved it. Frankly I didn't appreciate you rushing off in a huff. To say that I am "self-obsessed" was really below the belt. I spend my entire life thinking about others, whether it is you, Jens, mum, the boys, my team, etc etc. The reason I was whispering that to myself was part of Exec Bronze. Of course I love you, and your body too. You are fantastic. Goes without saying.

Please don't be cross.

See you tomorrow
I love you

Perky, who is still, if we are going to be 110 percent honest, a
tiny bit porky

7

JULY

My Funeral

JULY 1

From: Pandora@CoachworX!
To: Martin Lukes

Hi Martin,
Please find somewhere to read this where you are on your own.
It is imperative that no one interrupts you as you enter one of the
deepest stages of the Executive Bronze Program. Clear your mind,
and focus.

I want you to imagine that you are going to the funeral of
someone you love very much. Now imagine the church or the crematorium. Look at the faces of the other mourners, the flowers.

Next I want you to imagine yourself slowly going up to the
front and peeking into the coffin. Inside is . . . yourself! This is
your funeral, Martin. Look again at the people's faces, Martin.
Look at their sorrow and their pain. What sort of gap have you left
in their lives?

Now I want you to imagine that you pick up the program and
see there will be four speakers. The first is a member of your family. The second is a friend. The third is a work colleague, and the
fourth is from your church or any organization where you have
been involved in a giving role. Each one will talk honestly about
the role you have played in their lives.

Take your time to think about this. Your funeral is, after all, the ultimate wake-up call on what you have achieved, both in your relationships and your life.

What would it be like? What would those four people say about you?

I'm really looking forward to seeing what you are going to make of this, Martin.

This is probably the most life-changing exercise of the whole program!

Strive and thrive!
Pandora

From: Martin Lukes
To: Jenny Withers

Darling—fraid I can't go to Max's speech day this pm. I've got a big report to write for Atlanta, something v time sensitive that I need to crack on with. Tell him I'm sorry but I promise to come next year when he's at Eton.

Love you M

PS Quick question: what color would you wear to my funeral?

From: Martin Lukes
To: Jenny Withers

No need to be sarcastic . . . It is just an exercise I'm doing for Pandora. M

From: Martin Lukes
To: Max Lukes

Max—Really sorry not to be with you this afternoon, son. I'll be cheering you on from my desk, and expect to see a whole row of silver cups when I get home!!

Can I ask you something? Just suppose I popped my clogs in the next year or two . . . and suppose you had to say something about me at my funeral, what would you say?

Love Dad

From: Martin Lukes
To: Max Lukes

Forget it, doesn't matter. I just wondered if you'd mention the football games I've taken you to or me reading you Fireman Sam when you were little?

Love Dad

From: Martin Lukes
To: Keri Tartt

Would Pinky cry lots of piggie tears if Perky popped his clogs?

From: Martin Lukes
To: Keri Tartt

Cheeky message! I love it when you talk dirty like that . . . though maybe not a brilliant idea on work e-mail!

Come into my office now, we can pull the blinds down . . . per-fectly safe if we're quick . . .

Perky xxxxxxxxxxx

From: Martin Lukes
To: Graham Wallace

Ooops! What can I say??? That was a bit embarrassing! I suppose I should be pleased that it was you and not anyone else. . . . Shagging your secretary is a bit predictable and as you know, I specialize in the unexpected!! But Keri's not your classic secretary . . . she's a really amazing girl, shag of a lifetime, etc. But please please . . . NOT A WORD!!!

JULY 5

From: Martin Lukes
To: Pandora@CoachworX!

Hi Pandora

Can I be very honest with you? I've found it a highly emotional exercise. Cathartic, really. In fact thinking about my death made me break down and cry. It has been some time since that happened—last time was when Tiger Woods was beaten by that boring Fijian guy—but that wasn't quite the same.

So, here is how I envision my funeral.

Jens will be led into the church with Jake and Max on either side, holding her up. She won't be wearing black—she will have insisted that the funeral is not to be a sad occasion, but a celebration of my life, so she'll be wearing something bright. She'll be ashen faced. So will the boys.

My mother will be there looking unbearably sad, but not crying. She is a very strong person, who will do all her grieving in private. I've been trying to work out if my father would put in appearance or not. He walked out when I was 10. Basically, he was the sort of man who was always looking out for Number One. We've always been chalk and cheese—didn't get on even when I was a kid. On balance, I think he'll stay away—I don't think he'd have the guts to face the music.

My sister Katherine will come, though. She and I also haven't spoken for years, as she has serious issues around jealousy, and always complained that I was Mum's favorite. She had a series of breakdowns as a teenager, for which I think she blamed me. These days I don't even know where she lives. She'll arrive late at my funeral, and start crying hysterically. They say death is worse for people when there's unfinished business.

Keri Tartt will have organized the flowers. She will be standing leaning on Mary (Roger's PA) sobbing uncontrollably. Although we haven't worked together long, she not only respects me as a boss but also appreciates me as a human being. She will be in a black trouser suit, tight black T-shirt underneath—full mourning. A little detail that chokes me up: She will have taken the silver stud out of her tongue and put in a black one.

Jake will have made a slide show of all the photos of me—graduating from Durham, the one of me and Jens on holiday in Crete. I was looking very tanned and in very good shape. Jens will choose the music, which will be some of my favorite songs and things that remind her of me. Elton John's "Rocket Man." The Rolling Stones' "I Can't Get No Satisfaction." That brilliant bit of Wagner from Apocalypse Now. The Kinks' "Thank You for the Days." And "Stairway to Heaven" by Led Zeppelin. When Jens hears that she will start to cry, quietly but inconsolably.

The church will be packed. Standing room only.

Everyone from the UK board will be there. Cindy and Barry won't have been able to make it, but will have sent messages to Jens which will be read out by Keith. Barry's message will say I had one of the finest and most creovative™ headsets and warmest hearts of anyone he had the privilege of working with. It will be all American and totally over the top, but there will be a kernel of truth and sincerity in it too.

The odd thing is that I always thought there was something between Keith and Jens, but today she doesn't even look at him.

Max will read out my favorite poem, the one that goes "If you can keep your head, when all around you are losing theirs . . ." and then will say a few words about me. He's very good at speaking—he is head of the debating society at his prep school. He will tell them how I used to read him Fireman Sam as a child. How

I took him to football matches, and how, even though I was often at work, I always had quality time for him.

Graham will stand up and talk as my friend.

He will talk about the fun side of me. How mischievous I am, how I'm not frightened to break the rules. He would talk about how my handicap used to be higher than his, but how it is now lower, and how guilty he feels now about giving me such a hard time about it.

As I'm not a member of a church, and as I'm not really part of any charity thing, I'll have just the three speakers. Though if the funeral can be put forward a year or two I may be a parent governor of Eton by then, so maybe the Provost of the school would give a little talk about my added value in the school, and my attitude to the nonprofit sector in general.

Then afterwards everyone will come back to our house. At first the mood will the solemn, stunned. There'll be loads of bubbly and posh eats and people will start to talk, and laugh, and dance. It will be the best bash anyone can remember.

On my gravestone it will say:

MARTIN LUKES
A CREOVATIVE™ MIND AND A LOVING HEART WHO
NEVER STOPPED PUSHING THE ENVELOPE.

22.5 percent better than my very bestest
Martin

JULY 6

From: Barry Malone
To: All Staff

Howdy!

It's been a challenging first half! As you'll see from the attachment, our Q2 earnings are down 21 percent, as we've been hit by the continued competitive pressures in the economic landscape, by adverse currency fluctuations, and by falling demand in many regions.

*However, our underlying performance is strong, and we have
a strategy in place to transition us to our goal of Phenomenal
Performance—Permanently!*

*I am thrilled to announce that after three months of obsession,
love and determination by Keith Buxton and his team, we are
ready to raise the a-b glöbâl talent bar. Tomorrow all coworkers
will receive a letter at their home addresses letting them know if
they are an A, a B or a C.*

*Can I just say that the Cs who will be leaving our close-knit
family will be in our prayers. I would like to take this opportunity
to thank each of them individually for their talents and their dedication and wish them joy in whatever the future brings them!*

I love you all,
Barry S. Malone

From: Martin Lukes
To: Jenny Withers

Jens—I suggest you go in to work normal time, and I'll wait for
the postman . . .

M x

From: Pandora@CoachworX!
To: Martin Lukes

Hi Martin
    When I read about your funeral, I was deeply moved. However
there are some issues here. I want you to think about closure with
your sister and father. Is this something that you should try to get
while you are still alive?
    I'm also interested at the way you single out Keri, who as you
say hasn't been with you that long. Is there an issue here that we
need to visit?

My other concern is that your involvement with the community could be stronger.

Martin, in this life to achieve the goal of lifelong success and happiness, it is not what you take out, but what you put in that counts!!

Strive and thrive!
Pandora

From: Martin Lukes
To: Pandora@CoachworX!

Hi, Pandora,
Sorry—can't reply at present. I'm waiting for confirmation that I'm an A.

22.5 percent etc.
M

From: Martin Lukes
To: Jenny Withers

No fucking post and it's 9:45. The postal system in this country had gone down the tubes. The whole bloody lot of them should be fired. I'm going to give it 20 more minutes, then I'm coming into the office. M xx

From: Martin Lukes
To: Jenny Withers

HHOOOOOORAYYYYYYYYYYYYYYY!!!!! I'm an A!!!!!!!!!!!
!!!!!!
   Shall I open your envelope or shall I bring it in?

M XXXXX

From: Martin Lukes
To: Jenny Withers

Congratulations, darling. You are a B. Let's go out and celebrate somewhere really nice tonight. The Savoy?

Love you
M

From: Martin Lukes
To: Jenny Withers

Darling . . . There's nothing wrong with being a B! It's really good! Bs are high achievers who exit their comfort zone to go the extra mile!! Fine about dinner, if you don't want to. Quite understand. Must get into work now . . . I'll see you later.

M xx

From: Martin Lukes
To: Keri Tartt

Pinky—that's so sweet of you. Yes, I'm pleased, though obviously it's not the be all and end all. There are more important things in this life of ours! I'm glad you're dead pleased to be a B. One of the many things that I love so much about you is that you're so happy with yourself just as you are. What's that great Barry White song, "I love you just the way you are . . ." Ambition really screws people up. Just look at Jens—she's sulking about being a B as if it's some huge disaster.

Let's go out and celebrate—call the Ivy and get a table for two 8ish? I know it's a bit public there and there's a chance of people recognizing me, but I feel like making a splash. We'll just have to be a bit careful to keep our hands to ourselves during the meal . . .

Perky xxx

From: Martin Lukes
To: Keri Tartt

What do you mean they are fully booked??? Call them back and tell them I'm an A.

From: Martin Lukes
To: Graham Wallace

Bad luck, but at least you're not a C! Actually, I'm an A—probably a fluke! Have you heard about Rog or Faith??

Mart

From: Martin Lukes
To: Pandora@CoachworX!

Hi Pandora

Sorry not to have got back to you sooner, but everything's been going mad here. The powers that be have decided in their wisdom that yours truly is an A. Although I wasn't surprised, I was relieved, because in this place (as I have discovered to my cost!!) reward isn't always aligned with talent. Think Roger.

I've been thinking about some of your suggestions. I'm 145 percent in favor of giving something back to the community. It is a matter of finding the right fit.

RE my family, I've decided against touching base with my father, even if it was possible to find where he is. He's a C if ever there was one, and I can't see any value added coming from a meeting. Re Katherine, I'll mull it over. Closure might do us both a lot of good.

And re Keri—you're barking up the wrong tree there! She's a great gal, and a terrific PA, but that's about as far as it goes!!

22.5 percent better than my very bestest
Martin

From: Pandora@CoachworX!
To: Martin Lukes

Hi Martin

Just a quick note to congratulate you on being an A. But as your most sincere fan, I think you should view it as a baseline. You can go further. Ask what is the point of being an A? Is it an end in itself? Think of that eulogy. You are the creovative ™ guy who never stopped pushing the envelope. Go push that envelope! Give something back!

Strive and thrive!
Pandora

From: Martin Lukes
To: Bettina Schmidt

Bettina

I understand that you are upset, but I think we need to look at this calmly. First, any decision to make you a C did not emanate from myself. Your response is perfectly natural and is the first step of the SARAH cycle. When you hear difficult news, the first response is Shock and Anger. In time you may feel a little Resentment moving on towards Acceptance. The final H is either hope or happiness, can't remember which!

In the long term, you will discover that being a C is the right thing for you. It gives you the chance to be redeployed somewhere where the fit is better!

You might not believe this, but I can be pretty vulnerable myself, and have had one or two knocks along the way. SARAH has proved very useful to myself dealing with disappointment and moving on.

Martin

From: Martin Lukes
To: Graham Wallace

Rog is an A???? That is absolutely fucking bonkers. He doesn't possess any of the values at all—except obsession—about saving the marginal 2p. And Christo as well?? If they make idiots like that A, it really devalues the currency.

From: Martin Lukes
To: Keri Tart

My darling Pinky
Thank you for last night . . . you are so sexy and funny and lovely. I'm only sorry that the evening ended on a slightly off note. I realize that it is hard on you getting closer and closer to yours truly and then having to put up with the fact that I go home to Jens every night.

But I was speaking the total truth when I said the corporal hasn't been anywhere near her in ages. You are the only one for me (and him!!). The hanky-panky side of our relationship ended pretty much some time back.

You have to believe me when I say that I do want to be with you properly, I promise. Cross Porky's heart. But I can't leave her just now when Max hasn't even started at Eton yet. Give me time.

We would be brilliant together. We ARE brilliant together.

Love you very very very much
Porky

From: Martin Lukes
To: Phyllis Lukes

Dearest Mummy
Thanks for your message. You said you were sure I'd be an A— and guess what?? I am! Obviously v pleased though playing the diplomat here a bit as there are a lot of disappointed people about—Jens included!

Delighted you've settled in so quickly back home and that your knee is behaving itself. It's probably more restful being home than it was staying chez nous!!

Don't worry about Jake—I know he's drinking a bit—but they all do it after GCSEs these days. Look at Tony Blair's sons! At least last week Jake passed out in the privacy of his own house! Did I tell you Max scooped up all the prizes at prize day . . . rugby, maths, debating, he even got a cup for kindness!

Haven't got any other news except that Pandora has had me planning my funeral! Don't say anything mum—it was actually very revealing about myself. It got me thinking about Katherine and wondering if I should contact her. She always had issues with my overachievement, as she saw it. Which is ridiculous, really, because she was a bit of a slogger but always got there in the end, if my memory serves. Do you have an e-mail address for her?

I must go now, and earn my salary. We'll come down at the weekend. And if the weather's nice, might nip off for a game of golf at the RAC club as one of my colleagues just became a member.

Yr loving son
Martie

PS I can't believe that you're gardening again. Actually I can believe it knowing you!

JULY 12

From: Roger Wright
To: All Staff
IMPORTANT: PLEASE READ

I am very sorry to inform all staff that an incident of a serious nature has occurred re Project ABC. There is evidence that an individual or individuals have gained access to computer files and some of the appraisals have been tampered with.

This is an exceptionally serious matter and we have decided that we will be getting our IT experts to search the hard disks of every computer in the office. All e-mails and all files will be examined by myself, and by Jeff Grout, Director of IT.

In the meantime all As, Bs and Cs are considered only provisional.

I know I can count on your assistance in this matter.

Roger Wright
Acting Chairman

From: Martin Lukes
To: Graham Wallace

Who do you think it was?? I've got my suspicions. Frankly what concerns me are some pretty dodgy e-mails on the system I've sent to Keri . . . aarrgghh.

From: Martin Lukes
To: Max Lukes

Hi Max—

This is Dad again in my role as technical ignoramus!!! Max, you're the computer whiz of the family, and I just wanted to ask your advice on something. We've had a bit of a security breach here, and I'm trying to help the IT guys. Suppose someone had sent a load of messages on e-mail at work, and deleted all of them—would they still be there on the hard drive? And how easy would it be to delete?

Love, Dad

PS Probably best not to mention this to mum. She doesn't like it when I help out people in other departments. She says I should be more focused on my own priorities, and then come home on time!!!

From: Martin Lukes
To: Keri Tartt

Set up hotmail account for you. *Kinkypinky@hotmail.com* password: privatepussy.

From: porkyperky@hotmail
To: kinkypinky@hotmail

Dearest KP

From now on, HOTMAIL ONLY. NO MORE E-MAILS on the work system. We can't be too careful.

According to Max there is a way of removing all trace . . . he's got a couple of ideas but I need some access codes which must be somewhere in the IT dept. I need to get in at night when everyone's gone . . .

Pp xx

From: Porky Perky
To: Kinky Pinky

Pinky . . . you haven't got much faith in my IT skills, I'm pretty confident I can do it. The main problem is going to be explaining to J why I'm going out yet again . . .

Perky

From: Martin Lukes
To: Jenny Withers

Darling

Tim Zadek from Boogie Gargle Fink has asked me at the last minute to go to Glyndebourne tonight to see Carmen. You know I love Puccini, so I've said yes. He's only got one ticket . . . so fraid it's just me. Won't be back till v late. Hope you don't mind.

Love you
M xx

From: Martin Lukes
To: Jenny Withers

Bizet, whatever. I'll send a cab home to get my dinner jacket.

JULY 13

From: Porky Perky
To: Kinky Pinky

Disaster. Failed mission . . . don't want to go into details just now—Maybe a good idea if we don't see each other for a bit . . .

From: Porky Perky
To: Kinky Pinky

Sweetie . . . don't be like that . . . please . . . please understand my whole life is flashing before my eyes . . .

Worried Perky x

JULY 14

From: Martin Lukes
To: Pandora@CoachworX!

Hi Pandora—

I have a serious issue I need to share. Long story short, a low-key relationship has developed between myself and my PA Keri. All very casual, which is why I hadn't mentioned anything. If anything, my relationship with her has been very much in keeping with your teachings, about being with younger people to reduce my psychological age etc. Anyway we now have a situation where some idiot (I've got my suspicions) has been fiddling with the appraisals, and all e-mails are now being read.

Unfortunately there are a couple of e-mails on the system I've sent to Keri that might be misinterpreted. Obviously, now that I'm an A player, it's imperative that I am seen to eat, drink, breathe all six values 24/7. Quite apart from rocking the boat with J.

So I went in the office late last night trying to do a bit of deleting on the hard disk. Unfortunately I was seen by the head of IT who now suspects me of tampering with the grades myself.

Help!

Martin

From: Pandora@CoachworX!
To: Martin Lukes

Martin, most of the time, I just love being a coach. It is one of the most amazingly exciting jobs in the world, but sometimes it's one of the toughest jobs too. When I read your e-mail just now I felt my own energy levels depleted. I felt you had drilled a big hole in my colander, and I was literally watching the energy drain away.

Martin, I am saddened. You have not been truthful to me. Or to yourself. You have violated your values. If you lie to yourself,

you do not respect yourself, deep down. And without self respect you cannot generate self love.

I can't tell you what to do now. You must feel for the true path yourself. Let the GROW model help you do the right thing.

Strive and thrive!
Pandora

From: Martin Lukes
To: Pandora@CoachworX!

With the greatest respect, I don't think this is the time for a GROW model. I have sent some e-mails to my PA that would not look good if read by others. I am now wrongly suspected of fiddling with the ABC grades. My wife may leave me. I may be the laughingstock of the company. I may be fired.

No wins here, only some losses more totally horrendous than others.

Not better than my best at all
Martin

From: Pandora@CoachworX!
To: Martin Lukes

Martin—I quite disagree! There are HUGE wins here from doing the right thing. Remember NO FAILURE—ONLY FEEDBACK! To get back onto the track of being better than the best you can be takes great courage. And I know you have that!

Strive and thrive!
Pandora

From: Roger Wright
To: All Staff
Subject: IMPORTANT PLEASE READ

A meeting will be held this afternoon at 1500hrs in the staff restaurant to discuss urgent developments re ABC. It is imperative that every staff member attends promptly.

Roger Wright
Acting Chairman

From: Martin Lukes
To: Jenny Withers

Darling
    Could we do lunch today? There is something I wanted to talk to you about quite urgently. All Bar One on Canning Town High Street?

Love you, M xx

From: Porky Perky
To: Kinky Pinky

Pinky—I've got to tell her. I'm going to play it down as much as poss, say you were a one-night stand . . . that it's all over anyway . . . no big deal. Wish me luck. Perky

From: Porky Perky
To: Kinky Pinky

Pinky, you're not being very supportive. Don't you see how hard this is for me?

From: Porky Perky
To: Kinky Pinky

Keri—Jens has taken it very badly. She said I was a cretin, and all sorts of highly hurtful things about you—Tartt by name, tart by nature, moronic new age antipodean etc—I'll spare you the details.

Sweetie, what this means is that we are going to stop seeing each other. I'm totally gutted, but I really can't see any alternative. I know you are going to be upset, and I can't bear that, but what can I do? I want you to know that it's been really wonderful. I mean it. I'm going to miss you, but I think there is a time for doing the right thing . . . can't talk about it now . . . it's Rog's meeting now. Better go up separately . . .

Martin

From: Roger Wright
To: All Staff

I would like to document the proceedings of today's meeting for those staff members unable to attend.

We have discovered that the discrepancies in ABC rankings were as a result of statistical errors inputting data carried out by junior members of the team. There will be no further investigations into this matter.

Members of staff with incorrect grades will receive notification by the end of the week.

Roger Wright

From: Martin Lukes
To: Graham Wallace

I don't fucking believe it . . . I've just come clean to the ladywife (actually, not 110 percent clean as I said it was just a couple of flirtatious e-mails, and I had only kissed her once). Jens went nuclear, and I've split with Keri. And all for nothing—Great reward for honesty. If I am now downgraded to a B, I'm going to kill myself.

M

JULY 20

From: Martin Lukes
To: Keri Tartt

Hi Keri

Can you go through my schedule for next week, and get me a large latte. And please don't look like that. This is very hard for myself too.

Martin

From: Martin Lukes
To: Keri Tartt

Jesus Christ! I would have forgotten altogether . . . Thanks for reminding me! Catastrophe averted!!

M

From: Martin Lukes
To: Jenny Withers

Darling—Don't think for a minute I had forgotten your birthday! What do you want? Would really like to push the boat out for you a bit this year. M XX

From: Martin Lukes
To: Bettina Schmidt

Hi Bettina!

Well what did I tell you? I'm delighted that you've been upped to a B! So you won't be leaving us after all! No one could be gladder than myself!

I told you that the SARAH cycle ended in Hope, and I wasn't wrong, was I?

Best, Martin

From: Martin Lukes
To: Jenny Withers

Listen darling. I know you're a tiny bit cross with me and my brief silliness over Keri, so I've got you something lovely for your birthday—a luxury weekend to Champneys!! All the treatments . . . shiatsu, massage, facials, pedicures, you name it. You deserve the break, and I'll take the boys. I'd like to have a bit of quality time with them . . .

Hope you really enjoy it and destress a bit! It will show you that there's more to life than work . . .

Love you, M xx

From: Martin Lukes
To: Jenny Withers

Darling, that's great, well done! Did you get the letter just now? I must say I'm not at all surprised. I was sure you'd be an A—apart from anything it looks bad if none of the top women are A's. And I was sure Keith would look after you!

M xx

From: Martin Lukes
To: Graham Wallace

I'm feeling thirsty all of a sudden. Drink?

JULY 21

From: Barry Malone
To: All Staff

Howdy! Project ABC has been an astounding success! I am humbled by the hundreds of grateful e-mails I have received from Cs thanking me and telling me how they have been empowered to go forward and use their talents!

At a-b glöbâl we have passion for integrity. A passion for driving performance. But the greatest of all is a passion for the communities we live in.

We will never achieve Phenomenal Performance Permanently unless we think of our corporate heart, and of what we are giving back.

Everywhere I go within this company I meet co-leaders who say: what can I do to contribute? And we have decided our value added lies with the global under-16 community. Kids in every geography are our seed corn. They are our future. I have tasked

Cindy Czarnikow in Atlanta and Jenny Withers in London with heading up the Project.

I love you all
Barry

From: Jenny Withers
To: All Staff

Hi everyone
As you will have read from our CEO's memo, this week sees the launch of Project Global Seed Corn—our way of giving back to children globally. This is a phenomenally exciting initiative that will enable us to achieve our goal of sustainable triple bottom-line growth. This week I am asking every department to come up with ways of improving the lives of children, not in a one-time way, but as part of a long-term relationship that will grow the seed corn!

Jenny Withers

From: Martin Lukes
To: Jenny Withers

Darling! That was brilliant. Your e-mail sounded really professional, very can-do, as well as a cri de coeur. Well done, you.

I'll make sure my team does its bit! Will be home by 7 at the latest.

M xx

JULY 23

From: Martin Lukes
To: Katherine Lukes

Hi Katherine

I think you'll be pretty surprised to get this e-mail. It's been a long time.

Look, I'm not going to beat about the bush—basically, I thought it was time we met up. I think there are issues that you, and for all I know myself too, need closure on. I occasionally hear your news from mum who, btw, was a bit miffed that you didn't help more with the knee op, which I stumped up the dosh for so that she wouldn't have to wait.

Anyway I'd be very happy to buy you lunch or a drink or something in the foreseeable—it'd be good to catch up!

Best
Martin

JULY 26

From: Martin Lukes
To: Pandora@CoachworX!

This is going to have to be a quick report back on the month, as I am trying to get home on time. Basically I think you should be very pleased with me. I have contacted my sister, and have taken the courageous option and told Jens about my brief flirtation with Keri. Now I'm being the model supportive husband. I also plan to get my team to do something to support deprived local kids . . .

22.5 percent better than my very bestest
Martin

From: Pandora@CoachworX!
To: Martin Lukes

Hi Martin—
   Well done! You have done the really difficult thing! You have
told your wife, and are working to heal the damage. Hang on to
that view of your wife in the crematorium—ashen faced. Integrity
is one of the values that makes you an A. You are fighting for your
integrity, and that it is a hard thing to do.

Strive and thrive!
Pandora

JULY 29

From: Porky Perky
To: Kinky Pinky

I can't bear this. It's too painful, especially in the hot weather. The
corporal really misses his private. I'm sure we can carry on if we
are really, really careful. Fire escape in five mins?

From: Porky Perky
To: Kinky Pinky

Dearest Pinky . . . do you want me to beg? Look, tell you what. J is
away for her de-stress weekend at Champneys. I'm meant to have
the boys, but I can always bribe Svetlana to take them. Paris,
maybe?

Porky Perky xxxxxxxxxxxxxxxxxxxxxxxxxxx

8

AUGUST
My Work/Life Balance

AUGUST 2

From: Porky Perky
To: Kinky Pinky

Dearest sweetest sexiest loveliest Kinky Pinky

Thank you for the best night ever. Ever since I got home I've been pottering around the house singing the Hot Chocolate song that so reminds me of my pink: "You Sexy Thing." Max has told me to shut up—no respect at all. Trust Eton will see to that.

Must go now, as Jens is due back from Champneys any minute. Just wanted to say you mustn't worry about the future. We will be together one day. Porky promise.

Lots of kisses
Xxxx

From: Porky Perky
To: Kinky Pinky

Dear Pinky

It's 1am. Jens has just gone off to bed, stress levels not much helped by £700 of healing, palmistry, graphology, herbal medicine etc . . . It really pisses me off that she isn't more grateful seeing as she only gave me an orange squeezer for my b'day.

She went nuclear at me for not unloading the diswasher and at Max for leaving his cereal bowl on the table. She's still very angry about you—keeps making snarky remarks about "la Tartt."

Pinky, don't want you to take this the wrong way, but I've decided it'd be better for all and sundry if you stopped being my PA. It'd get Jens off my case, and would make it easier for us to carry on.

The best thing would be for you to work for Graham. His PA, Denise is on the verge of dropping her sproglet, and as he's in the loop re us, it'll make it easier. Bed now. I need my beauty sleep.

Love you
Porky

From: Porky Perky
To: Kinky Pinky

Pinky, I understand you're upset, but you really mustn't ring on my mobile—it's far too dangerous.

And I take exception to you saying I'm henpecked. It's so far off base that I'm not even going to waste words defending myself. OK, I know you don't like me going on and on about Jens all the time, but I do have to live with her, and I think you should be a bit more understanding of that.

I also think you should adopt a more positive headset towards working for Graham. I know it's a demotion for you working for a B rather than an A. But at least those lazy idiots in sales don't know the meaning of hard work, so you'll have more spare time to do little things for me—and the corporal.

Bed now. See you tomorrow.

Perky xxx

From: Pandora@CoachworX!
To: Martin Lukes

Hi Martin

This month we are going to focus in on balance. Like many of my coachees, you put your heart, your soul and your brain into your work. But are you going to turn around one day and wish you had put more into the rest of your life?

I am forwarding to you the StressBusta! RU Balanced? ™ test, which I would like you to do today.

Strive and thrive!
Pandora

From: Martin Lukes
To: Faith Preston

Hi Faith

Re your suggestion of Thelma Dowd as my new PA—she clearly has the right experience quotient, but does she have the energy profile? We're a very fast-paced team in marketing, and I wonder if she'd keep up.

Bestest
Martin

AUGUST 4

From: Martin Lukes
To: Graham Wallace

Graham—Have you seen the interview with Barry in Fortune? He talks such a load of crap sometimes. Makes me wish I worked for a British company. That journalist had her tongue right up his arse.

Btw have you spoken to Faith about Keri? I hope you're very grateful. You get a gorgeous 29 year old New Zealand physiotherapist. I'm getting Thelma Dowd—fat, 55. Can't wait.

Drink later?

M

AUGUST 5

From: Martin Lukes
To: Barry Malone

Hi Barry

Apologies for not touching base earlier—I just wanted to put on record how much I enjoyed the article in Fortune. In my experience, journalists usually get everything wrong—but this Janine Rosenholz sounds one smart cookie!

I also wanted to say what incredibly good sense your tips made to me. I hope you won't be offended if I suggest a 6th tip—Play Golf! I've thought deeply about this, and concluded that golf isn't just a game—it's a whole philosophy of life. As Jack Welch once told me, golf is about two things—people and competition—which is the same as being a CEO!

My bestest, and once again, congratulations on an excellent article!
Martin Lukes

From: Martin Lukes
To: Barry Malone

Hi Barry

Thanks for getting back to me so quickly. Delighted you buy into my golf idea! And yes, I'd be honored to come and play at Augusta!

My handicap's 15—would be lower if I took my own advice and played a bit more. But what with the pressures of work and family, we none of us get to play as much as we would like!!

Martin

From: Martin Lukes
To: Graham Wallace

Eat yr heart out Graham—BSM has asked me to go and play in the US company tournament at Augusta!! M

From: Martin Lukes
To: Jenny Withers

Darling—BSM has just asked me to go play golf in Augusta in two weeks. I hope you don't mind—it'll mean cutting our holiday short by a couple of days, but Florida is quite close . . .

Love you, M XXX

From: Martin Lukes
To: Jenny Withers

Jens darling. I know we've got our pact on spending more time together as a family—I'm 120 percent committed to that . . . But please understand, this is a massive big deal for me. M x

From: Martin Lukes
To: Pandora@CoachworX!

Hi Pandora

I've finally done the test and sent it off. It was very long, and I'm not sure how relevant some of the questions were. Actually I'm not feeling at all stressed at the moment. Energized would be a better word. Very bizarrely I think the person who is having more difficulty with stress levels and balance is Jens, who keeps taking on additional responsibilities, and has recently been put in charge of work/life balance for the UK company.

22.5 percent better than my bestest
Martin

From: Martin Lukes
To: Thelma Dowd

Hi Thelma—

Welcome to the marketing family! I think Keri has left you a list of tasks so that you can hit the ground running. As you see, we're a very young department—until now I've been the oldest by a wide margin, so I'm grateful to you for raising the average! A latte would be nice, if you're popping out later.

Martin

From: Martin Lukes
To: Thelma Dowd

Quite possibly they did brew up their own Nescafe in finance. But here in marketing we go for authenticity—so it's Starbucks lattes for us! Strictly speaking it may not be your job to get me coffee, but I always discourage my team from following the rule book. Don't worry, you'll get used to us in time!

Martin

From: Martin Lukes
To: Keri Tartt

Keri—how are you finding sales? Assume you're sitting there twiddling your thumbs. Can I ask a tiny favor? Don't dare ask Thelma . . . could you cash in my return air ticket from Orlando, for a ticket that stops off in Augusta?

My golf kit is also in need of upgrading . . . Basically what I need is a Callaway ERC II driver, some Callaway Hawkeye irons and the new Odyssey broom handle putter. Two-tone Footjoys size 10½. Some Hugo Boss golf-range shirts (size M) would be nice if you can find anything on special. Can you see if the UK sites can deliver them in two days, or buy from a US site, and get them delivered to my hotel?

Ta muchly M

AUGUST 9

From: Pandora@CoachworX!
To: Martin Lukes

Hi Martin—Challenging news, I'm afraid. I've just got back the feedback from your StressBusta! tests showing your stress levels are dangerously high.

Before I feedback the results to you, I should say that I am not surprised. This sort of result is not unusual for my high flying coachees.

People who score in this range cannot typically control and recognize their feelings or act on them appropriately. They can become bitter, angry and resentful.

Don't worry, Martin. There is hope!! You can decrease your level of burnout by rebalancing your life and following these tips.

1. Read books—try the classics—they're great!

2. Spend time loving your spouse.

3. Banish all negative thoughts.

4. Laugh!

5. Practice a random act of kindness every day.

6. Slow down! Martin, you are a speed junky. Take some deep breaths. Relax!

Let's start with some easy wins. I want you to keep a stress diary. Recognizing your big stressors is the best way to overcome them. I also suggest you buy 200 Bio Dots. These are stick on spots (you can buy them from us at CoachworX!.co.uk) that change color to record your stress levels.

Strive and thrive!
Pandora

AUGUST 10

From: Martin Lukes
To: Thelma Dowd

Where are all the papers that were on my desk? I'd appreciate it if you didn't move things around. Also why have you put all these internal meetings in my calendar? My strategy is never to commit to any meetings unless I can see easy wins coming out of it.

Martin

From: Martin Lukes
To: Pandora@CoachworX!

STRESS DIARY Day 1

Woke up to find that Svetlana had drunk the entire carton of blueberry and banana smoothies that I had bought to reduce stress. Comforted myself with the thought that she is sodding off back to Russia next week. Stress levels high. Got into work. Thelma starts talking to me about the weather.

The dot is dark purple, which is ominous.

Martin

From: Porky Perky
To: Kinky Pinky

I'm meant to be getting home at 7 this week as part of a new work/life balance jag that Pandora has me on . . . but if we're very fast, I think we could squeeze in a quick one. After all, now that you are not my PA you count as "life" not "work"!

See you fire escape half an hour?? P xxx

From: Porky Perky
To: Kinky Pinky

Oh dear . . . that made my bio dot go black—which is the highest stress you can have before you die! P xxx

From: Martin Lukes
To: Graham Wallace

I've just watched Thelma eating the large ham sandwich that she brings in every day. She opens her mouth very wide and leaves a rim of red lipstick on the white bread. Urgh. How are you getting on with Keri? Keeping your hands to yourself, I trust.

M

From: Jenny Withers
To: All Staff

I'm sure I don't need to remind you that this week is national Work/Life Balance Week! This year we are going to celebrate in style. Special features will include

- *Breakfast at 7:00am on Tuesday with the UK's number one stress guru, Professor Gary Copper. He is going to tell us how stress is this country's biggest killer, and share with us his 101 hottest stress-busting tips.*

- *On Wednesday we are also going to repeat last year's enormously successful Go Home On Time Day. However, we plan to make it even better by rolling it out across all departments, and posting a blacklist of coworkers who do not leave on time!*

- *I am also delighted to say that we shall be offering all coworkers an online grocery service. This will remove one of life's great stressors by allowing you to shop from your desk (outside normal working hours, please!!). Anyone willing to road test the service plse message me or Faith!*

Jenny

From: Martin Lukes
To: Jenny Withers

Darling—Would be delighted to do my bit for the WLB agenda . . . Why don't I share the platform with Copper and talk about my learnings . . . I think so often these things are women's ghettos, it would be refreshing to see a senior alpha male taking it seriously . . . Also count me in as a shopping guinea pig . . . what groceries do we need?

Best, Martin

AUGUST 11

From: Roger Wright
To: All Staff

I am pleased to inform all staff that a-b glöbâl (UK) has been short-listed for the British Telecom Work/Life Balance Award. On Tuesday we will have a team of judges from BT watching our work. For that day it is imperative that all staff arrive and leave promptly.

Roger Wright,
Acting Chairman

From: Jenny Withers
To: All Staff

Hi!
There are two minor amendments to our plans for this week. Gary Copper informs me that due to excessive work pressures next week he is not going to be able to make the breakfast. However Martin Lukes has kindly agreed to step in and talk to us about "Work/Life Balance—the holistic viewpoint." I have also been informed that many of you have evening Team building workshops next week, and so will not be able to leave work on

time. You will be exempted from leaving on time, and will NOT get black marks!

Cheers, Jenny

From: Martin Lukes
To: Keri Tartt

Pinky—sorry can't do tonight . . . am working on my breakfast presentation for tomorrow.

Perky

AUGUST 12

From: Martin Lukes
To: Faith Preston

Glad you enjoyed the talk!! As you know these are issues that are very close to my heart!

Martin

From: Martin Lukes
To: Help Desk

Can somebody come down NOW and help me get my computer linked up to this supermarket thing. The screen keeps freezing. Urgent.

From: Martin Lukes
To: Help Desk

WHAT THE BLOODY HELL DO YOU MEAN—YOU'RE GO-
ING HOME??? I WAS UNDER THE IMPRESSION THAT YOU
WERE THE HELP DESK. I DON'T CARE IF IT'S 5:30. I'M A
DIRECTOR OF THIS COMPANY SO GET DOWN HERE AT
ONCE!!!!

AUGUST 13

From: Martin Lukes
To: Jenny Withers

For Godssakes, Jens, calm down! I've no idea why they've delivered 8 six-packs of Grand Marnier chocolate mousse—I only
meant to buy one. The reason I ordered 6 packets of antifungal
shower cream was that it was on special—three for two. And you
should be delighted that I bought the Nutool cordless drill. You're
always moaning that I never do any jobs around the house.

Sorry about forgetting your Cranks sunflower seed bread and
the Olivio low fat spread.

Love you M xx

From: Roger Wright
To: All Staff

*I'm delighted to say that a-b glöbâl (UK) is the gold medalist in
the BT Work/Life Balance Day Award. The judges were impressed
by our "passionate commitment to balancing work and life at
every point along the value chain."*

*Congratulations to all staff who facilitated the attainment of
this prestigious award.*

Additionally, Martin Lukes was runner-up in the Individual

Contribution to Work/Life Balance category. The judges found his approach an "original contribution towards a wider understand of where WLB fits into a global HR footprint."

Roger Wright
Acting Chairman

From: Martin Lukes
To: Pandora@CoachworX!

Fantastic news—yours truly has won an individual WLB award! Will supply details later, but thought you'd appreciate a heads-up.

22.5 percent better than my bestest
Martin

PS Will do the stress diary when time permits.

From: Martin Lukes
To: All Staff

I just wanted to say a sincere "thank you" to everyone who has congratulated me on my award. In many ways, I am uncomfortable at being singled out for an individual award. I feel that it was very much a team effort, and so I'd like to thank my team for the fantastic backup they've given me. And I'd like to thank my lady-wife, Jens, who, as well as masterminding our brilliant WLB day, is the "balance" in my life!

All my very bestest
Martin Lukes
BT Outstanding Individual Contribution to Work/Life Balance (Runner Up)

From: Martin Lukes
To: Jenny Withers

Oh for Godssakes! What is wrong with the term "ladywife"??? I just can't get it right, can I? If I mention you, you get cross, but if I didn't you'd be even crosser. It would have been nice if you had congratulated me on my award . . .

I've got lots of stuff to sort before we go. Would you mind taking my Paul Smith chinos to the dry cleaners, and going to the bookshop to pick me out a couple of the classics. Pandora has prescribed it as beach reading.

Martin x
BT Outstanding Individual Contribution to Work/Life Balance (Runner Up)

From: Martin Lukes
To: Thelma Dowd

Hi Thelma—There is no need to keep sharpening my pencils nor to tidy my pens. I'm more creovative™ when the arrangement of my stationery is spontaneous.

Martin
BT Outstanding Individual Contribution to Work/Life Balance (Runner Up)

AUGUST 16

From: Porky Perky
To: Kinky Pinky

My dearest slinky pinky

I've bought you a necklace. Pandora says I must practice a random act of kindness every day.

P xx

From: Porky Perky
To: Kinky Pinky

Silly Pinky, of course it wasn't random . . . I didn't mean like that! And yes, I did put it on my credit card, but don't worry, Jens is far too busy with her midlife crisis and with her Professional/Personal Integration to be going through my things . . . though now I think of it, I think the receipt may be in my trouser pocket.

P xx

From: Martin Lukes
To: Jenny Lukes

Darling—forget about the dry cleaning! In my new role as work/life balance supremo, I'll do it myself!!

Love you
M
BT Outstanding Individual Contribution to Work/Life Balance (Runner Up)

From: Martin Lukes
To: Katherine Lukes

Hi Katherine

Great to get your e-mail! If I am 110 percent honest I had given up hope of hearing from you. Still—better late than never!

Glad to hear that life is treating you well. Sounds like being a social worker suits you down to the ground! You don't say what's happening to you relationship-wise. It's been years since you split with Geoff?/Gregg? . . . what's been happening since then?

You suggest I come down to meet you in Brighton. Unfortunately I'm a tad tied up before we go on hols (we're off wake-boarding in Florida!)—so let's be in touch again in September.

Bestest
Martin

From: Martin Lukes
To: Katherine Lukes

I see!! When you mentioned your friend Fiona, I didn't realize she was that sort of "friend"! I don't know why you thought I'd react badly . . . I'm very open-minded about these things. Maybe you and Fiona would both like to come up to London for a drink when were back from hols.

Martin

From: Martin Lukes
To: Phyllis Lukes

Dearest Mum
    Sorry I didn't make it last night. I was involved in some grocery scheme at work (don't ask!!!) now looks like I won't see you till we're back.
    I've just had a really odd e-mail from Katherine. Did you know about "Fiona"?? Why didn't you tell me?? It's all a bit of a shock, though I suppose fits in with the rest of her life.
    Sorry this is so brief . . . you'll be proud to hear that I've won an award for my work/life balance!

Your loving Son
Martie
BT Outstanding Individual Contribution to Work/Life Balance (Runner Up)

From: Martin Lukes
To: Jake Lukes

Jake—just seen your message. No you can't go to Reading pop festival. You are going on holiday with us. Frankly I don't care what Tarquin or anyone else is doing. I've spent an arm and a leg on this wakeboarding holiday and you are coming for the duration. I have hardly seen you this summer, and you are spending quality time with me whether you like it or not.

Dad
BT Outstanding Individual Contribution to Work/Life Balance (Runner Up)

From: Martin Lukes
To: Pandora@CoachworX!

STRESS DIARY Day 2
    Sorry I haven't been keeping the diary properly. I've been totally up against it workwise.
    The weird thing is that I'm finding the home section of my life very stressful at present. Jake is being impossible, threatening not to come on holiday. Jens is getting more difficult by the day. And just discovered that my sister is a dyke. Which explains a lot about her attitude to yours truly.
    The only part of my life that is not stressful is golf. I played at the weekend. My bio dots stayed yellow throughout.

22.5 percent better than my bestest
Martin
BT Outstanding Individual Contribution to Work/Life Balance (Runner Up)

From: Pandora@CoachworX!
To: Martin Lukes

Hi Martin

Remember I told you about words that drain your energy? Dyke is one of those. It is a negative judgment on the core values of others. You should welcome your sister's life choices, which are as equally valid as your own.

Can I also suggest a different way of communicating with your son? Often we are in too much of a hurry to realize the impact our words have upon children. Instead of blurting out, "You're so clumsy!" or "Why can't you be quiet?"—remarks that can powerfully undermine a child's sense of self-worth—try using humor to break his or her pattern. For example, you could say, "If you continue on this track, I might start getting a smidge cranky," with a smiling face.

Strive and thrive!
Pandora

From: Martin Lukes
To: Pandora@CoachworX!

Hi Pandora

I'm not sure you understand. Jake's self-worth is if anything too high. Last time I tried the softy approach he asked if I was gay. Do you have any children yourself?

And on the subect of being gay, you get me wrong if you think I have any negative baggage on that score. Whatever turns you on!

22.5 percent better than my bestest
Martin
BT Outstanding Individual Contribution to Work/Life Balance (Runner Up)

AUGUST 15

From: Porky Perky
To: Kinky Pinky

Darling Pinky

Hotel noisy, food ropey, and I'm already missing you horribly . . . I've tried wakeboarding with the boys, and I'm pleased to say I'm better than Max, but not as good as Jake. Though I've hardly seen him since the first day . . . he's found some gorgeous little French number. She looks 18, but turns out to be 13. Jake—like his father—turns out to have a penchant for the younger woman!!

love you, miss you . . . P xxx

AUGUST 25

From: Martin Lukes
To: Pandora@CoachworX!

I'm afraid the dots have been dark purple or black solidly since arrival. Jens is working flat out on a paper on our Personal/Professional Integration policy, so I've been doing more childcare than ideal. In the same hotel is the head of global marketing at L'Oreal—who might have become a very useful contact, only Jake has ruined everything by shagging his 13 year old daughter.

Max has started beating me at tennis, and J is so angry about my flying off to Atlanta she has stopped talking to me.

And Christo sends me almost hourly e-mails telling me how brilliantly he is coping in my absence.

Martin

AUGUST 26

From: Martin Lukes
To: Jenny Withers

Darling—Arrived safely in Augusta . . . Hope you all get back to London safely. E-mail me news on Jake's GCSEs.

Love you, M XXX

From: Martin Lukes
To: Graham Wallace

Augusta is **UNBELIEVABLE**—the course exquisite, most manicured in the world! I'm staying in the Log Cabin—my room is right next door to BSM and the others are all in an annex. Cindy C is here too—strutting her stuff disgustingly. I didn't even realize she played golf—turns out she's a single handicap!!!!

M

AUGUST 27

From: Martin Lukes
To: Jenny Withers

CHRIST! Didn't that bloody school teach him ANYTHING? I've spent an arm and a leg on his eduction. And WHY the HELL did you phone the headmaster without consulting me? It is much better that these approaches come from me. I'll e-mail him now.

From: Martin Lukes
To: Headmaster@MillgateSchool

Dear Mr. Pitman

I understand that my son Jake has achieved only two Bs and two Cs at GCSE. I also understand that you spoke with my wife this morning and informed her that you would not be able to offer the lad a place in the 6th form.

I believe that the boy has considerable creovative™ talents, and his poor results do not reflect a lack of ability, but issues around concentration.

He has grown up a lot over this summer, and I anticipate that these issues are now in the past. Going forward I see Jake being a member of your school community who would excel in all areas.

I therefore believe it would be in the interests not just of my son, but of the school, for the lad to be given a place in the 6th form.

I am currently in the US, at a top level meeting with our CEO. However I would be happy to meet with you on my return to discuss how we progress this.

Yours sincerely
Martin Lukes
Marketing Director
a-b glöbâl UK

From: Martin Lukes
To: Graham Wallace

Hi Graham—How goes it?

Yours truly has just played the game of a lifetime. The 12th hole is unbelievably tricky—and I got a birdie! And as if that wasn't enough, Cindy totally screwed up Amen Corner—topped the tee shot on the 12th and then sliced her second on the 13th into the trees!!! BSM obviously impressed—put his arm around my shoulders practically crushing me to death and said: "I just love this guy." You should have seen the look Keith gave me. I think we've got it wrong about Barry. He's tough when he has to be but he's actually very sincere and has even got a wicked sense of humor!

Janine—that Fortune journalist—was there too. She's rather sexy in that scrawny American way. She's working on another article—in which yours truly may figure!

Mart

From: Martin Lukes
To: Jenny Withers

Jens—

Pitman isn't playing ball and had the cheek to suggest that the reason Jake didn't do better in his GCSEs is that he doesn't have the support at home. I said that I didn't pay £13,000 a year to educate him myself. Everything great here. It was definitely a good call to come. Sat next to BSM in his private plane on the way back to Atlanta, had a fascinating chat about a-b glöbâl, the world, the universe, everything. I never realized what a really nice guy he is...

He's definitely got some big job in mind for me—not UK chairman at all, but something bigger here in Atlanta. Possibly Keith's job, which explains why Keith has been so short with me.

It'd be brilliant for the whole family to move here. It'd solve Jake's schooling issue. Max would come to visit us for the hols, and I'm sure you could always do something in the HQ press office. Whaddya think?

Love you, M XX

From: Martin Lukes
To: Keri Tartt

Your Porky is on his way home!!! Am coming straight in off the red-eye tomorrow. Can you book the Novotel for tomorrow pm? Corporal salutes you etc.

Perky xx

AUGUST 29

From: Martin Lukes
To: Barry Malone

Hi Barry, just to say the last few days have been a ball for me! I am now back in London incredibly energized and am already setting up a scheme to roll out our blueprint for personal and organization consciousness across the UK company. Will keep you in the loop!

Cheers, Martin

From: Martin Lukes
To: All Directors

I have just spent a fascinating four days with our CEO and would like to debrief you on the essence of the many conversations we shared. Top of Barry's mind right now is the issue of how to drive value creation in 21C while unleashing our spiritual mission. I have attached a memo outlining our thinking and would be happy to discuss how we make it actionable.

Martin

AUGUST 30

From: Martin Lukes
To: Jenny Withers

Oh Jesus. That's all we need. Has his passport gone too? I bet the randy little sod has gone off in search of Solange. Perhaps you'd better e-mail her father. On second thoughts, I'll do it. It'll look better coming from me, and my French is better than yours. M

From: Martin Lukes
To: Thelma Dowd

Have you got a French dictionary to hand?

From: Martin Lukes
To: Jean-MichelBon@loreal

Salut Jean-Michel!
    J'espere que vous etes en bon sante. Si vous avez aucunes questions sur les "marketing breakthroughs" n'hesitez pas de demander a moi! Je suis tourjous heureux de vous aider. J'ai un petit question pour vous. Avez vous aucune idee ou est mon fils? Il est disparu, et ma femme et moi-meme sont un peu inquietes. A-t-il dit quelquechose a Solange?

Mille mille mercis, Martin

From: Martin Lukes
To: Jenny Withers

Just got an answer (in JM's pathetic English) saying he's absolutely no idea about Jake's whereabouts, and that Solange is forbidden from having any contact with him. M

From: Martin Lukes
To: Jenny Withers

Well at least he's safe. Where did he get the money from??

From: Martin Lukes
To: Jake Lukes

JAKE—I AM BEYOND ANGRY. YOU HAVE STOLEN
MONEY, DISOBEYED ORDERS AND CAUSED YOUR
MOTHER AND MYSELF SERIOUS WORRY. YOU ARE
GROUNDED AND YOUR ALLOWANCE IS STOPPED UNTIL
FURTHER NOTICE.

YOU MAY BE INTERESTED TO KNOW THAT AS A RE-
SULT OF YOUR PATHETIC EXAM RESULTS YOUR
SCHOOL DOES NOT WANT YOU BACK. YOUR YOUNGER
BROTHER FACES A BRILLIANT FUTURE AT ETON.

YOU WILL DO WELL TO GET INTO TOOTING SIXTH
FORM COLLEGE. I HAVE FOUGHT FOR YOU UNTIL NOW,
BUT NOW FRANKLY YOU'VE GOT WHAT YOU DESERVE.

DAD

AUGUST 31

From: Martin Lukes
To: Pandora@CoachworX!

Hi Pandora

It's been a very odd month. Some humungous wins, and some
challenges. Basically I believe that I am now better placed than at
any point in my career to date—I think a huge job is in the offing
for me. Not Roger's job, but something bigger.

My stress levels have been high, but I've reached the conclusion that I am the kind of guy who likes stress. It just isn't a stressor for me.

We have had issues at home, but I think we have come through them and learned something along the way! I feel I have shared some of my experience with Jake and that he will grow from it going forward.

A reflection, if you will. Golf is the perfect form of work/life balance. It is half work and half life, and very balanced.

At the end of the day, I don't think your bio dots have anything to bring to the party. I am going to give them to Jens so that she can monitor her anger going forward.

22.5 percent better than my bestest
Martin

9

SEPTEMBER

My Development Opportunities

SEPTEMBER 1

From: Pandora@CoachworX!
To: Martin Lukes

Hi Martin!

This month we are going to peep onto the other half of your personal balance sheet and meditate on the areas that could be holding you back.

I would like today to contact some of the people who know you really well, and ask them where they think your less strong stengths lie. Then we'll have a baseline, and can move forward from there.

Strive and thrive!
Pandora

From: Martin Lukes
To: Pandora@CoachworX!

Hi Pandora

Absolutely no problem at all, only I'm not sure who you planned on asking. I don't think Roger has the emotional intelligence to be able to read other people. And Thelma hasn't had time to get to know me yet. If you want someone who really understands what makes yours truly tick, then Graham Wallace is your man.

Re my own take on my Development Opportunities—can I mull over for a day or two and get back to you?

22.5 percent better than my bestest
Martin

From: Martin Lukes
To: Jenny Withers

Darling—
I know you're up against it . . . you seem to be working on 5 million different projects . . . Why don't I take Max down to Eton for his first day of term?

Martin xx

PS If Pandora contacts you about my weaknesses, can you try to be a tiny bit nice??

SEPTEMBER 2

From: Martin Lukes
To: Phyllis Lukes

Dearest Mum
Thanks for your message . . . yes it was lovely to see you on Saturday. Hope the curtain rail is still up . . . as I said, I think your curtains are a touch on the heavy side, and the wall is a bit soft, but fingers crossed!
Took Max off to Eton yesterday. He looked great in his black tailcoat. Totally confident, as if he owned the place. Jake starts tomorrow at Tooting 6th form college, and seems fairly positive about it. He's got some working out to do about who he is and

where he's going, though that's not unusual for a lad that age. He finds his mother quite difficult, at the moment, but our relationship is quite strong . . . he just needs some space.

Your loving son
Martie

SEPTEMBER 3

From: Martin Lukes
To: Provost@EtonCollege

Dear Provost

I'm so sorry our conversation got interrupted yesterday—it was all a bit of a scrum. As I explained, I'm Martin Lukes, Marketing Director of a-b glöbâl (UK), father of Max, one of your scholars.

Following on from what we were saying, I'm a great believer in partnership between business and education. We should join hands to pool best practice and enjoy the synergies, if you will. From your brochure, I see that last term you attracted speakers from the "Arts World" including Jonathan Miller and Judi Dench, and on the sciences side you had Richard Dawkins (I have issues with his take on genetics, but that's another story). I would be delighted to assist by throwing some names into the ring—John Browne, CEO of BP, happens to be a personal friend, or my own esteemed CEO, Barry S. Malone, would be only too delighted to help. Alternatively, if you did not want a "Big Name" I myself would be honored to offer the boys breakout workshops on creovation™.

As you know most business people today are on the go 24/7/365, but I'm sure I could sort something out!

Yours sincerely
Martin Lukes

SEPTEMBER 5

From: Martin Lukes
To: Pandora@CoachworX!

Hi Pandora

Sorry for the delay. I always find it challenging thinking about my less strong strengths—but I've tried to be very honest, and really dish the dirt!

1. I have an issue around not tolerating fools gladly. If I sense someone is a lot less perceptive or forward-thinking than myself, I can seem a tad dismissive. Example? I suggested to the Provost of Eton College that the lads should be taught creovation™. He had some difficulty grasping the concept, and complained he couldn't find it in the dictionary!!

2. I have a low boredom threshold. Because I am interested in driving change, I can get bored and frustrated when change is too slow. Basically that's my issue with Roger. He's a boring guy. End of story.

3. Because I set the bar very high for myself, I can sometimes get a bit frustrated if other people don't live up to the same standards. This is an issue in my relationship with Jake—it also may be a problem with Thelma going forward.

If I think of any others, I'll let you know!

22.5 percent better than my bestest
Martin

From: Porky Perky
To: Kinky Pinky

Pinky . . . please don't put pressure on me. I WILL tell her. I'll do it when the time is right. I know I said as soon as Max had started at Eton, but I didn't mean immediately. I'll try to leave at 6 tonight and we can have a couple of hours before I go home.

Kisses and more
Porky

From: Pandora@CoachworX!
To: Martin Lukes

Hi Martin!
Before I feedback the—fascinating—results from the little exercise I've done, I want to share with you my disappointment.

Martin, you know what I feel about the negative. It has no place in Executive Bronze! We are NOT talking about your weaknesses! I never allow my coachees to say the w-word. All your characteristics are strengths, but some of them are less strong than some of the others!

Now the feedback. I've kept the responses anonymous because people were more prepared to be completely frank on a no-names basis.

One less strong strength that various people flagged up was listening. It seems that you have serious issues in listening to what other people are saying. Don't worry Martin. We can fix that!

Another issue is around anger. My feedback suggests that you can have a short fuse!

It was also suggested that there were other issues—around snobbery, envy, ego, cynicism, lack of attention to detail, laziness, status anxiety—however I think we will leave those for another day and zero in on anger for now.

Anger is something we feel when our values have been violated. So next time you feel angry, Martin, get a little curious, and ask yourself: why do I feel this? Then I want you to close your eyes and breathe. In—out—in—out—in—out. Ten times. When you have done that you are ready to draw your anger. This can help let the toxins out of your brain. Once the toxins are out, you can start to deal with it in a more positive way!

Strive and thrive!
Pandora

From: Martin Lukes
To: Pandora@CoachworX!

Who said all that??? Have you been talking to my wife, by any chance? Completely fucking typical (if you'll pardon my French) that she would bad-mouth me. You have probably sussed out that we aren't exactly getting on like a house on fire at the present moment in time. Who else has been slagging me off?

Martin

From: Pandora@CoachworX!
To: Martin Lukes

Remember, Martin . . . positive words only!! Expletives drain your energy source.
   As I said these are NOT negatives, and I don't feel it would be fair to name the people. They are all close to you, and all want to help you be better than your best!

Strive and thrive!
Pandora

From: Barry Malone
To: All Staff

Howdy!
  Over the past months we have taken many big steps towards our goal of Phenomenal Performance Permanently. The biggest of these is viewing ourselves as a global family that is truly world class. That does not just mean picking players from Atlanta, or London or Tokyo. It means picking peak performing players from every geography—in particular it means searching countries such as India for members to join our family.
  Many companies have taken the route of offshoring parts of their business. But that is not what we are doing. We are right-shoring. We are looking for the right shore to base certain business fuctions. We are looking for the right home for new members of our family.
  I shall be leading a small team to India next week to visit various sites, and will keep you notified of all developments going forward.

I love you all
Barry

From: Martin Lukes
To: Graham Wallace

Sounds ominous—though marketing isn't something that you can expect cheap labor in India to get their heads around. Sales much more vulnerable . . . last two months' figures totally tanking, so if I were you I'd be very afraid. We work our arses off here in marketing, but where does it get us if you guys don't get out and sell???

Btw did you tell a whole bunch of evil lies to Pandora re yours truly??

Martin

PS Drink?

From: Martin Lukes
To: Barry Malone

Hi Barry
Many thanks for your message! I would be delighted to take part in the Indian trip. The subcontinent has always been close to my heart, and I am strongly in favor of offshoring as much as economically feasible. Diversity is one of our greatest challenges, and obviously in India the entire population is diverse!

All my very bestest.

PS Please pass on my best wishes to your charming wife Randee.

From: Martin Lukes
To: Jenny Withers

Jens—very exciting . . . I've just been asked to go on Barry's road show to India next week!! This is bigger than ABC—and he wants me at the heart of it! Neither Keith nor Cindy are going . . . feels like I'm cruising past them on the inside lane . . .

Martin

From: Martin Lukes
To: Jenny Withers

How was I supposed to know you were going to the Diverse High Potentials symposium in Dortmund? I don't remember that being on the calendar. In any case it's only Jake at home, and he'll be fine with Svetlana.

M

From: Martin Lukes
To: Thelma Dowd

Hi Thelma—Can you Google "India" and "outsourcing" and get me some facts and figures? Also can you sort injections and flights, visa, security situation etc.

Ta muchly
Martin

SEPTEMBER 9

From: Martin Lukes
To: Thelma Dowd

WHY IN GOD'S NAME HAVE I BEEN SENT ECONOMY TICKETS??? Can you get them changed asap? Can you tell Rog that this trip is mission critical and that I'll have to hit the groud running.

Martin

PS I'm nearly out of business cards—will need more by tomorrow . . .

From: Martin Lukes
To: Pandora@CoachworX!

Hi Pandora—Anger situation over being sent economy air tickets. I've taken a deep breath and drawn a picture of myself cooped up all night in economy, which if anything has made me even crosser.

Martin

SEPTEMBER 10

From: Martin Lukes
To: Katherine Lukes

Hi Katherine
    Thanks for your e-mail. So sorry to hear you've lost your job—would love to help in any way I can down the road.
    Fraid I can't do the 12th for our grand reunion . . . I'm off on a trip to India with our CEO. Will be in touch on my return.

Martin

PS rgds to Fiona!

From: Martin Lukes
To: Thelma Dowd

WHAT'S WITH THESE NEW BUSINESS CARDS??? MINE IS COMPLETELY USELESS BECAUSE IT HASN'T GOT MY BLOODY TITLE ON IT. CALL STATIONERY AND GET THEM TO SORT IT OUT ASAP. M

From: Martin Lukes
To: Thelma Dowd

I don't believe I'm hearing this! They're MEANT to be like that? M

From: Jenny Withers
To: All Staff

I would like to explain the thinking behind our exciting new business cards, which you should be receiving today. You will notice that the section that used to bear a title is now left blank. This is because each individual member of the a-b glöbâl family is equally an ambassador for our company.

Jenny

From: Martin Lukes
To: Jenny Withers

NOT ONLY IS THIS MILES OUTSIDE YOUR REMIT . . . IT'S TOTALLY FUCKING LOONEY TUNES. YOU DON'T SERIOUSLY BELIEVE ANY OF THAT TWADDLE DO YOU????

From: Martin Lukes
To: Pandora@CoachworX!

Pandora

I'm totally fucking FURIOUS! I've drawn a picture of my feelings which was a great big scribble. It didn't make me feel any better, and all I've done is ruin the nib on my Montblanc pen. Now my wife is trying to scupper my career chances with an idiot change to business cards. Am going to do some breathing and compose a diplomatic message to Keith.

Martin

From: Martin Lukes
To: Keith Buxton

Hi Keith

Long time, no hear. Hope all is well in Atlanta. As you know I'm pretty snowed under ahead of the Bangalore trip, which promises to be interesting!

I wanted to contact you re the plan to remove titles from business cards, which my ladywife informs me she and your good self have been working on co-jointly.

As you know, I couldn't care less about who comes where in the hierarchy, but our external stakeholders need to know who it is they are dealing with. Withholding that information makes it impossible for us to do our jobs effectively.

Martin

From: Porky Perky
To: Kinky Pinky

Dinky Pinky . . . Don't sulk at me. This trip is make or break for me with BSM . . . I really need my beauty sleep tonight. Will bring you back a lovely pressie from India.

Porky xxx

SEPTEMBER 11

From: Martin Lukes
To: Graham Wallace

Hi Graham

Greetings from sunny Bangalore! Guess what I can see from my bedroom??? A beautiful golf course!! Sky is blue and it's 79 degrees. Barry was on the same flight from London—just as well I went economy—because he was in economy too. I didn't even see he was on the plane until I was well into my third g + t, a bit embarrassing as he was on the water.

He's brought that Fortune journalist Janine with him. Apparently she's writing an article about this too!

Cheers, M

From: Porky Perky
To: Kinky Pinky

Darling Pinky—Arrived safely, though knackered after the flight. For now it's the minibar and Terminator 3. Will msg tomorrow. Please don't be cross with me . . . Love you, Mxx

From: Martin Lukes
To: Jenny Withers

Darling Jens—Arrived safely, though knackered after the flight. For now it's the minibar and Terminator 3. Will msg tomorrow. Please don't be cross with me . . . Love you, Mxx

SEPTEMBER 13

From: Martin Lukes
To: Barry Malone

Hi Barry,

Great meeting just now with Sanjay Balasubramanian. I'm confident that by going the captive route we can ensure we get 210 percent buy-in to our core values. However, I do feel there are some communications issues and we need to be proactive in addressing these.

Suggestion. I feel it would be helpful if I sent a daily debrief to the folks at home—something quite chatty in style, a bit like a letter, to be posted on the intranet. This would facilitate wider ownership/comprehension of the global process.

Are you eating in the pavilion dining room later?

Bestest, Martin

From: Martin Lukes
To: Pandora@CoachworX!

Hi Pandora

Incredibly embarrassing thing happened last night. I was sitting on the edge of my bed with my eyes shut and chanting "I feel calm, I feel fabulous, I feel marvelous, I can do anything, I can be anything"—exactly as you told me, when Barry came in. At first I thought that was me done for. But it turns out that he does the same thing himself! He says that he started working with his coach on his own self-esteem 20 years ago!

22.5 percent better than my bestest
Martin

From: Martin Lukes
To: Graham Wallace

Graham

Stop press! Barry and Janine definitely an item. They keep disappearing together . . . he turns off his mobile . . . supposedly to conduct in-depth interviews . . .

Mart

From: Martin Lukes
To: Barry Malone

Hi Barry. Just seen your message. Never mind about supper tonight. That's fine for a 5:30am breakfast tomorrow. See you then—if I don't run into you in the gym beforehand!

Bestest, Martin

From: Martin Lukes
To: All Staff

Namaste! (as they say in these parts!)
This is Day Two of the right-shoring fact-finding mission fronted by Barry Malone and my good self. We felt it would be helpful to keep you in the loop with a daily e-mail. This morning we visited the captive operations of GE. The place was incredible—really quiet, really clean. The Indian can-do headset is totally mind-boggling. These people smile all the time, nothing's too much trouble.
They have no issues around pay, as low salaries are part of the unique culture. I have attached a paper from McKinsey on the economics of BPO showing that this really is win-win. Namaste!

Martin

SEPTEMBER 14

From: Porky Perky
To: Kinky Pinky

Dearest Pinky
Still no e-mails from you. And when I tried to call on your mobile it was turned off. Please don't sulk at me.
Sky is blue here, and everything fine, except that I am lonely in

my big hotel bed. I've bought you a beautiful sari at the hotel shop (cost an arm and a leg) and a Nehru suit for myself, so we can play dressing up when I get home. I thought you could wear it with no knickers and I'll unwrap you.

Love you, Perky

From: Porky Perky
To: Kinky Pinky

That's not very grateful! It's a lovely turquoise color, which I thought would be nice with your eyes . . . Actually, the Nehru suit is a great hit—plenty of positive feedback from the shop assistants!

Perky xx

SEPTEMBER 15

From: Martin Lukes
To: All Staff
Subject: Bangalore briefing note 2

Namaste!!
As I get to know this place better, I'm aware of how many profound misunderstandings there are about the Indian culture.
The first is about skillsets. These people are actually highly intelligent and educated! I had dinner last night with an Indian guy who was fascinated by my take on viral marketing. Not only did he speak really good English but has an MBA from Harvard!
The level of passion for work is really energizing.
The other observation is about corner shops—paradoxically there aren't any here at all! It's totally ironic that Indians have cornered (!) the market in corner shops in Britain, while the market here is wide open. An opportunity for some creovative™ entrepreneur!

Please don't hesitate to message Barry or myself if you have any questions.

Namaste!
Martin Lukes

From: Martin Lukes
To: Graham Wallace

Hi Graham

Thanks for your message. You're quite right—basically thousands of jobs will go in the US and UK, but only at junior level. For you and me, it'll be fine.

You'd love it here. Some of the girls are gorgeous, though not very available. The cute little thing who cleans my room gave me a meaningful smile last night, but when I reciprocated she didn't want to know. Ironic she should be so uptight when this is the home of the Karma Sutra! Believe me, it's a land of paradoxes.

Martin

SEPTEMBER 17

From: Martin Lukes
To: Thelma Dowd

Hi Thelma. Got back last night totally shattered. I'm off the caffeine, but a mint tea would be great if you can find such a thing . . .

Martin

PS I've got a gift for you—it's by your desk.

From: Martin Lukes
To: Jake Lukes

Jake—I understand that while I have been away you have failed to show up at college at all. Starting today, I am implementing the following remedial four-prong action plan.

1. You are grounded until further notice.
2. I have spoken with the principal of yr college. He will notify myself of your attendance daily.
3. Your allowance is cut to zero.
4. Your mobile phone is confiscated.

We will review the above on a weekly timeframe going forward.

Dad

From: Martin Lukes
To: Thelma Dowd

Oh dear, you weren't meant to see the card! You're right, I did buy it originally for someone else but decided to give it to you instead! Actually she's smaller than you—but the good thing about saris is it's one size fits all!

Martin

From: Martin Lukes
To: Thelma Dowd

Goodness gracious me (as they say in India!) I didn't mean to be size-ist. Though as a matter of fact I noticed many Indian matrons—

much larger than you!—who looked very good in saris. Where was that tea?

Martin

SEPTEMBER 20

From: Barry Malone
To: All Staff

Hi Co Leaders!
Following the hugely successful visit last week to Bangalore, we now have a road map in place for right-shoring as many of our functionalities as practicable. The intention is to aggressively realign our resources by opening two offshore satellite centers each of which will help deliver our goal of insane profitability.
I have tasked Martin Lukes with feeding back more detail from the trip.

I love you all
Barry

From: Martin Lukes
To: Barry Malone

Hi Barry
Can I just say what a highly inspirational memo that was! The tone was 140 percent spot-on! I believe there is now a window we can leverage to facilitate buy-in from those who have issues around right-shoring.
I plan to hold a creovative™ series of lunchtime masterclasses

with videoconferencing links to other geographies so that all our co-colleagues can share the learnings.

My bestest, Martin

SEPTEMBER 21

From: Martin Lukes
To: Christo Weinberg

Hi Christo
I've got a great opportunity for you! Would you like to take my place at the annual Maverick Marketing conference in Milton Keynes and give a paper on Customer Relationship Marketing. I can e-mail you the presentation I gave last year. It was way ahead of the curve then, so if you tweak it a bit, it should still be pretty leading edge this year.

Cheers, Martin

From: Martin Lukes
To: All Staff

Hi!
There has been a phenomenal level of interest in the trip fronted by myself and Barry to Bangalore. To enable everyone to take ownership of the process I shall be holding a series of lunchtime masterclasses entitled Breakthrough Bangalore! to address all key issues in a compelling and thought-provoking way. The first one is scheduled for Wednesday. There will be a live link to other geographies, featuring a guest appearance from Barry. Book early to avoid disappointment!

My best, Martin Lukes

From: Martin Lukes
To: Ameera Ali

Hi Ameera

We've never actually spoken, but I understand from Faith you're doing great things in HR! As you may know, I've just returned from a trip to Bangalore with our CEO. I wondered if you'd like to say a word or two at my masterclass. It'll be really informal—maybe you could share your personal experience of India—it'd be your chance for fame and stardom as the CEO himself will be joining in, hopefully!

Best, Martin

From: Martin Lukes
To: Ameera Ali

I see. Of course I realize you are British, but I didn't know your family originally hailed from Pakistan. Still I hope you'll come along and enjoy a samosa!

Martin

From: Martin Lukes
To: Keri Tartt

In haste—Corporal has got a plan . . . he could spend the whole night training with his Private on Tues. . . .

From: Martin Lukes
To: Jenny Withers

Darling—I'm going to be away from home for one night on Tuesday at the Milton Keynes conference. It'll be v boring but I'm obliged to show my face . . .

Love you M xx

SEPTEMBER 22

From: Martin Lukes
To: Jenny Withers

Jens—Have you seen my BlackBerry anywhere? I seem to have lost it . . . I am supposed to be going to McKinsey today for a mega session to kick around some ideas with their top guys on off-shoring . . . I can't be out of touch for the whole afternoon.

M xx

From: Martin Lukes
To: Thelma Dowd

Hi Thelma—Have left some data on your desk. Can you turn some of the data into nice color slides for my masterclass—I want a few charts, broken up with a few pics of smiling Indian people?

Martin

PS Could you nip up to the vending machine and get me some curry flavored Doritos?

From: Martin Lukes
To: Thelma Dowd

moron

From: Martin Lukes
To: Thelma Dowd

Frankly, Thelma, you've lost me this time. Industrial tribunal? What are you talking about? If you feel that strongly about it, I'll get the crisps myself. Martin

From: Martin Lukes
To: Keri Tartt

You sexy bitch. I want to fuck you right now!

From: Martin Lukes
To: Keri Tartt

Pinky, darling, you know I love it when you talk dirty like that . . . but what brought that on? . . . Actually not really feeling like it now as the corporal is a bit under the weather and I'm snowed under with this McKinsey outsourcing report. Tomorrow or day after?

Perky xx

From: Martin Lukes
To: Graham Wallace

Hi Graham—It's hormone city here. The women in this place are losing it. First Thelma flies off the handle about a bland memo I sent her. She's threatening me with legal action . . . and something's up with Keri. Does she seem normal to you today?

M

From: Martin Lukes
To: Roger Wright

dickhead

Sent from my BlackBerry Wireless Handheld

From: Martin Lukes
To: Roger Wright

Hi Roger. Sure, I'll come up now. What did you want to see me about? I hope it's not the India expenses? Barry has signed off on them, so they are all on HQ's budget.

From: Martin Lukes
To: Jenny Withers

I've got a wicked little secret that you don't know about. Would you like to know it?

Sent from my BlackBerry Wireless Handheld

From: Martin Lukes
To: Jenny Withers

Jens, can you help me here? You have ignored me since I got back from India, and now you send me a message saying "not particularly"? Not particularly what??

Martin

From: Martin Lukes
To: Martin Lukes

Liar, wanker, plonker

Sent from my BlackBerry Wireless Handheld

From: Martin Lukes
To: Jake Lukes

JAKE DID YOU JUST SEND ME A MESSAGE FROM MY BLACKBERRY?? FEAR FOR YOUR LIFE IF YOU DID.

From: Martin Lukes
To: Systems

Can you disable my BlackBerry now??? Urgent.

From: Martin Lukes
To: Jenny Withers

DISASTER . . . JAKE'S GOT MY BLACKBERRY . . . HELP!!!!

From: Martin Lukes
To: All Staff

Some individuals have been receiving bogus messages apparently from myself sent on my BlackBerry handheld device, which was stolen this morning. The thief has gained access to the security code and has been sending prankster e-mails. If you receive any such messages please ignore. I apologize for any confusion caused.

Martin Lukes

From: Martin Lukes
To: Jake Lukes

JAKE—I AM BEYOND FURY—SUGGEST YOU DO NOT AT-TEMPT TO COME HOME UNLESS YOU ARE PREPARED TO UNDERGO A ROOT AND BRANCH PERSONAL REBRAND-ING. I HAVE ALERTED EVERYONE IN MY ADDRESS BOOK TO IGNORE ANY "JOKE" MESSAGES FROM YOU SO THERE IS NO POINT IN SENDING ANY FURTHER. SHOULD YOU DO SO, HOWEVER, I SHALL CONSIDER THIS TO BE FRAUD AND ALERT THE POLICE.

DAD

From: Martin Lukes
To: Martin Lukes

Wow . . . I'm like so scared. Not. Though you should be, coz I'm just about to forward an interesting message out of your in box to mum . . . something about pinky? Sounds a bit fishy to me, dad . . . J

Sent from my BlackBerry Wireless Handheld

254.

From: Martin Lukes
To: Systems

I DON'T FUCKING CARE IF YOU ARE SHORT STAFFED TO-DAY. DISABLE MY BLACKBERRY NOW.

From: Martin Lukes
To: Jenny Withers

Here's a message from someone called "pinky" sent to someone called "perky." I think you might find it interesting.

Forwarded by Martin Lukes

From: Kinky Pinky
To: Porky Perky

My cutey, chunky, porky Perky
Pinky's feeling happy again!! Cool to spend the whole nite with u on wed . . . sorry I gave u such a hard time . . . it's just I love u and want us to be together—which I no we will be 1 day!! It's hard for little pinky going to bed on her own every night, knowing u are in bed with Jenny. Private P gets lonely . . . But I am going to be a big brave patient piggie.

Loveya loveya loveya loads!!
Pinky xxxx

Fishy, huh?

Sent from my BlackBerry Wireless Handheld

255.

From: Martin Lukes
To: Jenny Withers

Darling. This isn't what you think. We need to talk now. M xx

From: Martin Lukes
To: Thelma Dowd

Thelma—something has come up. I need to go home for a bit. Can you cancel the Bangalore masterclass?

Martin

From: Martin Lukes
To: Graham Wallace

Catastrophe—I've just been chucked out by the ladywife. Can I bunk down with you for a bit?

From: Martin Lukes
To: Jenny Withers

Darling . . . Please, can we just talk about it? I can really explain everything. Please. I'm sorry.

Love you
Martin

From: Martin Lukes
To: Graham Wallace

Not even for one night??? What's Lynne got against me?

From: Martin Lukes
To: Pandora@CoachworX!

Pandora. Something really terrible has happened. I would rather not discuss on e-mail. Can I come and see you?

Martin

From: Porky Perky
To: Kinky Pinky

Pinky darling—Jens has kicked me out. I'll bring my stuff round to you tonight as an interim arrangement, and then we can see how things go. Perky xx

From: Martin Lukes
To: Keri Tartt

Of course I love you and want to marry you, you know that. I just didn't want it to happen like this. Please give me a break. This is the worst day of my life.

SEPTEMBER 23

From: Pandora@CoachworX!
To: Martin Lukes

Hi Martin
   Sorry it took a while for me to get back to you. I'm so in demand at the moment!
   I'm afraid the Executive Bronze Program is only e-mail, so it would be irresponsible of me, under the terms of the contract, to

allow personal visits. But please e-mail me the issues, and I, as your greatest fan, will help you be better than your best!

Strive and thrive!
Pandora

From: Martin Lukes
To: Pandora@CoachworX!

Pandora

Yes I know Executive Bronze is only e-mail, but I thought you might have made an exception for an emergency.

Long story short? Basically I have been going on seeing Keri on an occasional basis. I feel she has been very helpful with New Me. It has been a good arrangement, with no one getting hurt.

Unfortunately my son Jake has issues with myself at present, has got hold of my BlackBerry and forwarded one of Keri's messages to Jens—who has totally flipped and chucked me out.

Obviously this is not what I need. I need to have the whole family behind me at the moment . . .

I'm moving in with Keri for now, but as I said, not ideal.

Martin

From: Pandora@CoachworX!
To: Martin Lukes

Hi Martin

You may feel pain now, because whenever you violate your core values the result is pain. I also sense a lot of confusion in your account—I think you are losing sight of your goals. It would do you a lot of good right now to do a GROW model.

It is time to revisit your core values, Martin. Say them out loud to yourself. Ask youself: which values have I violated? And how do I repair and renew?

Strive and thrive!
Pandora

From: Martin Lukes
To: Pandora@CoachworX!

Frankly, Pandora, I don't give a shit about my values right now. If you had ANY IDEA how bad I'm feeling right now you would not have dared suggest I do a FUCKING GROW model. My whole life is crashing around my ears. I am not in the mood for any of your other quick fixes.

I am going to see my mother (who is my genuine greatest fan), and I'm going to get some work done.

Martin

SEPTEMBER 27

From: Martin Lukes
To: Phyllis Lukes

Dear Mummy
    Can I come and see you on Saturday morning?

Love Martin

From: Martin Lukes
To: Phyllis Lukes

Dear Mummy

You ask if anything is up. I was going to wait until I saw you, but maybe I should tell you now. I know you never thought Jens was right for me, and maybe you were right. The bottom line is that she has chucked me out.

There is someone else, mum. I think you'd like her. She's very down to earth, calls a spade a spade. She's not the brightest cookie on the beach, but she's very intuitive and has been very good for me. She's called Keri and she's 29 and a New Zealander. Started to train as a physio, so she's very caring. But it's all too soon for me to get serious, especially as the situation with Jens is all rather up in the air. I need to talk to Jens about it, but she's being totally unreasonable—listening is not a strong point of hers, to put it mildly!!

Much love
Martie

From: Martin Lukes
To: Phyllis Lukes

Dear Mum, yes of course I'm thinking about the boys. But Max is at Eton, and Jake has basically done something that I find hard to forgive. And don't forget, this wasn't my choice. I'm not leaving. I've been chucked out. I had hoped you'd see this from my point of view . . .

See you tomorrow
Martie

SEPTEMBER 29

From: Martin Lukes
To: Barry Malone

Sure! Let's talk 11am your time . . . Sounds exciting!

Bestest
Martin

From: Martin Lukes
To: Barry Malone

Hi Barry

I just wanted to say again how incredibly excited I am about your offer. I feel this is just the right opening for me—and hopefully for yourself, as well. Truly win-win!

I love this company as much as you do. I am thrilled at this opportunity to serve it in a more pivotal role. I will send you soonest a memo detailing what should be front of mind for me as your chief of staff.

You mentioned relocation of my wife and children. I just wanted to flag up at this stage that my domestic situation is a bit fluid. So I am not sure that the whole family will be coming with me.

All my very bestest
Martin

PS Give my best to the lovely Janine.

From: Martin Lukes
To: Keri Tartt

Sorry darling, going to be back late tonight. Got an important memo to write to Barry. Something vv exciting has happened. Will tell you later.

M x

10

OCTOBER

My Money

OCTOBER 1

From: Martin Lukes
To: Jenny Withers

Jens

I know you said no messages. But I've got such BRILLIANT news, it puts our difficulties into perspective. I'm going to Atlanta as BSM's Chief of Staff!! This is my DREAM JOB—it's got power, it's got profile AND it's going to be intellectually stimulating . . . I've been catapulted into the hot seat right in the heart of the control room!

But this isn't just win-win for me—if you approach this with a more positive headset it'd be great for you and the boys too. I'd be well placed to get you whatever job you fancy—within reason! Lunch today to discuss? Or I could come round to my own home this evening?

Love you
M xxx

From: Martin Lukes
To: Jenny Withers

Did you get my message? What do you think?

From: Martin Lukes
To: Jenny Withers

Would a reply be too much to ask for?

From: Barry Malone
To: All Staff

Howdy!

I am today announcing some exciting changes to our corporate structure that will position us ahead of the curve in our goal of Phenomenal Performance—Permanently! To support my leadership platform and facilitate execution of new policy initiatives I shall be establishing an Office of the Chairman in Atlanta. The office will be headed up by Martin Lukes, currently Marketing Director of a-b glöbâl UK.

To those of you who do not know Martin, he has an unrivaled track record in creovation. He has a results-driven headset and a very British sense of humor! I know he is going to be a genius in his new role, and a best-in-class addition to our top team!

I love you all
Barry

OCTOBER 4

From: Martin Lukes
To: Pandora@CoachworX!

Hi Pandora

I wondered if we could be a little creovative™ about this module of the program and focus on money? I'd like your take on how to maximize my package. On merit grounds alone, I should be paid more than anyone in the UK, and more than Keith. And given my present domestic situation (don't ask!!) I may be running two homes . . . which is obviously going to cost me an arm and a leg.

22.5 percent better than my bestest
Martin

From: Pandora@CoachworX!
To: Martin Lukes

Hi Martin!

Sure! I have no problem coaching you on wealth! It is something I have helped literally thousands of coachees on in the past, with phenomenal success!

The first step is to understand true wealth isn't about money. It is about the joy you feel seeing the face of a laughing child. Or the beauty of a turquoise ocean.

But money can be an aspect of wealth—and that is what we are going to work on now. Martin, this month I am going to help you develop the millionaire's mind-set. Already in your mind, you have a collection of beliefs and emotions around money. We need to look at these before we can start increasing your wealth. Ask yourself: what does money mean to me? What would having more money give me that I don't already have?

Strive and thrive!
Pandora

PS Given your new responsibilities, now would be a great time to upgrade to the Executive Gold or Executive Platinum Coaching Program. Not only would this be more in keeping with your status, it would free up more of my time to help you be even better than your best!

From: Martin Lukes
To: Thelma Dowd

Hi Thelma—I've got a lot to do trying to sort my package today. Various members of my team want to talk to me . . . can you keep them all away?

Martin

OCTOBER 5

From: Martin Lukes
To: Pandora@CoachworX!

Hi Pandora
You ask what would money give me that I don't have already? Easy! I'd like an Aston Martin DB9. I'd also like to upscale my real estate. A substantial residence in Atlanta, with smaller pads in London, Antigua and Aspen, Colorado. I am not into being flash with money—I certainly would never want my own plane. But I

think I would like my own art collection, or something classy like that, which was as much about taste as money.

22.5 percent better than my bestest
Martin

PS Re Executive Platinum, I strongly agree, though I think the best strategy is to get my package sorted first, and then to ask for extras. Sure it won't be a problemo.

From: Pandora@CoachworX!
To: Martin Lukes

Martin—
I'm a teensy bit disappointed that you haven't grasped what this exercise is all about. I was asking what emotions—happiness, security, freedom—you thought money would get you.
Think again: why do you want more money?
The reason, Martin, has got to be: BECAUSE YOU'RE WORTH IT!!
If you don't believe that, you can throw away all your hopes of getting the package of your dreams. What is money? Money is a symbol of someone's confidence in you! If you want more money you are going to have to have Extraordinary Confidence in yourself, so that others will have Extraordinary Confidence in you!

Strive and thrive!
Pandora

From: Martin Lukes
To: Keri Tartt

Keri darling
I've been thinking about this, and I know I said I wanted us to be together. I do, obviously. But I don't think it would be a good idea if you come to Atlanta with me unless you have a job. Not

earning would be bad for your self-esteem. And if you had a job, if anything happened between us, you'd still have an income.

My plan is to import you as my PA. I'm sure I could wangle you more money and a grand title—something like Senior Administrative Assistant to Chief of Staff, Office of the Chairman. I'm going to need some people on my side, it's a vipers' nest out there.

Love you M xxx

OCTOBER 6

From: Martin Lukes
To: Max Lukes

Max old man

I hope school is going well—well done for coming top in the Latin test!

I don't know if mum has said anything to you about me, but I thought you had a right to know that she's a tad miffed with me at the moment. To be perfectly honest, she's gone on a bit of a bender and chucked me out (!), so I'm presently living with a friend. I do hope that this is a temporary situation and that she'll come to her senses and won't break up our fantastic family. Might help if you put in a word for your old dad next time you talk to her?

The other big news item is that I've been offered a really wicked job in the US with loads of money—I'll have a ginormous house with pool and private golf course. I hope you'll spend your Christmas holidays with me—you can have all the burgers and skateboards and iPods you ever dreamed of . . .

Love, Dad

From: Martin Lukes
To: Barry Malone

Hi, Barry

As you know I am blown away with excitement about my new position. I can't get started soon enough!

However, there are just a couple of details that I think we should iron out re package.

We haven't talked numbers, but I'm assuming that my pay would be in line with comparable senior executives. I would see myself coming in slightly north of Keith and Cindy, but not out of the ballpark. In addition, 100 percent housing allowance, school fees, cars for myself, my ladywife and my older son and all the other usual perks.

I understand that the job will not initially be a main board position, but that this would happen in the fullness of time. Could we nail down when that would be? I am also assuming that I can bring my PA, Keri Tartt, with me. A small pay raise for her would send a highly motivational message.

As I think I may have told you, there are some issues around the relocation of my spouse. At present she is in External Relations in London. To facilitate her transition I would like some career coaching and psychological counseling. Can we discuss these matters soonest?

My best, Martin

From: Martin Lukes
To: Keri Tartt

Keri—Sorry darling, I'm going to be late back—am working flat out on package negotiations.

I'm absolutely starving. Can you order a takeout curry for

about 9:30—and I'd also like some Ben and Jerry's (Cherry Garcia if poss, otherwise Chubby Hubby) for afters.

Love P xx

PS should be no prob at all getting you a great new job in Atlanta . . . but I'm insisting on monster raise for you.

OCTOBER 7

From: Martin Lukes
To: All Contacts

Hi everyone!

Apologies for not reaching out to each of you personally, but I wanted to tell everyone who I have had the pleasure of working in partnership with these last few years that I am moving on to pastures new!

From October 15 I shall be transferring to Atlanta to become Chief of Staff, Office of the Chairman. This is obviously a pivotal position, and I will be working directly with the legendary Barry S. Malone, who was recently named by Fortune as the 7th most respected business leader in the world.

It has been a great pleasure working with you in the past, and thank you for the deep interest you have always shown in my career. I hope you will feel able to continue your relationship with a-b glöbâl (UK) going forward.

My best regards
Martin Lukes
Marketing Director, a-b glöbâl (UK)
Chief of Staff, Chairman's Office (designate)

From: Martin Lukes
To: Jenny Withers

Jens darling

I didn't appreciate it at all just now when I came to talk to you in your office and you went on talking to your PA as if I wasn't there. I know that you are upset. Rightly so, as I'd be the first to admit! But this is going too far.

I've been doing some digging about possible jobs for you in Atlanta, and there are two suitable openings in the press office—none with a grand title, but you'd be a big fish in a big pond!

I'm playing hardball re money, and looks like we'll be able to afford whatever we want accommodation-wise—I'm thinking enormous house, obviously with pool, in a gated community with its own golf course.

We must talk about this . . . time is running out.

Martin

From: Martin Lukes
To: Jenny Withers

Yes I know you don't play golf. And please don't accuse me of going behind your back with Max . . . I simply told him what his life would be like with me in Atlanta. M

From: Martin Lukes
To: Jake Lukes

Jake—I think it is time for you and I to be highly honest with each other. I am still very angry at what you did. You are presently living with the consequences of your actions, and I hope you have come to experience some serious regrets.

That said, I am aware that you are going through a difficult patch in your life, and that you need the support of your father.

How about a drink before I go to the US? I shall come and pick you up from the house at 7pm Thursday night.

Dad

OCTOBER 8

From: Martin Lukes
To: Jenny Withers

Jens—Before you bite my head off for contacting you again, this is a legit business e-mail!

I've decided to write a lighthearted Q&A press release that could work as a diary piece—Brit Hits the Big Time in the US. The business pages are always looking for something a bit different, a bit humorous!

I'm planning to take Jake out for a drink next week. He hasn't honored me with a reply. Can you make sure he is in, and ready on time? M

With which historical figure do you identify most closely?

Einstein. He was the original creovative™ guy!

Which living person do you most admire?

My mum, who taught me to appreciate the little things in life! And Barry S. Malone for teaching me not to understand the word "impossible."

What was your biggest break?

Getting this job. Oh, and meeting my wife, Jens.

What or who is the greatest love of your life?

That'd be telling! Seriously, after my own family, I love the extended family that is a-b glöbâl.

What is your greatest weakness?

Bounty bars!!!

What keeps you awake at night?

Nothing! I believe in work hard, play hard. I
don't take my worries to bed with me!
What was your proudest moment?
Leading the award-winning a-b glöbâl rebranding
initiative. And getting a birdie on the famous
12th at Augusta.
What is your most unappealing habit?
You'd have to ask my ladywife. She might mention
something I do with the toothpaste tube!!!
How would you like to die?
As I have lived—giving 110 percent.
What would be your epitaph?
A creovative™ talent who never stopped pushing the
envelope!

From: Martin Lukes
To: Jenny Withers

What do you mean it's naff?? It's actually really funny and it helps
people get to know me quickly. And what do you expect me to say:
that my wife has kicked me out and is refusing to come to Atlanta
with me???

M

OCTOBER 11

From: Martin Lukes
To: Barry Malone

Barry—I've just had a message from a Kimberly Warp in HR outlining my package. I have serious issues with some of the detail.
She says the only benefit I am entitled to is healthcare insurance,
and that I cannot bring my PA with me. I guess I can train up a lo-

cal hire as a PA, but I need confirmation that she has made an error over the benefits question.

All my bestest, Martin

From: Martin Lukes
To: Pandora@CoachworX!

Hi, Pandora
Alas, your technique isn't delivering the desired package. This isn't a confidence issue—I've got loads of that! The problem is that some idiot in HR begs to differ. Any advice?

Martin

From: Pandora@CoachworX!
To: Martin Lukes

Hi Martin
Can I share with you a little story about myself? When I was in my 30s, I was in debt, I was living in one room, and my self-worth was so low I could hardly get up in the mornings.
A few months later I began creating money everywhere I looked! Within a few years I had become a millionaire. Because I had changed myself and my perception of the world, money came flowing to me!
Your mind is like a magnet, Martin. You must create the millionaire's mind-set. Make a scrapbook and stick in it all the things you would like to own. Imagine you own them already and one day you will!

Strive and thrive!
Pandora

From: Martin Lukes
To: Thelma Dowd

Hi Thelma—can you organize my leaving drinx for Thurs? Find out what Rog will swallow expense-wise—I don't want to be left with a sodding great bill!

Could you also reduce these Aston Martin pictures on the color printer so that they'll fit into this notebook? Then cut them out and stick them in.

Martin

From: Martin Lukes
To: Keri Tartt

Darling Pinky—going to be v late home—problems on the package front. Atlanta's playing silly buggers. There's been a hitch re yr job, but I'm fighting your corner—worry not! M

OCTOBER 12

From: Martin Lukes
To: Phyllis Lukes

Dearest Mum—just a quick message to say I'm definitely coming on Saturday, and will bring Keri. She is very young, mum, and she's also a bit nervous about meeting you, as I've built you up into a bit of a wonderwoman! We'll try to arrive in good time for pre-prandial drinkies. Fraid she's a vegetarian, but don't go to any trouble.

Your loving son
Martie

From: Martin Lukes
To: Barry Malone

Hi Barry

I wanted to share with you some creovative™ thinking I've been doing around Monday's Q3 results. My idea is a live webcam for staff and investors featuring you talking through the figures. But instead of seeing you in your office—been there, done that, got the T-shirt!—we could have you playing a few holes at your club. This would be visually sensational and the message would be unforgettable!

As you introduce yourself, you could be teeing off—you could then talk about the importance of winning, of playing the game, and having fun! As you discuss the hostile economic landscape, we could see the ball going into the sand—and so on, and so forth.

What do you think?

Cheers, Martin

From: Martin Lukes
To: Jake Lukes

Hi Jake—really good to catch up with you last night. A man-2-man chat like that was really useful for both of us. As I said, do hope you and Max will come out at Christmas—there's lots of young female talent—I think you'll like the look of my boss's daughters!!

Dad

PS That was a joke, btw, I don't want you to get any ideas!!

From: Martin Lukes
To: Keri Tartt

Pinky Darling

Bad news . . . those idiots in Atlanta have said no to your transfer for now, but I'm still working on them! What I suggest is that I go over without you initially, and that you can always come out later and join me when I've sorted something. I know it's a blow, but I think we should look at it positively. We both need some space.

Don't wait for me this evening . . . I'm going to be a tiny bit late . . .

Would you mind taking all my suits to the cleaners and make sure they're ready by Friday, as it now looks like I'm going to be off on Saturday night, a couple of days earlier than we thought?

Love you
Martin

From: Martin Lukes
To: Keri Tartt

Pinky, please don't be like that. Of course I still love you. You'll always be my dinky winky kinky pinky! I know the corporal has been a bit tired recently. It's so stressful trying to get this package right. I only have one shot at it. I'll take you out to dinner tomorrow night. Porky promise. xx

Love you Perky xxx

From: Martin Lukes
To: Graham Wallace

Yes to drink, though it'll have to be a swift one as Keri is now getting funny about me staying late. Had a massive row with her last night about the US—she seems to think she can come as my partner, and live the life of Riley without lifting a finger. All v awkward, esp as I think Jens will eventually back down and come . . .

Only good news is that I'm getting all my options repriced and the way the share price is tanking, it means a nominal additional £358,796.32, which can't be bad. Also planning to get an Aston Martin DB9 . . . eat yr heart out.

Martin

From: Martin Lukes
To: Thelma Dowd

Hi Thelma
Can you e-mail a list of all the things you do for me to my new PA—she's called Sherry Zook(!). Ta muchly. Can't believe Rog is being so tight about the party—I don't see why I should pay for a big bash out of my own pocket . . . I'll buy the team a round at the local after work tomorrow. M

From: Martin Lukes
To: Sherry Zook

Hi Sherry
This is Martin Lukes in London. I'm delighted that you're going to be working with me as my assistant—I am sure we're going to be an unbeatable team! I'll be flying in on Sunday night at 22.45 EST. Can you arrange a car to pick me up from the airport, and reserve a suite at the W? I have asked my PA Thelma Dowd to e-mail you a list of tasks—which hopefully will make your learning curve less steep!

All the bestest
Martin

OCTOBER 14

From: Martin Lukes
To: All Marketing

Team!

A reminder: everyone's invited for drinx tonight at the Dog and Duck to celebrate my departure Stateside! Let's make it a night to remember!

Martin

OCTOBER 15

From: Martin Lukes
To: All Marketing

Team!

Thanks for the great send off last night. I've certainly got a thick head this morning!

I just wanted to say that you have been a terrific load of people to work with these last few years, and together we've been producing some of the best marketing projects the company has ever seen and we've had a load of fun on the journey! I'll miss you, but obviously we'll keep in touch, and I'll take a keen interest in your work from afar.

All my very bestest
Martin Lukes

PS Many thanks for the book of golfing jokes. I'll never be at a loss for a way to begin a speech!

From: Martin Lukes
To: Christo Weinberg

Hi Christo

I just wanted to put on the record how very much I think you've grown into your role in the last ten months, since being my mentee. You've shown that with the right leadership you have genuine creovative™ promise.

Although obviously I won't be able to mentor you from Atlanta, I'll always be happy to help on an informal basis!

Cheers, Martin

PS It was good to meet your friend Sven, last night. Hope I didn't say anything out of line. He obviously doesn't realize what a joker I am . . .

From: Martin Lukes
To: Katherine Lukes

Hi Katherine

Really sorry but I'm afraid I'm going to have to cancel on you again tomorrow. My news—I'm moving to Atlanta to be the Numero Duo in the whole company, globally!!!

I don't know if mum mentioned to you that there are also some issues in my marriage, though I hope not too serious.

As for your news—wow! I think bringing up sproglets is one of the most important things one can do in this life. A warning though. Bringing up children, even in "conventional" families, can be quite a struggle, so I think you should think carefully before embarking! Let's keep in e-mail touch. It's always good to hear what you're up to (or not up to!!) and we can see each other on one of my visits back to these shores.

Best
Martin

From: Martin Lukes
To: Phyllis Lukes

Dearest Mum

Thank you for saying that! You'll find this hard to believe, but no one else has had the decency to say that they'll miss me. In fact everyone seems to be against me at the moment. Jens is, obviously. And she's being very unfair with the boys and trying to talk them round to her point of view.

Most of my colleagues are so jealous of my new job they are being really weird—even my mates can't be happy for me.

And things with Keri are pretty difficult. I'm sorry you and she didn't hit it off a bit better, I think she was a bit nervous meeting you. That was why she was doing that silly laugh all the time. She isn't like that normally. She's actually a very sweet person, but I've decided that for now it's best if I go to Atlanta on my tod.

Your loving son
Martie

PS I was meant to be seeing Katherine tomorrow, but have had to cancel, and have even had a huffy message from her—so she's cross with me, too! Btw what do you think about her news on the adoption front? I'm pretty skeptical, though obviously I tried to put it very positively to her, as you know how touchy she can be. But the bottom line is that it's not really fair on the kid to be raised by two lezzies. Try explaining that in the playground!

From: Martin Lukes
To: Jenny Withers

Jens—Arrived safely last night. Have attached all my contact numbers in case you felt an urge to speak to your husband.

M

From: Martin Lukes
To: Graham Wallace

Graham—Just spent the day at the Malone mansion. Totally amazing—really vast, luxurious and even quite tasteful. I didn't realize how cultured Barry is. He's passionate about art, and has got a Picasso drawing and two Matisses! He gave me a tour of all his pictures, and told me how much everything cost. I kept a running total, and I think I got up to $96m!

Randee was really friendly—all over me, in fact. She's in amazing shape given that she must be in her late 40s. Don't think she has any idea her husband is humping a tasty young journalist . . .

Must go to bed now to be fresh for the filming tomorrow. Barry gets into the office before dawn, and I think I should try to get in first. M

From: Martin Lukes
To: Barry Malone

Hi Barry, I just wanted to thank you and Randee for a really wonderful day. It was great for me to feel so welcomed into your family, and to get to know your beautiful daughters. I felt particularly privileged to see your sensational art collection. Like you, I've always been a huge fan of the "art world." My favorite artist is probably Jack Vettriano—have you thought of buying any of his? I'm told they're a great investment at the moment.

Have arranged for the camera crew to meet us at the golf club at 8:30am for a run-through. See you in the office before that. I normally get in at about 5:30am.

Martin

OCTOBER 17

From: Barry Malone
To: All Staff

Howdy!

I would like to welcome to Atlanta Martin Lukes, who today commences his new job heading up my 35-strong personal office.

His first task here will be spearheading the rollout of our PPP program, and masterminding our annual conference in Paradise Island, Bahamas, next month, the very first under the new a-b glöbâl brand.

I love you all
Barry

From: Martin Lukes
To: All Staff

Hi!

First up I would like to say a humungous thank-you to Barry for making me feel so welcome here. The task is a big one, but people who know me well are kind enough to say that I have always embraced a challenge! Being a-b glöbâl's first chief of staff is a huge privilege. This is only Day One for myself, but already,

thanks to the sheer drive of our CEO, I feel as if I've been here forever. I mean that in a good way, obviously!

All my very bestest
Martin Lukes
Chief of Staff, Office of the Chairman

From: Martin Lukes
To: Sherry Zook

Hi Sherry
   Great to meet with you just now. If you'll forgive a personal
remark, that green sweater really goes with your eyes!
   I'm confident that we can sort out any issues around the nature
of your role. You may be used to a different way of working, but if
you are prepared to fasten your seat belt, working for me is going
to be really stimulating and a load of fun!
   Question. Do you have issues around getting coffee for your
boss? I realize that this is something many PAs are concerned
about, and if you do, no problem. However if you are comfortable
with this, mine's a tall latte with soya—I'm on a dairy free diet at
the moment, and am finding it very beneficial.

Martin

From: Martin Lukes
To: Sherry Zook

Seems we're both on a steep learning curve! With all due respect, I
just meant to be pleasant. Can you help me on another small matter? I wanted to find out how to get Georgia customized license

plates for my car, which I shall be importing from the UK. I would like the plates to say CREOV8.

Best, Martin

PS So where is the nearest Starbucks?

From: Martin Lukes
To: Sales@AstonMartin

Re my order.

Dear Sir

Thank you for your e-mail confirming the order of my Aston Martin DB9. I am ordering customized license plates for my car but would also like the customized plaques on the sills to read: Driving Performance with Martin Lukes. As discussed, I have sent you a swatch taken from the inside of my favorite Paul Smith leather jacket. I would like the seat uphostery to be matched exactly.

I note that the delivery is September next year, which I assume is an error. I require the car asap. I understand that these highly individualized cars are not built overnight, but I would like to remind you that we live in a Just in Time marketplace. In my business if we do not deliver extraordinary service with extraordinary speed, we'd go out of business.

Martin Lukes

OCTOBER 20

From: Martin Lukes
To: All Staff

Hi everyone

This morning at 10am EST we will be broadcasting a live web-cast with our chairman and CEO, Barry S. Malone, who will be taking us through the background to our Q3 figures. It is essential that every co-colleague takes the time to watch it. Not only is it humungous fun, it contains some very powerful and uniquely motivational messages for the future of the company.

Bestest
Martin Lukes
Chief of Staff, Office of the Chairman

From: Martin Lukes
To: Barry Malone

Hi Barry—that went brilliantly! You delivered the lines perfectly! Total triumph!

Martin

From: Martin Lukes
To: Graham Wallace

Graham—Did you see it? What did you think?? That bit where Barry deliberately topped the ball on the fairway while talking about the one-time costs of Project ABC was really inspired. I wrote the entire script myself—Barry might be a business genius but he's not much of a wordsmith. Shares seem to be down quite a lot. Which shows the market doesn't understand these results. Good for my options though . . .

Mart

PS How's Keri behaving? I think she's sulking at me again, but I don't have the mental capacity to deal with it right now.

OCTOBER 21

From: Martin Lukes
To: Graham Wallace

This was in the Financial Times this morning. Journalists are such bloody idiots. They know bugger all about the real world.

Â-B GLÖBÂL SHARES TUMBLE ON RESULT

a-b glöbâl, the US-based multinational, yesterday disappointed markets with a 35 percent drop in revenues and a 42 percent fall in operating profits for the year to September. The figures come just a month after a-b glöbâl's chief executive, Barry S. Malone, was named among the most highly respected in the world by *Fortune* magazine. In a broadcast to staff and investors, Mr. Malone said yesterday that this was a temporary setback and that the earnings outlook was strong: "We are taking the economic medicine today to oil the wheels for a blue-sky tomorrow," he said. The broadcast, in which he was seen playing a round of golf, was yesterday criticized as "inappropriate" by Wall Street analysts. "What the hell was he doing playing golf while Rome burns?" said one. A spokesman for a-b glöbâl said: "This broadcast was concrete evidence of our creovation. It has had huge

impact as a communications tool and proves we are
never scared of pushing the envelope."

From: Martin Lukes
To: Barry Malone

Hi Barry—Can I offer my perspective on this morning's press coverage? I think there are two key learnings we can take out from this. It is vital to bear in mind that the market and the media are incredibly conservative, and they take a long time to recognize a creovative™ way of communicating. The second message is that we are becoming victims of our own success. The market had decided that you can walk on water. That means if our numbers come in slightly below analysts' figures, they totally overreact. I think you are 210 percent right to keep a steady hand on the tiller. Shares have already bounced back a bit this am. This is just a blip.

All my very bestest
Martin

OCTOBER 24

From: Martin Lukes
To: Cindy Czarnikow

Hi Cindy! Thanks for your offer. A potluck brunch on Sunday would be great. I'm hoping that Jens will be over at the weekend. She'd love to see you too!

Best, Martin

From: Martin Lukes
To: Pandora@CoachworX!

Hi Pandora

Sorry I haven't touched base until now. I've been so in demand, you wouldn't believe it. The job is a blast. Totally energizing—I'm still not over the jet lag, and am only sleeping about four hours a night, but I've never felt better. Will e-mail properly when I get a window.

22.5 percent better than my bestest
Martin

From: Martin Lukes
To: Barry Malone

Hi Barry

I've been thinking outside the square on the name for our PPP conference and I think we need to brand it so that people will realize that we haven't simply changed our name to a-b glöbâl, but we are embracing change across the spectrum. I suggest we call it One Family! What do you think?

I've drawn up a list of internal speakers and have had a coup in getting Tom Peters. I felt he hit a stale patch a couple of years back, but his Re-imagine! Stuff is extraordinary!

Bestest
Martin

From: Martin Lukes
To: Jenny Withers

Darling—I have personally argued the case for you to give a plenary address at our conference on Storytelling—this is going to be a mega opportunity for you to make your name.

In return, why don't you come out for the weekend—Cindy is

giving a brunch for me, and it'd give you the chance to get to know
Barry and Randee?

Martin

PS Give my love to the boys and tell Max I'll get him a top of the
range iPod for his b'day.

From: Martin Lukes
To: Jenny Withers

I have been trying so incredibly hard to be nice to you. In return
you are cold and sarcastic. If I wasn't such a basically decent guy I
would can your speech.

Martin

From: Martin Lukes
To: Keri Tartt

Hi Pinky darling
    Sorry I haven't e-mailed for a day or two. The pace is crazy
here! Haven't had time to job hunt for you properly, but I've got
an idea. Why not come out for a long weekend next weekend?

Love Perky xx

OCTOBER 27

From: Martin Lukes
To: Cindy Czarnikow

Hi Cindy

Much looking forward to Sunday. What's your address? Unfortunately Jens isn't going to be able to make it. A young former colleague of mine might be passing through Atlanta, so I might bring her.

Martin

From: Martin Lukes
To: Graham Wallace

Hi Graham—Big article in NY Times about Barry's affair with Janine, implying that his Number 7 position in Fortune rankings was a stitch-up, and that Randee is going to take him to the cleaners.

I told you something was up.

M

OCTOBER 28

From: Martin Lukes
To: Barry Malone

Hi Barry

First up can I offer my sincere condolences at all this recent publicity. I strongly believe that your private life concerns only your good self (and Randee and Janine, of course!). I know you to be a man of the highest integrity, and if these stories persist, I suggest we retaliate with stories about all your charity work.

On a more personal level, can I say how strongly I empathize with your position, being personally embroiled in something similar myself!

Bestest, Martin

OCTOBER 31

From: Martin Lukes
To: Keri Tartt

Dearest Pinky
Did you get back home safely? I realize the weekend was a bit difficult for us both, and sorry if I was a tad distracted.

Perky

From: Martin Lukes
To: Keri Tartt

Pinky—yes of course I want us to carry on! I do love you a lot Pinky. I just need a bit of space at the moment. Sorry I didn't tell Cindy and everyone that we were an item. I was waiting for the right time. But then you got so pissed . . . it was all highly unfortunate.

P

From: Martin Lukes
To: Keri Tartt

Keri—please don't! Please give me another chance . . . I really don't see why we can't carry on . . . you've totally got the wrong end of the stick in thinking that this is just a sex thing for me. Obviously the corporal appreciates you (!!) but I really love you as a holistic person. Going back to Kiwiland is way too extreme.

From your busy but very loving Porky

From: Martin Lukes
To: Barry Malone

Do you ever think women are more trouble than they're worth?

From: Martin Lukes
To: Barry Malone

No, I don't either! I agree they are beautiful too—some more than others!! And yes, I'm getting on with the synopsis for the One Family! conference, which I'll have with you shortly!

Bestest Martin

From: Martin Lukes
To: Jenny Withers

Dear Jenny
When we talked on the phone just now, I felt that you had no interest in hearing my side of the story. So I have decided to write this e-mail to share my feelings with you. You say you want a divorce, and if that is what you want, I'm not going to stand in your way.

However I think that before we go down that road, you should think about what this would do to the boys. You should also meditate on where you are now, and how you got there.

You seem to think that somehow I'm in the wrong. But it does take two. Deep down, I think you know that.

As I have decided to be totally honest, I should also say how angry I am with you. Relationships are hard work, Jens, and it deeply saddens me that you are not prepared to put that work in. I've been thinking outside the square on this one, and it seems to me that marriage involves give and take. And frankly at the moment you only seem interested in taking.

I made a mistake. Not only have I put my hand up and said sorry, from the bottom of my heart. I have also grown from my mistake. I have a saying that has helped me a lot in the past 10 months: No failure, only feedback. Neither of us has failed. We need to concentrate on the learnings out of this, and see if we can grow as people from them.

I have also decided that there is no place for Keri in my life. I doubt if she and I will ever speak to each other again. It never meant anything, Jens. She was my midlife crisis, if you will, and I'm now ready to move onto the next level.

No need to reply at once. I want you to read this message and think deeply about it. Read it again. Sleep on it. And then tell me—are you prepared to walk the extra mile?

Jens—I've talked the talk. But now I am going to walk the walk. You must believe me.

Your husband
Martin

From: Martin Lukes
To: Pandora@CoachworX!

Pandora

A lot has happened in the last two weeks that I should debrief you on. Basically, first and foremost, the job is all I wanted and more. Totally pivotal, totally powerful, and Barry and I make a perfect partnership. I'm the Yin to his Yang, if you will.

I've got the Aston Martin DB9! Since I put one in that scrapbook, and focused on how much I really did want one, it's come true. (Or rather, it will come true when the guys at the AM factory move their lazy arses and make it for me!)

I think the car will be well aligned with my leadership brand . . . Already Barry sees me very much as the Brit maverick. The DB9 is the perfect car for that.

On the domestic front, you'd be very proud of me—I have sent Jens a long e-mail putting down all my feelings, and encouraging her to challenge her own. No reply as yet, but I told her to take her time.

22.5 percent better than my bestest
Martin

11

NOVEMBER

My Relationships

NOVEMBER 1

From: Barry Malone
To: All Staff

Howdy!
   *Next week our 300 most senior leaders will assemble in the
beautiful location of Paradise Island for this company's 16th annual management conference.*
   *This year is going to be uniquely special. For the first time we
are gathering under our new a-b glöbâl identity, united as One
Global Family with One Prayer, One Misson and One Set of Behaviors. It is the first year that we have committed to our goal of
Phenomenal Performance Permanently.*
   *We have traveled a very long way in the past year. We have a
lot to celebrate.*
   *If I had one wish, it would be that all of our 30,000 leaders
could join hands and celebrate together. And so for the first time I
have arranged to have my plenary address at Paradise Island
beamed by satellite to every location globally, so that we will all
be able to share the moment and rejoice together.*
   *I have tasked Martin Lukes and Cindy Czarnikow with send-
ing out a schedule for the conference. Please reach out to them or*

to me if there are any issues, any questions or any thoughts to share!

I love you all
Barry

From: Pandora@CoachworX!
To: Martin Lukes

Hi Martin—
   It is Month Eleven, and you are ready to binge on life!
   There is one more thing to do first. You need to think about your relationships with other people and ask yourself: are my relationships aligned with New Me? If not, it may be time to let them go.
   In essence there are three sorts of relationship—
   The energy draining relationship—you do not want these people in your life!
   The energy dependent relationship—there is balance here but it's not extraordinary.
   The energy exchange relationship—this works like a rocket, where the other person's energy will help catapult you to being better than your best. You must make some choices, Martin. I want you to be really honest and think of your relationships. Which ones drain you, and which ones blast you into space like a rocket?

Strive and thrive!
Pandora

From: Martin Lukes
To: Pandora@CoachworX!

Hi Pandora
   Will analyze relationships soonest. Am feeling a tad below par this morning—I am having issues around sleep. Basically I go to sleep fine—a couple of glasses of whiskey do the trick—and then wake up around 3am and can't get back. Went to the doctor last

week who gave me some pills, but they don't make much difference, so I'm going back today for something stronger.

Maybe my body is just adapting to my turbocharged lifestyle. Margaret Thatcher was also on the go 24/7/365 and she only slept four hours a night. And she thrived on it!

22.5 percent better than my very bestest
Martin

From: Pandora@CoachworX!
To: Martin Lukes

Hi Martin

Alcohol and drugs are a no-no!! When you have true self belief, you do not need crutches that give you a chemical high. Your brain is a powerful tool, Martin. You should be able to use it to make you feel deep profound relaxation. Before you go to bed, dim the lights, sit on the side of your bed and close your eyes. I want you to imagine a sword of white light slowly penetrating your body from the top of your head, running down to the base of your spine. I want you to start chanting your core values to yourself, over and over again, until you feel a deep sense of peace and well being and are ready to lie down and to sleep.

Strive and thrive!
Pandora

NOVEMBER 2

From: Martin Lukes
To: Keri Tartt

Pinky—I do wish you wouldn't sulk—I have enough of that with the wife. Please send me a message and tell me when you're going to come and see Perky. He misses you.

xxxx

NOVEMBER 3

From: Martin Lukes
To: Pandora@CoachworX!

Hi Pandora

Alas, still no sleep. I did try the white sword but nothing doing. I know you don't like them, but the new pills the doctor gave me are brilliant.

Re relationships—hard one, this. Off the top of my head, I'd say my relationship with Barry is definitely a rocket. We both give the other something—together we are much stronger than apart. My mum is probably a rocket too. With her I feel I can go to the top. Pandora, although we've never shared face time, I'd say my relationship with you has some rocket-like qualities too!! I hate to say it, but Jens does definitely sap my energy. But then she is my wife, so maybe that's different.

I think Keri is energy dependent. In the past I thought she might be a rocket, but now I'm not so sure.

It's all food for thought . . . must get on with the speech now.

22.5 percent better than my very bestest
Martin

From: Martin Lukes
To: Barry Malone

Hi Barry, I've drafted your speech. I've made it as inclusive as I can, and I've put integrity center stage. Hope you like it!

Bestest Martin

From: Martin Lukes
To: Barry Malone

Hi Barry
    Thanks for the honest feedback! I agree 230 percent. I'll give it more thought and come back to you, soonest.

Martin

From: Faith Preston
To: All Staff

Hi—Keri Tartt is leaving our shores for NZ at the end of the week. If anyone would like to sign her card and contribute to her gift—it's on my desk.

Cheers, Faith

From: Martin Lukes
To: Keri Tartt

Keri—Frankly, I am surprised that I get to hear through Faith that you have decided to leave. You and I have always communicated very openly with each other, and so I thought you would have the decency to tell me yourself.

However, it's all probably for the best, and I hope that we can remain friends.

My best
Martin

From: Martin Lukes
To: Keri Tartt

I don't get it, Keri. I send you an extremely nice message, and you accuse me of being a cold selfish bastard only interested in myself . . . blah, blah. Two can play at that game—I actually think it was extremely selfish of you to end our affair because you didn't think I was paying you enough attention. If you hadn't been so wrapped up in yourself you would have noticed that I have been given the job of a lifetime which is very stressful and is more than a 24/7 commitment. Frankly our relationship was an energy exchange—you didn't enhance my energy levels, and if I'm going to be totally honest, I should say I deserve a lot more.

Martin

From: Keri Tartt
To: All Staff

Hiya!

Thanx 2 everyone for the gr8 card and the generous M&S vouchers!!! I'm going to have loadsa fun spending them! It's been so cool working with ya! I'll take many happy memories back to NZ with me! And if u r ever in NZ come and c me!!

Cheers
Keri

From: Martin Lukes
To: Barry Malone

Hi Barry

I've re-dreamt your speech, and this time I hope you'll agree it's sensational!

My Big Idea is to set up your address like a pop concert. There will be a flashing strobe and the Sister Sledge song "We Are Family" will be playing very loudly. I shout over the PA—"THE GUY YOU HAVE ALL BEEN WAITING FOR . . . BARRY MALONE!!" and you come running onto the stage and the crowd then gets up and whoops.

You march up and down on the stage shouting I LOVE THIS COMPANY! WE ARE ONE FAMILY!! I'll get the crowd cheering, and then you ask: What are we? We'll shout back: ONE FAMILY!! You'll say: WE ARE UNITED BY INTEGRITY. WHAT ARE WE UNITED BY? We will shout back: INTEGRITY!!!

This will get everyone on their feet, and get the conference off to an exceptionally high-octane start.

If you think this is the way to go (and I hope you will!!) then I'll draft the rest of it tonight.

Bestest
Martin

From: Martin Lukes
To: Barry Malone

Hi—Thrilled you love it!! I am totally pleased with it myself! Will have the rest of the address with you soonest!

Martin

PS Brunch on Sunday would be great. It's a bit lonely for me here with no family, so I much appreciate the hospitality!

Martin

NOVEMBER 8

From: Martin Lukes
To: Barry Malone

Hi Barry
  Thank you for an energizing day! Can I congratulate you on the charm and beauty of your daughter? I'd lock her up if I were you! Also congratulations on having found in Janine a woman who not only cooks the perfect eggs benedict but plays such excellent golf!

Martin

From: Martin Lukes
To: Graham Wallace

Hi Graham
  Went over to BSM's house again yesterday. Randee not there this time. Janine was there instead . . . v friendly to yours truly. Actually I've changed my mind on her—she's very bright, and we had some good intellectual discussions! Afterwards we played a fourball with a gorgeous daughter, who is 15 but looks 25. I played pretty well.
  Barry has just bought a painting for $2.5m that he says is worth twice as much. Not sure how he managed that . . . and when I asked, he went all funny. Most of the time I know exactly

what Barry's thinking, but sometimes he plays his cards v close to his chest.

Cheers, Mart

PS What's the London gossip? Feeling a tad out of the loop.

From: Martin Lukes
To: Phyllis Lukes

Dearest Mum

So sorry not to have been in touch for yonks. Everything going mad here. Thanks for your message. Glad you went to have Sunday lunch with Jens and the boys.

Try not to worry too much about Jake—teenage boys always look pale and thin—they don't get out in the fresh air that much . . .

You didn't say anything about Jens. Did she mention the D word? She seems to have stopped talking about divorce, though if I'm totally honest, she's stopped talking about anything at all. Her coping strategy is to bury herself in her work—which worries me as it isn't the best thing for the boys.

Did I tell you that it's over with Keri? At the end of the day she decided she wanted something more serious than I was prepared to give at the present moment in time—I was upset for a bit, but then I figured that the two of us didn't have a lot in common—but I think you worked that out for yourself!

Work is fantastic, never been better.

Will e-mail or ring later in the week.

Yr loving son
Martie x

From: Martin Lukes
To: Jenny Withers

Jens

Mum says Jake's looking terrible. He doesn't reply to my messages, or speak on the phone. What's going on? Is he on drugs again? You really do need to keep me in the loop.

I hear you're working flat out, and frankly I worry that not only is that bad for the boys, it's not good for you. Love, Martin x

From: Martin Lukes
To: Jenny Withers

J—No I can't possibly come back this w/end. In case you hadn't noticed, I'm doing the most important project this company has ever undertaken. I'm under a lot of pressure . . . and you aren't helping. In case you are interested, I'm not sleeping at all . . . M

From: Martin Lukes
To: Jenny Withers

Jens—thank you for your "considerate" message. This is a very stressful time for me and I don't appreciate getting messages about my "double standards" and "dysfunctional behavior." I do NOT need therapy. If anyone needs it, it's you. By refusing to come and join me in Atlanta you are hurting yourself, myself and the boys. You are also draining our funds . . . I'm still in a hotel waiting on a decision from you on what sort of house to buy. The minibar bill for a week alone is the same as our annual gas bill.

I know what you think of Pandora, but I've been doing some interesting work with her on my relationships, and looking at the ones that drain my energy compared to the ones that boost it. My relationship with you, regrettably, falls into the first camp. Pandora clearly thinks we should split up—you aren't bringing anything to my party, if you will. Frankly I'm beginning to see where she's coming from.

Martin

NOVEMBER 11

From: Martin Lukes
To: All Staff

Conference Update!
    Attached is the schedule for Phenomenal Performance Permanently at Paradise Island. This year the theme is One Global Family! Please note that the dress code is Smart Casual (no suits required). Evening events casual with a Bahamas theme. Feel free to dress colorful!

```
AGENDA DAY ONE
Meeting Location: Ballroom
5pm-7pm CEO's Address: WE ARE FAMILY!
7pm-8pm Cocktails and canapes
8pm Banquet—poolside

DAY TWO
7:30 Breakfast
8:30-9:30 Martin Lukes: THE ART OF CREOVATION™—FROM
    LITTLE WOW! TO BIG WOW!
10:00 Keynote speaker—Tom Peters: RE-IMAGINE!
10:00-12:00 BREAKOUT WORKSHOPS LED BY A-B GLÖBÂL (UK)

These will be themed around a traditional Bahamas
festival, Junkanoo, where the people get together and
lose their inhibitions. At these workshops all co-
colleagues will be invited to check their existing
```

headsets at the door and free-associate! It's going
to be a ton of fun!

1. Christo Weinberg: BUSKING THE LGBT AGENDA—how
   lesbians, gays, bisexuals and transgenders grow
   the bottom line

2. Jenny Withers: AROUND THE CORPORATE CAMPFIRE—
   the magical art of storytelling

3. Roger Wright: DELIVERING ON BUDGET—zero tolerance of cost overruns

4. Faith Preston: UNLEASHING THE HOLISTIC HEADSET—
   the HR/Business Strategy Partnership

1:00–2:30 Lunch
2:30–4:00 Keith Buxton: RAISING THE TALENT BAR—key
learnings from ABC
4:00–6:00 Afternoon activities—golf, spa, healing
therapies
6:00–7:30 Conference wrap-up, Cindy Czarnikow: THE
WEAKEST LINK VISION AND VALUES QUIZ!

If you have any questions or issues or inspirations, please do
not hesitate to touch base with myself.

Martin

From: Martin Lukes
To: Keith Buxton

Hi—yes I have scheduled your talk for the after-lunch slot. And
no, it is not going to be possible to swap with mine. A huge
amount of thought has gone into the logistics of this and I believe I
have come up with a best of breed outcome.

I gave you the so-called "graveyard slot" because I thought

you'd deliver a presentation compelling enough so that people stay awake!!

Bestest
Martin

From: Martin Lukes
To: All Staff

Hi!

A reminder to all co-colleagues who will NOT be present at Paradise Island that Barry's speech will be broadcast live on the Web. Large screens will be erected in all geographies and co-colleagues are encouraged to watch it together in order to ensure maximum impact!

Bestest
Martin Lukes
Chief of Staff, Office of the Chairman

NOVEMBER 14

From: Cindy Czarnikow
To: Paradise Island delegates

Welcome to this island paradise!! For the next few days we are going to bond and to brainstorm. Today everyone should swim, soak up the scene and enjoy a lite lunch in the Jungle Bar. I recommend the plantain-crusted Nassau grouper creole. Yum!

Make sure you're well rested and refreshed ahead of Barry's extraordinary motivational plenary address at 5pm. And sharpen your wits for the Vision and Values quiz tomorrow! I shall be test-

ing everyone on our mission, our prayers, our behaviors and our dreams. You don't want to be The Weakest Link!!!

Cheers, Cindy

From: Martin Lukes
To: Jake Lukes

Hi Jake—Just seen your message. No I don't know where your mother is, she hasn't arrived yet. And no, I can't send you more money. You get 200 quid at the beginning of the month. Would appreciate an e-mail/phone call from you before then with some news in it, rather than just requests for dosh.

Dad

Text message to Jenny. Sent 14:23

Jens—are u here? Why haven't u checked in? M x

Text message to Jenny. Sent 14:46

Why have you got a separate room??? I booked a double suite for both of us. M

From: Martin Lukes
To: Barry Malone

Hi Barry
     Just wanted to say good luck, and remind you to let your natural warmth come through. Let your charisma fill the auditorium!
     The sound system is brilliant so the music will be very, very

loud. I've positioned a couple of cheerleaders in the audience who know when to clap, when to whoop, and when to stand up and stamp their feet. The rest of the audience will take their lead from them. Give it all you've got, and good luck!

Martin

From: Martin Lukes
To: All Staff

Welcome!
Everyone gather for Barry's address in the Ballroom now! Starting in 15 minutes!

Martin

Sent from my BlackBerry Wireless Handheld

From: Martin Lukes
To: Barry Malone

Hi Barry—
WHOOOOOAA!!! Your performance just now was amazing!! I haven't seen a crowd shout so much since I went to a Led Zeppelin concert when I was 17! You have taken the family concept and breathed life into it. THEY ALL LOVED YOU!! After you bounded off stage there was a feeling of real passion in the audience. People were crying and hugging each other. Amazing. An example unto us all!! WE ARE FAMILY!!!

Martin

Sent from my BlackBerry Wireless Handheld

NOVEMBER 15

Was upset u sat with Keith at breakfast. Can we have lunch? Am off to give my speech now. Fingers crossed. Best of British with yrs later . . . M xx

From: Martin Lukes
To: Barry Malone

Thank you very much! Yes when I was standing at the podium I felt this terrific current of positive energy coming from the audience. I've had some fantastic feedback for my speech, but to me it just proves that your strategy for uniting and re-energizing this company is delivering results already.

Bestest, Martin

Sent from my BlackBerry Wireless Handheld

From: Cindy Czarnikow
To: Paradise Island delegates

Sawat-dee-kha!!!!
   The Weakest Link quiz was a blast! Congratulations to Jenny Withers who knows all our visions and values down to the last letter! She was the fastest to name all our key behaviors, and to be able to list them in order. Well done Jenny!!! You win a free shiatsu massage in the health spa!!

Cheers, Cindy

Sent from my BlackBerry Wireless Handheld

Where r u? There's no one in the bar . . . I haven't found anyone to drink with all evening. Don't feel like bed yet . . . want to do some more celebrating . . . am in the mood for some action . . .

NOVEMBER 16

Text message to Graham. Sent 08:23

Arrgh. I'm so hungover. Can't face golf. C u later.

From: Martin Lukes
To: Jenny Withers

Jens—I'm very sorry about last night. I was very pissed—this insomnia thing is making me drink quite a lot. Anyway I didn't mean to barge into your room and hope my advances weren't entirely unwelcome! Can we have a drink by the poolside tonight to make amends. I'll have to be on call in case Barry needs me, but we should have a chance for a chat . . .

M xx

Sent from my BlackBerry Wireless Handheld

From: Barry Malone
To: All Staff

Howdy!
We've just concluded a weekend where every director of this company gathered in the Bahamas' beautiful Paradise Island for our annual conference. The theme was We Are One Global Family, and we showed that we are stronger than ever, united by love, values and belief.

I would like to thank Martin Lukes, whose passion and dedication to making it the weekend of a lifetime knew no bounds.

Also Jenny Withers in London, whose speech Storytelling— Around the Corporate Campfire gave us all so much to think about. It's a long time since I read the classics, but her speech has inspired me to go back and take a peek!

It is these stories, not just in books but by word of mouth, that we pass down to each other, that bind us together, to our past and our future. We are great apart. Together we are unbeatable.

I love you all
Barry

From: Martin Lukes
To: Jenny Withers

Sorry you dashed off to get your plane without saying good-bye. You see what an amazing couple we are—both singled out. Great apart—together unbeatable?

Mxx

From: Martin Lukes
To: Barry Malone

Hi Barry
   I see there have been a few more muckraking stories in the papers while we have been in the Bahamas. Can I make a suggestion? This is the moment to put out an internal announcement relating to your integrity, something that will reinforce your brand values. I have in mind something that is totally authentic to your character, but will distract attention from any further press reports on your divorce and Janine.

Bestest, Martin

From: Barry Malone
To: All Staff

Howdy!
   As everybody close to me knows, I do not rest easy knowing that there is injustice in this world. Every day I try to fight for compassion, against greed. It is for that reason that I have decided to give a significant percentage of my bonus this year to the Boy Scouts of America. The gift means some personal hardship for my family, but they understand that in tough times those at the top must make hard choices and hard sacrifices.

I love you all
Barry S. Malone

From: Martin Lukes
To: Barry Malone

Hi Barry
  Another Big Wow! That was just right. M

From: Martin Lukes
To: Graham Wallace

Graham—Frankly your carping pisses me off. Contrary to what you say, Barry does deserve his bonus. It's particularly generous of him to be giving money away when his wife Randee is suing him for $98m . . . Cheers M

NOVEMBER 23

From: Keith Buxton
To: All Staff

Hi
  I am delighted to announce that Christo Weinberg has been appointed Marketing Director in London. Christo has an exceptional creative talent, and I'm sure will breathe new life into this most important department.
  An announcement on a new permanent chairman of a-b glöbâl (UK) will be made shortly.

Keith Buxton
Global Chief Talent Officer

From: Martin Lukes
To: Keith Buxton

Keith

Why wasn't I consulted about this??? Christo Weinberg is a very bright lad who has hugely benefited from my mentoring over the past year. But no way is he ready to head up such an important department. And when you say "breathe new life" into the department, what exactly are you driving at?

Re the UK chairman: I'm glad a decision is imminent though sad you did not see fit to consult myself. With respect, I should be kept in the loop.

Martin

NOVEMBER 24

From: Barry Malone
To: All Staff

Howdy!

This morning I received notification from the SEC that it is investigating movements in the a-b glöbâl share price in the period leading up to Q2 and Q3 results. However, I have no reason to believe that this is any more than routine. There is no question of any wrongdoing by anybody inside this company.

I love you all
Barry S. Malone

From: Martin Lukes
To: Graham Wallace

Hi Graham

What are people saying in London about the insider trading story? I think it's definitely a storm in a teacup—though BSM seems a bit paranoid about it all. I caught him shrieking at his PA just now, an attractive little number called Stacey.

Mart

NOVEMBER 25

From: Martin Lukes
To: Barry Malone

Hi Barry,

I suggest we do something to take people's minds off the insider trading story. Just been looking at the outsourcing figures. Looks like we'll be cutting 6,000 jobs globally. Do you think now might be a time to get some of that bad news into the open to distract attention, if you will? You suggest I send out a message to put an end to the rumors. I've thought hard about this and wonder if we might do better to sit tight and wait for it to blow over?

My best, Martin

From: Martin Lukes
To: Barry Malone

Sure, on second thought I think you're 250 percent right. Will do soonest.

Martin

From: Martin Lukes
To: All Staff

Hi!

Our CEO, Barry S. Malone, has asked myself to touch base re the stories in the press relating to insider trading. Most of these bear little relation to the facts, which are as follows. An individual has been taken in for questioning for alleged insider trading in a-b glôbâl shares. We believe her to be a Manhattan-based art dealer. She has a large portfolio of stocks which she trades actively. Barry is a renowned art collector but has never met this individual. There is no link between the two whatsoever.

Martin Lukes
Chief of Staff, Office of the Chairman

From: Martin Lukes
To: Pandora@CoachworX!

Hi Pandora

Sorry I haven't been in touch—huge drama here on insider trading. Could be very serious, but I think we are controlling the agenda skillfully, and it'll probably blow over . . .

22.5 percent better than my bestest
Martin

NOVEMBER 28

From: Martin Lukes
To: Stacey Stone

Oh my God I don't believe it. Where is he now?

From: Martin Lukes
To: Keith Buxton

Keith—have you heard anything?

From: Martin Lukes
To: Graham Wallace

Fucketyfuckingfuck—Barry's been taken in for questioning. I just don't bloody believe it. The total complete and utter idiot. This is a personal CATASTROPHE for me—I need a drink NOW. Wish u were here . . . M

From: Martin Lukes
To: Keith Buxton

As bad as that? I must say I'm not altogether surprised. As I got closer to Barry I realized something was up. I never really bought into the integrity thing. In fact I was so suspicious about his art dealer person I had planned to check her out. Let's meet soonest to limit damage.

Martin

From: Martin Lukes
To: Katherine Lukes

Hi Katherine
    Got your SOS. Sorry you have split with your partner. But I'm in a worse crisis of my own. Will message when things calmer.

Martin

From: Martin Lukes
To: Pandora@CoachworX!

Pandora—
Malone has quit. He's been feeding insider information to this art dealer.

Fuckfuckfuck . . . I've been much too close to him . . . what shall I do? Help help M

From: Pandora@CoachworX!
To: Martin Lukes

Martin—Can I remind you that crisis management is a coaching service only offered with the Executive Gold Program. Unfortunately as you have not upscaled from Executive Bronze that means that I am not able to offer you in-depth coaching through this.

However, I can suggest as a start that you try to make a paradigm shift in your headset. Take some deep breaths. Put your hands in front of your mouth, or find a bag and breathe into it. This will stop you from hyperventilating. When the going gets tough, the tough get tougher . . .

Strive and thrive!
Pandora

From: Martin Lukes
To: Pandora@CoachworX!

For fuck's sake Pandora—I may be about to lose my job. Now is NOT the time to start breathing into a paper bag. Do you have any USEFUL advice on what I should do now??

Martin

From: Pandora@CoachworX!
To: Martin Lukes

As I said, Martin, I shouldn't really be offering you this, but I do it out of the goodness of my heart.

Ask yourself some questions. Is my relationship with Barry really a rocket? How do I protect my personal brand? The GROW model will help you, Martin. Remember this is a time to make sure that whatever you do is aligned with your values. If you ignore your values, you will damage your brand.

Strive and thrive!
Pandora

From: Martin Lukes
To: LucyKellaway@ft

Hi Lucy,

Long time no speak. Trust all is well with you and yours. We spoke back in February when I was doing a project giving back to the homeless. I remember the Financial Times was the only newspaper that handled the story responsibly.

I wanted to touch base to offer an exclusive on the a-b glöbâl story. You'll have seen on the wire that our CEO Barry S. Malone resigned this morning. Many newspapers will be running with the story that a-b glöbâl had not kept proper checks and balances on him. This actually is not the case. It was becoming clear to myself, as Malone's chief of staff, that he did not meet my own, or the company's, exceptionally high standards of ethics. In particular my suspicions had been aroused by his art dealing. The day before he was taken in for questioning, I challenged him personally. He did not give me a satisfactory answer, and I had that day considered contacting a support group for whistle-blowers. I can offer you an exclusive interview.

All my very bestest
Martin Lukes

From: Christo Weinberg
To: All Marketing

Hi!

Day One for me as Marketing Director has certainly been exciting! In case anybody has not yet seen it, the following story appeared in the London Financial Times this morning. Particularly direct your attention to my predecessor's angle on P17.

A-B GLÖBÂL CHIEF QUITS IN SHARE SCANDAL
By Lucy Kellaway

a-b glöbâl, the beleaguered Atlanta-based multinational, was plunged into crisis last night following the forced resignation of CEO Barry S. Malone after allegations of insider trading. Mr. Malone, who is a renowned art collector, is alleged to have passed insider information to his art dealer in return for works of art. Mr. Keith Buxton, chief talent officer, takes over as CEO pending the announcement of a permanent replacement. Earlier this year Mr. Malone was named by *Fortune* magazine the seventh most respected global leader. Last month Randee Malone, Mr. Malone's fourth wife, filed for divorce, following allegations of her husband's affair with Janine Rosenholz, a *Fortune* journalist.

Full Story, page 2
'My agony as whistle-blower', page 17

From: Martin Lukes
To: Keith Buxton

Keith—How DARE you accuse me of lying??? I was simply protecting the company, and correcting a few misconceptions about myself being a BSM groupie. Yes, I did send an e-mail out defending Barry before the shit hit the proverbial fan. But the thinking behind that was complex, and this has been a fast-moving situation.

Martin

From: Martin Lukes
To: Janine Rosenholz

Hi Janine
   Just seen your messages. I realize you are upset by the article in today's newspaper, and I hope in the fullness of time you will understand that, as a champion of the highest ethical standards, my first duty is to do what is right.

All my very bestest
Martin Lukes

NOVEMBER 30

From: Keith Buxton
To: All Staff

Hi everyone,
   First up I would like to say how honored I am to be given the opportunity to lead this company until the board has finalized a permanent CEO appointment. This is a time for firm leadership, and I would like to make two things very clear. It is imperative that no member of staff speaks to the press without prior authorization from myself and from our legal team. I cannot stress how essential this is. There have been some unfortunate incidents in the past few days, which we do not want repeated. I would like to reassure everyone that the company's strategy of delivering astounding value to all our stakeholder groups remains as strong as

ever. The only short-term policy shift is to abandon the rollout for the new office of the CEO. In the current climate we do not feel such extra resources to be justified. Individuals already recruited to this team will be encouraged to apply for jobs elsewhere in the group.

All my very bestest, Keith Buxton

From: Martin Lukes
To: Keith Buxton

KEITH—DID NO ONE EVER TELL YOU IT IS NOT A GOOD IDEA TO SACK PEOPLE BY PUBLIC E MAIL??? AND WHAT THE HELL JOB AM I MEANT TO BE APPLYING FOR????????

MARTIN

From: Martin Lukes
To: Jenny Withers

Jens—Don't you start, as well. I gave that interview for good reasons. I might have hoped you, as supposed media maestro, would understand that. My position here is untenable. I'm on the plane home tomorrow, and my first call will be to our solicitor. This is a cut-and-dried case for constructive dismissal. Keith hates me, and frankly the feeling is mutual. He's not going to get away with this. Would appreciate if you came to meet me at Heathrow.

From: Martin Lukes
To: Sherry Zook

Sherry—I'll be out for the rest of the day, and tomorrow I'm flying back home. If anyone wants me, tell them whatever you like. It's been great working with you, and next time you're in London do look me up.

Best, Martin

From: Martin Lukes
To: Jenny Withers

You can't keep this up. I've had a very very serious blow. This is the biggest disaster that has ever happened to me in my life. It is so unfair . . . Let me come home now. Please.

Love you M x

12

DECEMBER

Welcome Home

DECEMBER 1

From: Pandora@CoachworX!
To: Martin Lukes

Hi Martin
Congratulations, Martin, you have almost finished Executive Bronze! You are a wonderful person, with incredible gifts, talents and strengths beyond your wildest dreams. Take that thought and feel its warmth. Now double it. Double it again. And again. And smile. Because you know, deep down inside it is time to reclaim your birthright. It is time to return to your true self. WELCOME HOME!

Strive and thrive!
Pandora

From: Martin Lukes
To: Pandora@CoachworX!

Pandora
Can I be totally honest with you? I read your message with a growing sense of disconnect. Has it escaped your notice that I am NOT home?? I am actually staying at the Novotel Canning Town

for the foreseeable future and am living out of a suitcase. Neither am I "home" career wise. At the moment it is not clear whether I have a job at all. I came into the office this morning, expecting to return to my position as Director of Marketing, to find Christo Weinberg at my desk. I have nowhere to sit. I have no PA. I have no idea what I am supposed to do. Not only is my wife ignoring me, everyone is ignoring me. I might have gifts and talents beyond my wildest dreams, but no one gives a monkey's. If this is New Me, frankly I would like to reconnect with Old Me.

Martin

From: Pandora@CoachworX!
To: Martin Lukes

Hi Martin!
Whooaa! Looks like you need a refresher on some of the key learnings to date! I know that there have been some issues around your departure from Atlanta. But Martin, you must not take these personally. Have you forgotten the mantra, NO FAILURE ONLY FEEDBACK? You haven't failed. You are the same You who was Chief of Staff. Martin, I want you to think about the events of the last week. What happened? Why did it happen? What are the learnings you can take out from it?

Strive and thrive!
Pandora

From: Martin Lukes
To: Pandora@CoachworX!

Pandora—There are no learnings in this. I backed the wrong horse, and now I'm paying for it, big time. The only issue for myself is what next?
Basically, there is one thing that I want now and that is to be made Chairman of a-b glöbâl (UK). There is a humungous

problem—and that is Keith Buxton. He has issues around envy re yours truly, and frankly, it's going to be hard for me to persuade him to appoint me. If you have any concrete suggestions on this I'm in the market for them.

Martin

DECEMBER 2

From: Martin Lukes
To: Graham Wallace

Hi Graham, thanks for the invite, but no thanks. I think I'll just take it easy this weekend. In any case my clubs are in my luggage which is in storage.

Cheers, Mart

From: Martin Lukes
To: Graham Wallace

Yes, I'm feeling fine. Just because I don't feel like playing golf doesn't mean that I'm heading for a nervous breakdown. On Sunday, I'll probably be seeing the family . . .

Cheers, Mart

From: Martin Lukes
To: Jenny Withers

Dear estranged wife

I know you are beyond such normal emotions as human sympathy, but you may be interested to know that I have this morning started bleeding from my arse.

You might also like to know that I am planning to go to Eton this weekend to see Max, who is now the only member of my family who responds to my messages.

Your husband
Martin

DECEMBER 6

From: Martin Lukes
To: Sales@AstonMartin

Dear Sir
   Re order 245.
   Due to an unforeseen change in my circumstances I no longer require my car to be assembled as per the US market. I will take delivery of it in London, and require the steering wheel on the right.
   All the other customized details remain unchanged, except that I would like the customized plaques on the sills inscribed "Driving Performance with Martin Lukes" on pewter rather than brass. I have ordered British customized number plates CREOV8, which was fortunately also available, which I will deliver to you closer to the time.

Yours sincerely
Martin Lukes

From: Martin Lukes
To: SebastianFforbesHever@HeidrickFerry

Hi Sebastian!

Long time no hear! I expect you will have been following shenanigans at a-b glöbâl in the media, and will know that yours truly has been a key player!

Just to keep you in the loop, since we spoke I was appointed as Barry Malone's chief of staff in Atlanta, basically the second most powerful job in the company.

However, following the recent upheaval, I'm back in London considering various challenging openings here. Could we have lunch/coffee soonest to kick around some ideas on what's happening in the "outside world"?

All my very bestest,
Martin

DECEMBER 7

From: Martin Lukes
To: SebastianFforbesHever@HeidrickFerry

Hi Sebastian

Did you get my message? Don't know if you've been trying to reach me on my office phone. My extension has changed, it's now X4096.

Cheers, Martin

From: Martin Lukes
To: Graham Wallace

Graham

I don't know how much more can go wrong in my life . . . Christo is undoing all my good work in marketing and bloody Aston Martin say it's too late to put the steering wheel on the right-hand side, so I'm going to have to drive around in a car that will be a daily reminder of the job I don't have . . . When you're shelling out £103,000 you expect a bit more in terms of customer service . . .

Am just composing a missive to one of my headhunter friends, and then can we have the largest drink you've ever had?

Cheers, Mart

From: Martin Lukes
To: Jenny Withers

Hi Jens—Just seen yr message. Why do you need to go to Atlanta at such short notice? And why do you think I can just drop everything and help out??

You say you want a divorce because I'm "totally obsessed with myself." Then you turn around and ask me to move back in as a babysitter. Can I point out that YOU are the one who is selfish—your career obsession knows no bounds.

I don't believe in playing silly games so I am going to help you, not because you deserve it, but because I miss the boys, and I actually care about their welfare. I am their father and they are badly in need of my input.

Martin

From: Martin Lukes
To: Jake Lukes

Jake

I'm moving back in for the weekend when mum's away. Would be good to have some quality time together. We could rent the new Star Wars movie have a takeout curry and a couple of beers? What do you think??

Dad

From: Martin Lukes
To: Max Lukes

Max old man

Mum's off to Atlanta on some job jaunt this weekend, and I'll be holding the fort chez nous. Your housemaster has given special permission for you to come back for the weekend—Let's do something really wicked!!

Dad

From: Martin Lukes
To: Max Lukes

You want to go to CHURCH? Why???

DECEMBER 10

Text message to Jenny. Sent 22:14

Jens—Can u call me NOW??? Jake's been picked up by the police for possession of Ecstasy. Am heading down to Wimbledon police station now. M

Text message to Max. Sent 23:35

Max—am still at the station. Has mum called? Tell her to get on the first plane. Dad

DECEMBER 11

From: Martin Lukes
To: Jenny Withers

Jens

We're back home, all in one piece. I've sorted everything on my own, so there's no need for you to come back early. They've released Jake, who is presently sitting in front of the TV. He's very quiet and sullen. Still half off his head, I suppose.

The policeman was unusually bright and was pretty impressed when I said I personally would be responsible for Jake's future good behavior. I explained that the lad had been under a lot of pressure because you were working flat out and because of issues between us.

Looks like they're not going to press charges—worst case, I think he'll get away with a caution.

M

From: Martin Lukes
To: Jake Lukes

Dear Jake

The reason I'm putting this in an e-mail rather than waiting until you get up and saying it face to face is because I often find it easier to express myself in writing than verbally.

Basically, you deserve the biggest bollocking of your life. By being such an idiot and taking those drugs you have not just let yourself down, but you've let your mother and myself down. If it wasn't for me, you might be facing a 7 years prison sentence—which frankly would be the wake-up call you need.

However, I have decided not to punish you. When you were in the police station last night I had one of those eureka moments—I realized that at the end of the day what really counts is family. You, Max and, obviously, your mother.

I'd like to share something with you that you may find surprising. When I was your age, I got into a spot of trouble too. One day a gang of mates and myself got pissed on a bottle of Armagnac (I still can't drink it to this day!) and then we went into an Ann Summers shop and yours truly nicked a lacy bra! I got caught, and the store detective threatened me with the police but then let me go. I was terrified he would tell granny, though luckily he didn't. So I totally understand what you're going through, and I hope that you will confide in me going forward.

Jake, I know we've had issues in the past. It's true that you've been a disappointing son in many regards. You did something very, very wrong with my BlackBerry. You've performed exceptionally poorly academically, you've been lazy and you've not chosen friends of your own caliber. And now you are taking Class A drugs and getting caught. It doesn't look very good on paper does it??

But I want to say that I'm your father, and I'm 110 percent here for you. You are my oldest son. You are like myself (for your sins!!) in many regards. Moving forward, if you put your creovative™ streak to work, you won't go far wrong.

Your loving Dad

DECEMBER 13

From: Martin Lukes
To: Graham Wallace

Who told you that?!!? Yes, Jens has gone to Atlanta. I just spoke to her 5 minutes ago and she didn't say anything about being offered a job. I know that Keith has always had a thing about her, but even he wouldn't do that . . .

M

From: Martin Lukes
To: Jenny Withers

Thanks for your message. Jake much better this morning. He grunted at me in a slightly less hostile way. I've also sent him a long e-mail establishing some new ground rules. There is going to be one big win out of this—my relationship with him is going to be a lot stronger.

Btw Graham has heard a rumor that you're in the frame for Roger's job!!!???

M

From: Martin Lukes
To: Jenny Withers

WHAT??? That is the most stupid thing I've ever heard . . . You do realize I couldn't possibly work under you, don't you??

When u coming back? We must talk about this NOW!

M

From: Martin Lukes
To: Jenny Withers

Jens, sorry if my message just then sounded a bit negative. I've thought about it some more, in a very logical way, and reached the conclusion that this is a lose-lose situation. You lose because you would be doing a job that is not well aligned with your skillsets. Being chairman would make you totally stressed and miserable.

The company would lose because you would not be the right person and might start making sub-optimal decisions. I would lose because it is very unhealthy working for one's wife—or ex-wife, as you certainly would be if you took the job—and I would be left with no choice but to leave the company. Ergo, the company would lose again.

Most important, the boys would lose, especially Jake. If he had a mother who was around more, he would be much less interested in drugs. Max needs you around too. I was really shocked over the weekend at the change in him. He spent most of Sunday morning in church, did the washing up, took all the skateboarding posters down in his bedroom, and has stuck up some nightmare poster featuring a cheesy picture of Jesus. He's clearly in a bad way.

Mull it over, and you'll see I'm right. Please don't think I'm making these points out of self-interest. I'm not. I'm just standing back and looking at all the issues in the round.

Martin

From: Martin Lukes
To: Jenny Withers

No Jens, I'm not trying to blame you for the boys. As their father I realize that I'm responsible too. It's just that until now you have been closer to them. Yes of course I realize that at the end of the day, it's your call.

Well at least can you promise me one thing . . . that you'll think about it for a few days before deciding? Let's talk about it when you're home tomorrow. When's your flight?

Martin

From: Martin Lukes
To: SebastianFforbesHever@HeidrickFerry

Hi Sebastain

Don't know if you got my e-mail of last week. I'm attaching a copy of it in case not. Would be good to meet up soonest to kick around a couple of ideas.

Martin

From: Martin Lukes
To: Stewart@harleystreetclinic

Dear Dr. Stewart

As I told your secretary on the telephone, I have been finding traces of blood in my stool. Obviously this is a serious matter and tends to confirm—what I suspected at the time—that the bowel cancer man you sent me to missed something serious.

I also have a fast-beating heart, sometimes leading to palpitatons and chronic insomnia. I am tending to sweat more than usual, and am tired all the time, and sometimes irritable. This is not at all like myself, as I am usually very controlled.

Would appreciate an appointment at the earliest opportunity.

Yours sincerely
Martin Lukes

From: Martin Lukes
To: Max Lukes

Dear Max

Thanks for your message. It's kind of you to pray for me, but really old man, quite unnecessary. It was good to see you at the weekend, and so sorry that thanks to Jake's theatricals we didn't have much in the way of quality time.

Though if I'm being completely honest with you I'm a bit

worried about this Alpha course malarky. It just doesn't seem very you.

Love Dad

From: Martin Lukes
To: Max Lukes

Dear Max

I didn't mean to be dismissive! I quite agree with Jesus re tolerance and belief. Of course, at the end of the day we all have to do what's right for us as individuals. Thanks also for sending me the material on Alpha course in the workplace, all looks v interesting, but I'm not sure that a-b glöbâl (UK) is quite ready for it at the present moment in time!!

Love Dad

DECEMBER 14

From: Martin Lukes
To: Phyllis Lukes

Dearest Mummy

Thanks for your message, and sorry I haven't been able to nail down Christmas plans . . . To be perfectly frank, you and I might be spending it on our own at your place. Things with Jens are beyond bad—you were so right when you said it was a disastrous idea for her to work at the same place as me. You're not going to believe this but it looks like she's going to wind up as my boss.

It's all taking its toll on me physically. I went to see the doctor this morning, and it turns out I have piles. He says I'm depressed, which frankly I don't accept, but I've decided to take the pills anyway—which means I'm now on Temazepam, Prozac and Anusol.

Don't worry about the boys. They are both fine.
Can I come down and stay with you this weekend?

Martie

From: Pandora@CoachworX!
To: Martin Lukes

Hi Martin
Can I make a suggestion? Although Executive Bronze usually only runs for one year, there is no reason why in your case we shouldn't extend into next year. I feel this could be helpful as there are some outstanding issues we could address. I do not feel happy signing off on my coachees until they are at least 10 percent better than the best they can be. I am, as you know, your greatest and sincerest fan. It deeply pains me to know that you are letting your self-belief slip. Martin, please let me help you get to the top and stay there!

Strive and thrive!
Pandora

From: Faith Preston
To: All Staff

Hiya!
    This year at the Christmas party we are all going to play Secret Santa!
    Pick a name out of the hat, and you get to buy a present for this person! All gifts must be under a fiver! It's going to be a load of fun!!

Faith

From: Martin Lukes
To: Graham Wallace

Guess who I've picked out? Jens! Nightmare. She always hates my presents. I don't think Secret Santa really expects that you will be getting gifts for your wife who wants to divorce you . . .

DECEMBER 15

From: Martin Lukes
To: Graham Wallace

BELEAGUERED A-B GLÖBÂL APPOINTS WOMAN IN NUMBER ONE JOB

a-b glöbâl, the troubled Atlanta-based multinational, which was last month rocked by allegations of insider dealing, yesterday appointed Cindy Czarnikow (48) as its new chief executive.

Ms. Czarnikow, who currently holds the position of Chief Morale Champion, has worked with the company for 10 years. She takes over from Mr. Keith Buxton who was appointed only two weeks ago as acting CEO.

"I am humbled at the humungous responsibility that has been placed on me," she said yesterday. "This is a much storied company with a fine history, and I have pledged to return it to profitability within 12 months."

Last month a-b glöbâl announced a loss of $4.6b, the biggest in its history.

Asked if there would be a role for Keith Buxton, Ms. Czarnikow said, "Keith Buxton has many wonderful talents, and I will be speaking with him to see how best they can be leveraged going forward." Analysts yesterday questioned whether Ms. Czarnikow would be tough enough to make the mass redundancies needed to return the company to profitability. However one source close to her said, "Underneath the sweet manner is one tough cookie."

Cindy Czarnikow is the second woman to run a Fortune 500 company after Carly Fiorina of Hewlett-Packard.

Graham—have you seen this in the FT today??? I knew that Cindy and Keith didn't get on, but didn't realize it was that bad. Cindy's an idiot, but it's still good news for us—as Keith had it in for me. And there's no way Cindy is going to promote Jens—she'd be too much like competition.

Martin

From: Cindy Czarnikow
To: All Staff

Hi
First up, thank you for your trust. It means a lot to me.
I believe that miracles are within our grasp. I want each one of you to come into work every day believing you are about to do something miraculous. If you do that, we will exceed our goals within months! Can I ask you all to join hands in this holiday season and take a minute to think about the journey we are going to travel together.
I have two announcements to make on my top team. Keith will sadly be leaving us and I'd like to take this opportunity to thank him for the love and passion he has devoted to this company, and wish him the best on his travels, wherever they may lead him!
Roger Wright, who has done a best of breed job in leading the UK company through turbulent times, is appointed to be chairman of a-b glöbâl UK on a permanent basis.

I'm smiling at you
Cindy

From: Keith Buxton
To: All Staff

Hi everyone
It is with mixed emotions that I announce my resignation from a-b glöbâl. It has been a tough decision, but I have decided to pursue other options and spend more time with my wife and family. I would like to thank everyone here for making the last few years so enjoyable. I feel privileged to have worked with you and wish you everything good in continuing a-b glöbâl's proud legacy.

Very truly yours
Keith

From: Martin Lukes
To: Jenny Withers

Jens
    We are quits now. I've lost my protector and you've lost yours. Don't feel badly about the job. It's all for the best. M

From: Martin Lukes
To: Jenny Withers

You had already turned it down??? Why??

From: Martin Lukes
To: Jenny Withers

THAT'S FANTASTIC NEWS!!!!!!!!! When were you planning to tell me??? Did it happen that night in the hotel in Paradise Island? Can we have supper tonight to celebrate a new start?

M xx

From: Martin Lukes
To: Jenny Withers

PS Just reassure me—it is mine, isn't it?

DECEMBER 16

From: Martin Lukes
To: Cindy Czarnikow

Hi Cindy
 Can I be the first to say congratulations?? As you know, I have always had the greatest respect for your work and have always got a terrific buzz out of working with you. I'd also like to say that I share your respect for Roger, and have every confidence that he is the right man to lead us into calmer waters! However, his skills are more on the finance/cost side and would be complemented by someone who is more on the vision/strategy side. I am proposing myself in the new role of Director of Marketing and Strategy. Can we talk about this?

All my very besteset
Martin

From: Martin Lukes
To: Roger Wright

Hi Roger, many congratulations on your appointment. Very well deserved, if I might venture so bold.
 Can we have some face time re my position? I am prepared to move back to Marketing, but would like some additional scope to deploy my big-picture creovative™ skills.

Best, Martin

From: Martin Lukes
To: Roger Wright

Hi Roger

Director of Special Projects??? Not sure I like the sound of that. How many people would be on my team? Unless the job is clearly senior to Marketing Director, I don't feel at all inclined to accept it. In fact if that's all you can offer myself, you leave me no choice but to pursue options in the "outside world."

Martin

From: Martin Lukes
To: Jenny Withers

Darling

How are you feeling? Hope you're not tiring yourself.

I'm being offered Director of Special Projects, but I've turned it down. I've said that if they call it Director of Special Projects and Strategy I might consider it. Team is minimal, but I would be allowed to do almost unlimited blue sky thinking. Rog says that the position has been created specially for me, and it would be up to me to make my mark on it. What bothers me is that Christo may think he's senior to me. I couldn't take that . . .

Martin

From: Martin Lukes
To: Phyllis Lukes

Dearest Mummy

I've got some very big news for you. Jens is pregnant . . . I am totally over the moon, obviously. I think it means that I'll be moving back home soon, though Jens wants to take it very slowly. We are going to see a counselor next week to sort out a couple of issues, but should be for the best.

Your loving son
Martie

From: Faith Preston
To: All Directors

Everyone congregate in reception at 6:45 in your best 70s fancy dress, and we'll go together to the London Dungeons!!

DECEMBER 17

From: Martin Lukes
To: Graham Wallace

Great party last night! I saw you ogling that new trainee on your team—she can't be more than 21!!!

Odd turnup for yours truly—this must be the first Christmas party on record where I spent the evening trying to get off with my ladywife. Didn't altogether succeed; she said that my vintage 1970s lilac ruched shirt and brown velvet jacket made her feel sick. But at least she is talking to me again.

Martin

Hair of the dog later?

From: Martin Lukes
To: Jenny Withers

Jens, darling—I've been thinking . . . let's have our usual Yule party. It's been an amazing year, and we've got a lot to celebrate.

What do you think? It needn't be that much work. In view of your condition, let's push the boat out and get caterers in. I'll look after the booze, but they could do a seasonal finger buffet. How about doing it on the 22nd?

Love both of you (!) M x

From: Martin Lukes
To: Pandora@CoachworX!

Hi Pandora

I'm happy to say that won't be necessary to prolong Executive Bronze as things have taken a turn for the better chez nous—most surprising turnup is that we're having another baby!

I've also been offered a job here which I think I'm going to accept. I've been thinking about my core values, and I think it plays to all of them.

As a combined "thank you" and a "meet and greet" I wondered if you'd be able to attend our annual Christmas Party on Wednesday night? For obvious reasons it's all very last minute, but I do hope you can make it. It'll be very informal—just a few really close friends. 37 The Avenue, Wimbledon. Finger buffet, champers and Martin Lukes' famous lethal mulled wine! Any time from 7pm—hope to see you then!

Cheers, Martin

From: Martin Lukes
To: Katherine Lukes

Hi Katherine

Sorry to hear that you're still feeling so low after the breakup with Fiona. It's been quite a year for that sort of thing. Are you sure it's wise to go ahead with the adoption on your own?

Looks like Jens and I are back together, and we're having a party to celebrate. Do hope you can come. You'll meet the whole family in one go. Details and map attached. Hope you see you then!

Best, Martin

From: Martin Lukes
To: Graham Wallace

Very short notice, but we've decided to have our traditional Yule knees-up after all this year. 22nd. Hope you and Lynne can make it.

Mart

DECEMBER 23

From: Martin Lukes
To: Graham Wallace

Glad you enjoyed it! Am feeling v rough this am, but I think everyone had a good time.

Was it the hallucinatory effects of my punch, or did you disappear upstairs at one point with Svetlana? She certainly doesn't believe in playing hard to get!!! Even Jake had a go at her at one point . . .

Cheers, Martin

PS What did you think of my speech? Went down like a lead balloon with Jens, but I was pretty pleased with it.

From: Martin Lukes
To: Graham Wallace

Thanks, yes I thought you'd get the joke! Jens has been giving me a v hard time about it—when everyone had finally gone home last night she went ballistic that I had announced the impending birth of our little one—she says that she hasn't told anyone at work yet, that it's all early days etc etc. She also didn't think my comparisons with the virgin birth were at all funny.

Btw I think it's a great idea for Pandora to coach you next year. Did I overhear her saying that she's your #1 fan?? I should warn you she says that to all her coachees!!

You'll find that although some of what she says is bullshit, basically she's very sound. On balance, she's been cathartic for myself over the past year but now is the right time for me to move on. I've signed up with Steven Roberts from 4-Dimensional Leadership, who specializes in coaching people at the chief exec level. He's a bit more expensive than Pandora, but hopefully worth it to me at this juncture in my career.

Have a good one
Mart

From: Martin Lukes
To: Katherine Lukes

Hi Katherine

It was great to see you last night after all this time. You haven't changed a bit. Once I got used to your new hairdo I could see you are just the same little sis! Obviously there's a bit more of you than there used to be, but then I'm spreading out a bit myself!

It was good of you to spend so much of the evening chatting to Jake. Most adults have difficulty in seeing the positive side of him. Not sure you should have been encouraging him with the mary jane though!!

Great that you got on so well with Pandora. Did I ever tell you that it was she who suggested that I make contact with you, as she said you'd benefit from closure with me? Hope you don't mind, but I took the liberty of telling her that you had just come out of a long-term relationship, and that she might be able to help you work through some issues on rejection. I've found her very useful on matters personal.

Actually, it was very weird for me meeting her, as until last night I had never clapped eyes on her. I've been e-mailing her all my innermost thoughts for the past year so there's very little about yours truly that she doesn't know intimately!!!! I couldn't get over her appearance—I was expecting her to be petite and forceful and sexy. So you can imagine how shocked I was at the reality!

Have a terrific Crimble. Let's meet up in the new year a deux to have a natter about old times.

Cheers, Martin

From: Martin Lukes
To: Phyllis Lukes

Dearest Mum

Sorry you couldn't make it to the party. It was a huge success. Weird seeing Katherine after all this time. At first I didn't recognize her at all. She's aged a lot and put on weight. The red spiky hair is a mistake.

It was also very odd meeting Pandora. She's hugely fat and was wearing a pink shell suit, and kept on nipping out onto the loggia for a fag. It's very hard to believe that she was ever a ballerina . . . She was all over Katherine, and the two of them shared a cab home afterwards. The thought occurred to me that she may be inclined that way too. Which would make a lot of sense. I suppose neither of them, for different reasons, ever met the right man.

Jake and Katherine really bonded, and as I said to Jens afterwards, there are a lot of similarities between them. Both of them have lived in the shadow of brilliant siblings, which has definitely left scars. K's asked Jake to go and stay in Brighton in the New Year at her place and experience some of the counterculture there, which was nice of her.

As for Max, his new religious jag is really getting to me. He stood on the sidelines looking disapproving as we all got merry. Drinking is what Crimble is all about. I'll drive down and pick you up tomorrow morning. Really looking forward to a lovely family Christmas xx

Your loving son
Martie

DECEMBER 27

From: Martin Lukes
To: Graham Wallace

Hi Graham

How was yours?? Ours pretty good, though Jens feeling sick and very bad tempered. Jake and I went for a long Boxing Day walk, and although he's still monosyllabic I think relations between us are improving. Max spent most of the morning at church, and the afternoon doling out soup in some hostel. And mum was happy as Jens let her cook the turkey. Slight friction when Mum said Jens should stop work and 43 was an unnatural age to have a baby. I could see where she was coming from, but it wasn't exactly tactful.

Still I was allowed back into the marital bed—though no hanky-panky as yet due to the nausea. Jens gave me the South Beach Diet for Crimble, and I've said I'll start in the New Year. I think it allows me to drink but only red wine. Pint of Guinness in an hour?

Martin

PS Did you read in the papers over Christmas that it looks like BSM may get locked up for some time? Serves him right.

From: Roger Wright
To: All Staff

Re: Staff changes
    Martin Lukes is to become Director of Special Projects and Strategy, effective immediately. This is a main board position, reporting to myself. Martin will be in charge of a broad range of projects and will work closely with other directors and members of staff. He will continue to be responsible for our right-shoring project. I wish him every success in his new role.
    Thelma Dowd has been appointed his assistant.

Roger Wright
Chairman

From: Pandora@CoachworX!
To: Martin Lukes

Hi Martin
    This is the last day of Executive Bronze and the last day of our journey. I have said many words to you over the year, and I have only two left.
    Martin, I want to say: Thank you. Thank you for making the journey. Thank you for growing. It's been an incredible year. Thank you for sharing it with me. You have come a long, long way and I now can officially declare you to be 22.5 percent better than your best! As your Number One fan I would like to say:
    Martin, keep striving and keep thriving!

Pandora

From: Martin Lukes
To: All Staff

Dear friends, co-colleagues, mentors and mentees,

After some gut-wrenching soul searching with family and friends, I have come to an important decision re my career at a-b glöbâl. Over the holiday season I have pondered whether to pursue some exceedingly interesting opportunities in the "outside world," or whether to stay here at a-b glöbâl.

You will have seen from Roger's announcement what my decision has been. However, I'm sure that you will all be curious about the thinking that went into this decision, and so I have decided to share it with you.

I'm staying because I've been given the freedom to be the creovative™ genius I aspire to be

I'm staying because the people I work with are uniquely talented

I'm staying because I never have to say, "can I be frank?" I just always am

I'm staying because I continuously want to see "what's around the corner"

I'm staying because I think we can make this company a better place to work, and I want to be part of that

I'm staying for these reasons and many more. But, most importantly, I'm staying because when I meet someone on an airplane or at a dinner party and they ask me what I do for a living, I'm extremely proud to tell them that I am a Director of a-b glöbâl.

All my very bestest
Martin Lukes

From: Cindy Czarnikow
To: All Staff

Hi everyone!

Wow! Thank you Martin for your honesty in sharing something so personal with us. I know that many hundreds of a-b glöbâl employees will be so grateful to you for expressing—so eloquently—exactly what each of them was feeling.

Next year is going to be a great one for all of us. I can just feel it.

I'm smiling at all of you
Cindy

From: Martin Lukes
To: Graham Wallace

Meet you downstairs now. I've got a raging thirst. M

From: Martin Lukes
To: Thelma Dowd

Hi Thelma
What's this urgent message from Sebastian Fforbes Hever? Did he say what he wanted?

Martin

From: Martin Lukes
To: Thelma Dowd

Off for a drink with Graham. Happy New Year. Have a good one.
If Sebastian calls back, I've got my mobile, pager and Black-Berry with me.

Martin

Authors' Acknowledgments

At the end of the day, a book is basically all about teamwork. *Who Moved My BlackBerry?* was no exception.

First up, we would like to celebrate the contribution of Jasper McMahon, who brainstormed, thought outside the box, and sweated the small stuff. Kathryn Davies and Sathnam Sanghera had many key inputs to bring to the party, as did Edward Lucas.

Juliet Annan and Clare Alexander gave 120 percent all the way.

And above all, sincerest gratitude to my coach, friend, and mentor, Michael Skapinker, for his unstinting creovative assistance each week for my column in the *Financial Times*. Credit is also due to Richard Lambert, who had the guts and vision to see that *FT* readers would be interested in the weekly antics of one Martin Lukes! It is no exaggeration to say we could not have done this without any of you. Cheers.

Last but not least, we would like to thank our loving better halves, Jenny Withers and David Goodhart, who helped by reading the chapters, and for being there for us 24/7. Thanks to our children, Jake, Max, Rosie, Maud, Arthur, and Stan, for sharing in the tears and the laughter and for pushing the envelope until it almost fell off the table.

MARTIN LUKES AND LUCY KELLAWAY

Pandora's Acknowledgments

I would like to celebrate the work of my friends and mentors from the coaching community who have taught me so much, and whose teachings I have passed on to Martin and to many coaches down the years.

Above all I would like to mention Steve Covey, whose funeral exercise is one of the most profoundly moving and revealing lessons of all. I would also like to thank David Taylor, Laura Berman Fortgang, Paul McKenna, Pam Richardson, Antony Robbins, and Arielle Essex for the inspiration I have garnered from you and your books. I have learned more about life from you than you will ever know.